BLOOD IN THE SAND

Asleep further on down the beach that deadly July morning, in what he called his "driftwood condo," a homeless man was shocked into wakefulness by the noise.

BLAM! Then, BLAM!

Throwing his plastic tarp roof off to see, he scanned the beach in all directions. He saw nothing in the dark and fog.

The man's life of hard luck and abuse had made him vigilant and alert. His friend had been kicked to death by a bunch of drunk high school kids while sleeping in the park. So, he took special notice of potential danger.

Just as he was about to settle down, BLAM! A third explosion.

"Goddam kids," he muttered. Less than two weeks had gone by since the Fourth of July, and probably some of the local brats were using the last of their hoarded firecrackers. After a while, the homeless man couldn't see or hear anything, decided that the hubbub was over, and settled back down in the warm, dry sand.

A hundred yards or so up the beach, a young woman and her male companion lay facedown with bullets in their heads.

In the driftwood condo, the homeless man never got back to sleep.

TRUE CRIME

ALAN GOLD

BERKLEY PRIME CRIME, NEW YORK

THE BERKLEY PUBLISHING GROUP
Published by the Penguin Group
Penguin Group (USA) Inc.
375 Hudson Street, New York, New York 10014, USA
Penguin Group (Canada), 10 Alcorn Avenue, Toronto, Ontario M4V 3B2, Canada
(a division of Pearson Penguin Canada Inc.)
Penguin Books Ltd., 80 Strand, London WC2R 0RL, England
Penguin Group Ireland, 25 St. Stephen's Green, Dublin 2, Ireland (a division of Penguin Books Ltd.)
Penguin Group (Australia), 250 Camberwell Road, Camberwell, Victoria 3124, Australia
(a division of Pearson Australia Group Pty. Ltd.)
Penguin Books India Pvt. Ltd., 11 Community Centre, Panchsheel Park, New Delhi—110 017, India
Penguin Group (NZ), Cnr. Airborne and Rosedale Roads, Albany, Auckland 1310, New Zealand
(a division of Pearson New Zealand Ltd.)
Penguin Books (South Africa) (Pty.) Ltd., 24 Sturdee Avenue, Rosebank, Johannesburg 2196, South Africa

Penguin Books Ltd., Registered Offices: 80 Strand, London WC2R 0RL, England

TRUE CRIME

A Berkley Prime Crime Book / published by arrangement with the author

PRINTING HISTORY
Berkley Prime Crime edition / February 2005

Cover design by George Long.
Cover art by Mark Tocchett.
Interior text design by Stacy Irwin.

For information address: The Berkley Publishing Group,
a division of Penguin Group (USA) Inc.,
375 Hudson Street, New York, New York 10014.

ISBN: 0-425-20115-5

BERKLEY PRIME CRIME®
Berkley Prime Crime Books are published by The Berkley Publishing Group,
a division of Penguin Group (USA) Inc.,
375 Hudson Street, New York, New York 10014.
BERKLEY PRIME CRIME is a registered trademark of Penguin Group (USA) Inc.
The Berkley Prime Crime design is a trademark belonging to Penguin Group (USA) Inc.

PRINTED IN THE UNITED STATES OF AMERICA

10 9 8 7 6 5 4 3 2 1

AUTHOR'S NOTE

This novel is based on the murders of Gabriella Brooke Goza, 26, and Frank "Kacy" Nimz, Jr., 36. The two were shot in the head on July 14, 1997 in the town of Seaside, Oregon. It is said they were on the beach waiting for the sunrise.

They were slain by Jesse Carl McAllister and Bradley Charles Price, who were roommates both about twenty-one years old at the time of the killings. The two were obsessed by a TV miniseries of Truman Capote's *In Cold Blood*, which they had rented four times just before the killings. The story concerns a Kansas family murdered by two drifters, apparently for no good reason.

The Oregon victims were chosen at random, literally in the wrong place at the wrong time. The morning of the crime, McAllister phoned a friend and told him that they did it "just for the hell of it."

Like the murderers in the Capote book, McAllister and Price took off for Mexico, and were on the lam for more than a year. They got jobs in Mexico City and stayed there until McAllister decided to return to the U.S. He was spotted by Ernie Tijerina, chief inspector for U.S. Customs Service at Brownsville, Texas. McAllister was crossing from Matamoros, Mexico, walking and carrying a military duffel bag at 8 a.m. Most people crossing drive or take a taxi.

"You pick people out of a crowd. You can't check them all, but with experience you learn what to look for. They don't appear to fit the norm, you check a little." Tijerina found McAllister's Oregon driver's license and Social Security card in the bag, along with his clothing and a notebook. A computer check discovered an outstanding warrant for his arrest.

He called the FBI in Portland to confirm that McAllister

was still wanted. "They said, 'Yes, we do want him, we want him bad. We'll come for him.' "

McAllister had showed no reaction when he was told of the warrant. Tijerina said McAllister "was calm. Calm enough to take a nap." He found McAllister sleeping in the security room when he went to check. As Jesse Carl McAllister was being extradited from Texas to Oregon, his accomplice, Bradley Charles Price, was arrested in Mexico City, the FBI said. McAllister arrived at Portland International Airport flanked by a Portland FBI agent, Oregon State Police and Seaside police, and was taken to the Clatsop County Jail in Astoria, Oregon. He was arraigned on 2 counts of aggravated murder. Price was arrested by Mexican Interpol police at the Mexico City disco where he worked, FBI agents said. Despite being charged with aggravated murder, the death penalty was off the table for Price because Mexico will not extradite a murder suspect to a country where prosecutors seek execution.

McAllister pleaded guilty to two counts of aggravated murder to escape the ultimate penalty, and confessed to the shooting.

Glorea Guritz, mother of Gabriella Goza, was against the idea of the death penalty for her daughter's killers. "I'm just not a killer. I don't think two wrongs make a right, or you should pay an evil with an evil. Look at Christ. He laid down his life for us even though we are sinners." Guritz brought photographs and other mementos of her daughter's life in a collage to court for the sentencing.

Frank Nimz was against the death penalty for other reasons. "Death, and quickly, would be too easy for you. I want you to rot in hell. He was a human being, not just a statistic." Nimz brought a video tribute to his son to court, including photographs of his son as a baby and as he grew up.

Price asked for a bench trial: no jury, judge only. He pleaded guilty, and blamed the shooting on McAllister. He claimed that they cruised the beach looking for victims, and that some people were saved because of the presence of witnesses. When they came upon Nimz and Goza, on the beach, he said that McAllister began waving the gun around. "I don't think there was anything I could have said to him at that point. He wasn't asking me any more." He admitted that he had done nothing to stop McAllister, and fled to Mexico out of fear.

The judge stated that Price "was more than just passive; he was an active participant."

During the separate penalty phase, the judge sentenced Price to life in prison with a possibility of parole in thirty years, the year 2029.

In October of 1999, McAllister was moved to isolation because he stabbed another inmate in a fight. He will be in prison for the rest of his life.

It was rumored that one or both of the aggrieved parents sought help from a psychic to help find the murderers.

These notes were compiled from various newspaper and TV news stories, and with the help of Clatsop County District Attorney Joshua Marquis, who is nothing like fictional DA Tom Knight.

The Crime

July 14, 1997

At 4:40 in the morning, even in high summer, the only light in the sky over Seagirt was electric light reflected back by the clouds. It was very still, just the sound of the surf, and while people slept and seabirds huddled on the sand, two lovers planned the rest of their lives together. Neither was a kid any longer, and both had a history, and none of that mattered.

They talked of a wedding, a house, and a future free of the mistakes and bad associations of the past. It had taken them a long time to get to this point, and they were ready to spend the rest of their lives together.

They didn't know, couldn't know, that the rest of their lives amounted to less than five minutes.

They were so intent on each other they noticed no one approaching. They were so caught up in their own happiness, they did not sense the presence of doom, or even that they were no longer alone on the beach.

The first dim light of dawn was shaded by the craggy Coast Range and diffused by the mists. It was just another summer morning on the Oregon coast.

The surf slid almost silently along the broad beach and under the fog. The fog absorbed the soft sound of the surf, along with the sharp sounds of raised voices and screams, and rose to meet the clouds somewhere above the beach, carrying the mingled messages to the dark sky.

Then, at 4:45, came the explosions.

BLAM! Followed by another BLAM! Then, after a while, a third BLAM!

The lovers lay facedown, shot to death in what the newspapers would call execution style. Their blood ran into the damp sand, dark halos spreading into one another, mingling. He had never even gotten to show her the engagement ring still in his pocket.

A couple of hours later, early dog walkers, carrying insulated metal mugs of coffee, found the victims, and the parade of onlookers began.

SECTION ONE

No Day at the Beach

1. Rude Awakening, July 14

Asleep further on down the beach that deadly July morning, in what he called his "driftwood condo," a homeless man was shocked into wakefulness by the noise.

BLAM! Then, BLAM!

Throwing his plastic tarp roof off to see, he scanned the beach in all directions. He saw nothing in the dark and fog.

The man's life of hard luck and abuse had made him vigilant and alert. At his age, and in his condition, he couldn't take the beatings or the ugly treatment anymore.

His friend had been kicked to death by a bunch of drunk high school kids while sleeping in a park. The man might not have lived his life in the best way possible, but he wasn't going out like that, so he took special notice of potential danger.

Just as he was about to settle down, BLAM! A third explosion.

"Goddam kids," he muttered. Less than two weeks had gone by since the Fourth of July, and probably some of the local brats were using the last of their hoarded firecrackers. After a while, the homeless man couldn't see or hear anything, decided that the hubbub was over, and settled back down in the warm, dry sand between a driftwood log and a small dune. He pulled the tarp back over his burrow, and tried to fall back to sleep.

A hundred yards or so up the beach, a young woman and her male companion lay facedown with bullets in their heads. In the driftwood condo, the homeless man never got back to sleep.

2. A Visit to the Shore

The Sunset Highway runs from Portland to the Oregon coast. Lou Tedesco poked along behind an elderly couple in an out-of-tune RV, waiting for the passing lane, headed for Seagirt, about eighty miles from Portland, west on the Sunset Highway and over the Coast Range from the Willamette Valley. His life would soon be intertwined in the aftermath of the two corpses on the beach.

He was on assignment, but also under orders to take it easy. He would be unable to follow those orders.

In Portland, Oregon, as in most cities of any size, there are weekly newspapers struggling to provide an alternative to the single daily paper. Lou Tedesco worked for one of these papers, the *Stumptown Weekly*. It was not the oldest, or the most successful, but it was the best. At least Lou thought so.

The offices of the *Stump*, as it was known, occupied a floor of a loft building in the industrial area on the east side of town, across the Willamette from downtown, and therefore cheaper. When all your revenue comes from the ads for small or marginal businesses, the best thing to do is to run cheap. This means paying your staff as little as possible, so

Lou lived not far from the newspaper office in another loft. He feared that gentrification would spring across the river, or move west toward it from the nearby residential area, to swell his rent and drive him out.

Lou cared mostly about music, movies, and food. He was a music critic and restaurant reviewer, and did the odd movie review for the *Stump*, and life was as good as it had been for a long time.

That morning, as he entered his office at the paper, he noticed a scrawled note on his chair. He set down his coffee cup. The message was recognizable as the hieroglyphic hand of owner/editor Blanche Perry.

Lou, sweetie, I am forced to cover the city council meeting because I fired the Toad.

So, I have to listen to the mayor and her crew run their jaws for a few hours. I don't know how long this thing will run, but I'll call later. Please have some restaurant reviews for me, and I'll have a surprise for you.

Blanche (the Boss)

In truth, the firing of the *Stump*'s longtime political reporter was a surprise in itself.

The phone rang.

Lou jumped, startled. He picked up the receiver.

"Weekly, Tedesco."

"Hey, Lou. It's Blanche." Lou could hear the echoing sounds of an enormous space in the background.

"Jeez, you scared the crap out of me. Actually, it may have been the sudden memory of the food I'm writing about."

"Poor Lou. Victimized by the food industry yet again. You should probably stay home some night and cook a meal."

"Please! Would you deprive me of my only pleasure in life?"

"You're a good writer, maybe a talented one. But, I think

that you haven't found your niche, yet. Sure, you like music, and can write perceptively about it. Same with movies. And your restaurant reviews are the only honest ones in town."

"Yeah," Lou interjected, "which is why we never get any restaurant ads."

"It would help if you would like a few places that could actually afford to advertise, but at least we're not boosters or shills. Anyway, I've been thinking that you should take a few days off, maybe go to the coast."

"I can't believe you fired the Toad." Lou tried to change the subject.

"Yeah, it was about time. Last week he attended a city council meeting drunk after lunch. He passed out and snored until they threw him out. It feels good for me to be back reporting the news.

"But let me finish that last thought. There's an old theater, a movie palace, reopening out there, somewhere. The Bijou or something. The town is having a festival this weekend for the opening. Old flicks, Lou, the real stuff. Bogart, Jean Harlow, the Marx Brothers . . ."

"Wow," Lou drawled, "that's really tempting."

"Charge it to the paper, and pop into a few joints out there to take in the chow. We can do one of those hokey 'weekend dining at the beach' things. You get to rest, see good movies, we get some feature stuff, and the whole thing gets written off. What do you say?"

"Anything else?" Lou asked, knowing there was.

"Yeah. Think about what you want to do when you grow up. You know, walk on the beach, listen to the gulls, dodge the surf and contemplate your navel. See what you find, besides sand."

Lou looked at the computer screen, up at the ceiling, and back at the phone.

"Okay."

"Good," she purred.

• • •

"Damn!" Lou swore. He had missed the passing lane as his mind drifted, and would have to endure a few more miles behind the wheezing, lumbering RV, whose back panel was soot black from oily exhaust.

He shrugged. He was in no hurry.

An hour later, after he ditched the shlepper in the RV, he approached the mountain pass bracketing the freeway. He could see the tops of clouds beyond the low range. On a typical summer day, the clouds would burn off about noon, leaving bright blue skies until late afternoon, when the mists would begin to gather again.

When he pulled into the coast town, he began looking for lodging, but No Vacancy signs seemed to be everywhere. Odd, he thought, middle of the week, festival not until the weekend, and plenty of rooms for handling the spring break crowds. What gives?

He finally found a small, much older motel, the Saltaire, on the north side of town, east of the main drag. Old, but it appeared acceptably kept.

Lou parked the car, and ambled into the office. A middle-aged woman in hair curlers and a print housedress smiled at him from behind a painted plywood counter.

"Howdy," she chirped, "if you're lookin' for a room, I got one left. Number six."

"I'll take it, sight unseen."

"I haven't had all my rooms rented in a while. Must be the . . ." and here her voice trailed off ominously.

"The what? The theater opening?" Lou's interest had piqued.

She looked around, shook her curlered head, and said under her breath, "The *killings*." Her eyes grew wide. "There's reporters and TV from Portland, Seattle . . . maybe San Francisco."

"Plural?" Lou's eyebrows went up. "More than one killing?"

"Two," she nodded, a sad expression on her face. "And local people, too."

"Did you know them?"

"Mister, in a town this size, everybody knows everybody. I went to high school with the girl's mother."

"A girl was killed?"

"Well, late twenties. She's a girl to me. Her boyfriend was maybe ten years older. Shelley Korta and Larry Narz. Poor kids . . ." She shook her head. "All that stuff they went through, and now this."

"Whereabouts did it happen?" Lou was definitely interested.

"Oh, not far. Maybe ten blocks down the beach, back toward town."

"When did this happen?"

"Oh, my, just last night, maybe early this morning."

"Okay, look," Lou snapped into functional mode, "I'll take the room. How much?"

"For—uh, sixty dollars a night."

Lou scowled; she smiled a sheepish smile.

"Done," he capitulated. "Credit card okay?"

She nodded, curlers waving atop her head.

The room was pretty comfortable, had a small color TV with a cable hookup, and a minikitchen. He threw his suitcase on the bed, and unpacked into the old dresser, which housed only one small spider. Then, he set up the booze and poison right in front of the dresser mirror.

Finally, Lou unpacked his computer, grabbed a couple of pads, and made ready to go.

"Mr. Tadusky?"

Lou jumped, startled. It was the clerk in curlers.

"Wow, you scared me. What is it?"

"Sorry, don't wanna scare a paying customer."

She chuckled at her little joke, sounding like a Lily Tomlin character.

"I forgot to tell you that we have coffee service in the morning." She grinned.

"Thanks. I may avail myself."

She insinuated herself deeper into the room, doing a quick eyeball survey.

"Avail? You one of those writers?" she asked.

"Guilty as charged."

"You here for the *killings*?"

"Believe it or not, no. I'm here for a working vacation, and the Bijou opening. I'm really a food and music critic, and I do the occasional movie."

"Oh," she said, encroaching yet further, "remind me to give you that flyer about our local musicians." Her eyes settled on two bottles. One was a bottle of cheap vodka, the other a small brown vial with a handwritten label.

"You drink vodka?"

"Not anymore."

"Well . . . ," she began.

"It's a long story, and I have to run."

"Sure, okay. What's in the other bottle."

Lou thought for a moment, then decided it was better to have it out in the open.

"It's cyanide. Another long story, but it's there in case I need it."

She went pale. "You're not gonna . . ."

Lou shook his head vigorously. "No worries. I'm going now."

"Well, okay." It was not okay, if the look on her face was any indication, but, she left him, slipping out the open door. He followed, making sure the lock was engaged.

Lou hopped in the car, drove west toward the beach, and south when he got to Shore Road. He saw the commotion blocks away, and found a place to park.

Walking out to a beach access, he made his way south in the direction of the crowd. The soft sand exaggerated his limp, acquired from a second-base crash during his prior career in minor-league baseball.

This was his first media circus and he was appalled.

There were dozens of news people, cameramen and women, and perhaps hundreds of gawkers. Print reporters dressed sloppy-casual stalked around looking for some vantage point. Radio reporters carrying tape decks and microphones milled around trying to find someone to talk to. TV reporters did their stand-ups with the crime scene in the background, fighting the wind. He saw a few he knew, including the attractive young Asian-American woman he liked best on the Portland news.

Her hair flew in one direction, her papers, clenched in a small fist, in another direction, and her skirt, to her embarrassment, whipped over her hips. If she tried to hold her skirt with one hand, she couldn't read her copy, and the microphone was in the other hand. Eventually, she gave up, got her camera guy to shoot her from the waist up, and drew quite a crowd. Lou felt sorry for her, but didn't walk away for a while.

The one thing he couldn't see in all this was a police presence. He angled closer.

Finally, he saw an area enclosed with yellow police tape. It seemed inadequate, too small for a crime scene, if his knowledge from cop shows and mystery novels meant anything. And, the surrounding beach was trampled with the prints of uncountable shoes.

Two cops were inside the tape: a gruff, thick-chested, cigar chomper and a tall, much younger and gangling Barney Fife type. Lou guessed chief and deputy, in that order. There was also a guy with an elaborate camera rig.

There were two bodies on the beach, with dark stains in the sand around the heads, and the impressions in the sand of hands and feet nearby. Lou shuddered. These were the first murder victims he'd ever seen.

Reporters were flinging questions into the taped-in crime scene in bursts, and the chief would answer a couple, wave them off, then try to get back to the job. During one of the chief's rants to the press, Lou signaled the younger cop, who sidled over keeping one eye on the chief.

"Yes, sir?" His nameplate read "Loober."

"Officer, uh, Loober is it? I was wondering. Have you isolated enough of the beach for a crime scene?"

Pondering a second whether to answer, Loober replied, "Well, probably not, sir. But, by the time we got wind of this, most of this area was already messed up pretty good.

We're lucky no one walked right over to the victims. Some dog did, though."

"Dog belong to the killer?"

"No, uh-uh. Belonged to the couple that found them."

"Gar, for Christ's sake, get back here!" the chief bellowed. "I can't do this myself."

"Sorry," Loober blushed, "I gotta go."

"Yeah, sure. Thanks for talking to me."

Loober waved and headed back. Lou shrugged and decided to walk down the beach.

Oregon beaches are underpopulated by the measure of the East Coast beaches Lou knew as a kid. Except for the burgeoning masses at the crime scene, Seagirt's beach was near empty.

As he angled toward the surf, Lou noticed two lines of footprints heading away from the crime scene at approximately the same angle he was moving. What caught his attention was the tread of the shoes. They were identical. Two sets of footprints, one kind of shoe. Funny.

And, one set was different from another, as though one foot of one set were heavier than the other.

On a whim, Lou looked north up the beach towards the other side of the "event," and started walking north along the shore. He found a similar set of two angling up from the shore and toward the crime scene. One set coming and one set going.

Probably just another pair of rubberneckers, he thought. But, just in case . . .

Lou walked back up to the yellow tape. He gestured toward Loober, who came over as the chief was haranguing the press on the one hand, and the photographer on the other.

"Yes, sir?"

"Officer, there's two sets of footprints approaching the scene, and two sets going away. Both sets are wearing identical shoes."

"And?"

"Well, I don't know if it means anything, but it might be worth looking at."

The long, tall deputy slipped under the tape. "Show me."

Lou walked Loober down to the prints.

The deputy looked carefully at the prints, and said, "Sir, please do me a favor. Don't let anyone walk all over these. I'll be right back."

In a few minutes, Loober came back, leading the photographer. They shot several pictures, a few at low angles, almost down at beach level. Loober held a mirror to reflect light across the prints for certain shots.

"Did you say there were some more of these somewhere?" asked the deputy.

"Yup. Just fifty yards or so, up the beach."

They trudged to the second set, and repeated the process, with Loober taking copious notes, including shot numbers supplied by the photographer. After the deputy was satisfied, he dismissed the photographer, and looked at Lou.

"Please come with me, sir." It wasn't an order, but Lou understood that it was not optional.

When they got to the crime scene, Loober lifted the tape, and indicated that Lou go under it. They walked up to a red-faced and sweating chief.

"Chief Lester Green," Loober gestured, "this is Mr . . ."

"Tedesco, Lou Tedesco." Lou offered his hand; the chief ignored it.

"He a witness?" asked the chief.

"No, sir, but he did see . . ."

"Loober, if he ain't a witness, then he's just a citizen, or worse, a reporter. Get him out of the crime scene."

"Chief, he found footprints on the beach identical to the one next to the bodies." At that, even the chief had to listen, an activity for which he was long out of practice. Loober explained what he had done with the photographer.

Lou started to walk over to the bodies. He noticed the footprint in question, and a deep handprint up near the head of one of the victims, Larry Narz. Then, Green yelled at him.

"Hey, Tedesco, get the hell outta there!"

"Is that the handprint of one of the killers?"

"No, goddamit. Now get over here. I didn't tell you you could dance all over the crime scene."

"It already looks like the Rockettes did the Easter show here." Lou was tempted to say it out of the corner of his mouth. "So, whose print is it?"

"The vic's, I guess." Green shrugged.

"His, or hers?"

"Uh, his. He probably broke his fall with it."

"No sale," Lou shook his head. "It's much too big for hers, true, but it isn't his either."

"And, how do you know that?"

Lou looked up at the chief. "You're kidding, right? The male victim has the top joint of his right index finger missing. The print has all five fingers intact."

Loober looked away, with what might have been shame on his face. Green seethed.

"There any witnesses I could talk to?" Lou asked blithely.

"Who the hell are you?" asked Green.

"I'm with the *Stumptown Weekly*, back in Portland."

"I knew you were a friggin' reporter. Get the hell out of here."

"How about the couple who found the bodies?" Lou pushed his luck.

The chief reached for his gun, and Loober said, "Easy, Chief. I'll escort him out."

When Lou slipped under the tape, Loober whispered, "Thanks for the tip on the footprints. We might get this solved, yet,"

Lou walked back to his car whistling "My Gal Sal." He felt a rush of blood in his face, and got light-headed, when he realized that he had challenged a police officer on the cop's own turf, with no more credentials than he had to be a restaurant critic: namely, none. It was one thing to find fault with an overcooked crème brûlée, quite another to butt into a murder investigation.

What he needed was some seafood. He stopped at a little

restaurant for fried razor clams and a house salad. He was amazed at his own lack of nausea, given his sudden qualms.

He was not amazed that the restaurant, which should have known better, ruined the clams. Overbreaded, like chopped veal in a faux Italian chain joint, and deep-fried in grease that hadn't been changed in a while, the clams were limp, greasy, and tasted off and the Roquefort dressing was bottled, with chunks of domestic blue cheese standing in for the Roquefort.

Now, he was *really* amazed at his lack of nausea. He began to compose a review in his head.

When he got back to his motel room, he loaded his portable boom-box with a CD of the original cast of *Bells Are Ringing.*

"I need a dose of Judy Holliday," he said out loud as he fired up his laptop and wrote a review. It was entitled, "Delusions of Adequacy."

> It's one thing to expect fresh seafood, cooked with respect for the noble creature and for the hopeful diner, in the Middle West. Fresh seafood is limited to what they can catch or farm in the lakes and rivers. Fresh crappie, sure; fresh razor clams? Nope.
>
> So, it was with the hope of the naive that I entered Melly's in Seagirt to order the bivalve, literally a short walk from a beach where the fresh razor clams are dug. Unlike the East Coast clams of my youth, which could be eaten raw, razors must be cooked, preferably, if you don't have elevated cholesterol, sauteed in butter with a light dusting of seasoned crumbs.
>
> I didn't expect fresh; the harvesting season is over. But I didn't expect razors not so much cooked as tortured to death. One had the image of an army of razor clams laying siege to a castle, and being drenched from the parapets with boiling oil, thirty-weight, if my guess is right.
>
> One imagines the clam raiders reeling with the shock, and falling limp to the ground never to rise again. Then,

one imagines Melly, if such a fiend exists, gathering the tiny victims to serve in his cathedral of bad cuisine.

Shame, Melly.

Oh, and the french fries were lousy, too.

3. A Career Move

Later that night, Lou walked down to a strip mall nearby and called Blanche. Something about Chloe, the motel desk attendant, made him seek out a neutral phone. He told Blanche about the murders, and the local constabulary.

"Lou, cover the story! You're right there. We've never had anything like this before."

"Blanche," Lou sighed, "I am not a crime reporter. I do bare justice to the reviews I write."

"Come on, Lou. You used to do investigative reporting for my dad. You were good at it. Your skills can't have deteriorated *that* much.

"Besides, change is in the air. I'm a political reporter again. Let's get the *Stump* back in the big boys' game."

"Blanche, I just don't have the heart . . ."

"Save it, Tedesco. By the authority vested in me as owner and publisher, voilà! You are now a crime reporter. Consider it a career move."

Lou knew when the fight was lost. "Okay, but if it comes out sounding like a description of *dim sum*, blame only yourself. That reminds me, any suggestions for places to eat in Seagirt? I should get a Purple Heart for the lunch I had today."

"People are always telling me about the Dunes Café. It's supposed to be the home-cooking heaven of the Oregon coast, and the waitresses call you hon."

" 'Servers.' 'Waitresses' is sexist."

"See? I knew you were the right guy for the job. You're sensitive to nuance."

"And you're full of crap. Call you tomorrow."

When Lou got back to the motel, he looked up the café in the slender phone book, and drove over. It was a one-story, gray-painted, cinder-block building, with large, plate-glass windows on three sides. It looked dark from the road, and it had a hand-lettered sign inside the glass door reading, "CLOSED FOR DEATH IN FAMILY."

Lou shrugged, and went down to a Wendy's nearby. At least, he thought, I know what I'm in for here.

Afterward, Lou drove down the main drag, Highway 101, fabled in song and story. He was looking for the Bijou, and assumed that it was on that road.

It wasn't hard to spot. Lou was impressed. It was a smaller version of the grandiose film temples that graced America's cities in the pre-multiplex past, like the Roxy and the Majestic.

Smaller, but magnificent still: Xanadu strained through Art Deco. Pseudo-Persian decoration, two cupolas on towers at the corners of the facade, lots of gold paint. A real box office at the front. Whatever effort had been put into its renovation had paid off. The place was a gem.

The marquee blared, "Grand Opening! Movies the Way They Were Meant To Be Seen! Opening Night, *To Have and Have Not*. Bacall Gives Bogie Whistling Lessons! Plus, Cartoon and 1948 Newsreel!"

Very cool, Lou thought.

Opening on Friday! proclaimed a banner stretched across the entrance. Lou stopped his car and made note of the number to call for more information. One way or another, he would get a story out of this trip.

Back at the motel, fighting off heartburn, Lou called the Bijou number.

"Bijou Theater," said a young, male voice, "home of real movies in a real movie house."

Lou introduced himself, and the young man said he was Anthony John, proprietor of the Bijou.

Lou praised the theater's renovation and asked for an appointment.

"What time works for you?" Anthony asked. "I'm here most of the day, and will be for the foreseeable future."

"How about tomorrow? Middle of the day?"

"Excellent. See you soon. Just knock on the big doors, and I'll be close enough to hear."

Lou rang off, and went to bed.

The next morning, Lou tried again and the Dunes Café was open.

When the bell on the back of the door jingled, a glum group of locals and employees snapped around to look at the door. The counter ran along the right side of the place, and there were eight tables to the left of the front door. The kitchen door was straight back from where Lou stood.

Three women in servers' uniforms, and one in a chef's apron, leaned on the counter. A half dozen others sat at the Formica counter, coffee cups and plates of nibbled pastry scattered among them.

"Uh, are you open?" Lou hesitated.

A collective sigh, and a "Yes, sir," from the staff.

Lou walked over to the counter. The customers shifted down a seat to give him room.

"I noticed you were closed last night. Are you related to one of those poor kids?"

They looked at each other for a second, and the presumed chef, a middle-aged woman with iron-gray hair and sun crinkles around her eyes, spoke.

"Not exactly. Shelley worked here for a long time until

she got her beautician's license. We're pretty close here, and she was like a sister to us."

"Yeah," said a tall woman in a server's uniform, "she was finally gettin' her act together, too. She was real happy."

"A damn shame," said another, and they all murmured agreement.

Lou sat down, ordered coffee, and asked, "How old was she?"

The tall woman drew the coffee and set it down. "Thirty, maybe."

"No," said one of the women at the counter, "no more than twenty-eight. She went all through school with my Margie, and she was never left back. She was a smart kid, until she . . ."

Her voice trailed off. The group sighed again.

Lou cleared his throat. "My name is Lou Tedesco. I'm really here to cover the Bijou opening, maybe do restaurant reviews for a Portland paper . . ."

"Uh-oh!" someone said, and the chef held up her hands in mock horror.

Lou laughed.

"No, no, relax. I've been re-assigned to cover this, um, tragedy."

"I'm Hetty Conrad," said the chef, "and I own this place. This," pointing to the tall woman, "is Ronnie Sims, that's Connie," a younger version of Ronnie, "and that's Phyllis," indicating a stout, grandmother type. "They all work here, and Phyllis has been here as long as the café."

"Hell, I'm older than Eve's undies," Phyllis said with a wicked grin. The crowd laughed.

The women at the counter seats all introduced themselves to Lou: Betty, Flo, Jean, DeeDee, Darla, Carmen. A general discussion of the sad state of the world ensued, but Lou's stomach growled ominously.

"Hmmm," said Hetty, "sounds like I need to feed you. Need a menu?"

"Nah, just a couple of eggs, over easy, home fries, and some crisp bacon."

Hetty nodded. "Hash browns do?"

"You bet. And," looking at Ronnie, "another cup of coffee, please."

As Hetty made for the kitchen, and Ronnie poured coffee, Lou tested the waters.

"Forgive me for being nosy, but I got the impression that Shelley had been through a few things. True?"

One of the customers, Jean, a feisty look on her face, shook a finger at Lou. "You're not gonna drag that poor girl's name though the mud, are you?"

"Whoa, back up! No, ma'am. I'm just getting some background." Lou sought a way to recover. "I used to be a drunk, and I understand the value of a person who picks herself up by her own bootstraps. I promise to stay out of her personal life."

The group looked at each other for mutual agreement.

Jean shook her head. "I don't know . . . Just leave it at this. She made a few real bad choices in her life, and snapped out of it a couple of years ago. All the girls here," and she swept her arm to indicate the café, "bent over backwards for her."

She lowered her voice. "They lent her the money to study cosmetology. They fed her when she was broke. They put her up when she had nowhere to live. I wish the whole world was like these girls."

Ronnie teared up and Connie comforted her.

"When she started seein' Larry Narz, we worried a little," sniffed Ronnie. "Larry was a wild boy himself. But, he stopped drinkin', and bought his own boat. Started makin' some money. Bought a little house up by Eighteenth Avenue, and fixed it up."

"How did he lose his finger?"

"Lotsa fishermen have parts or whole fingers missing," Ronnie made a face, then went on. "Line gets wound a round a finger, sudden pull on the net, or the boat lurches, *zip!* There goes a fingertip.

"So, we figured Larry had grown up, too. He was a few years older, but all the unmarried young people here kind of hang out together. They each had a past to get rid of, and it looked good for 'em."

"She was in here just a day ago," Connie said. "Told me that she and Larry were goin' out, and that he might propose."

Ronnie sniffled, and Connie patted her shoulder.

"That's probably why they were out so late," Ronnie said between sniffs. "Those are the kind of nights you don't want to end."

Hetty emerged with a plate of steaming breakfast. "I gave you sourdough toast. Okay?"

Lou smiled, "Fabulous." After dousing his potatoes with ketchup and his eggs with hot sauce, he dug in.

It was quiet for a while as he ate. After swallowing a mouthful, Lou asked, "I guess this is the question of the day: Who would want to kill them?"

Shrugs and mumbled puzzlement all around.

"Nobody had it in for them?" Lou persisted.

Same response.

"Well, is it possible that it was just Larry or just Shelley, and the other one was in the wrong place at the wrong time?"

Quiet, and stone faces. Jean, especially, had her jaw set, and a wary look on her bulldog face. Lou shrugged, "Okay. Thanks."

Talk turned to general topics: weather, tourists, gossip. Lou paid for his breakfast, set down an extravagant tip, and left.

The women watched Lou exit. Jean looked at Ronnie and said between clenched teeth, "Can't you keep your damn mouth shut? We don't know this guy, and we don't need our dirty linens out in public."

Ronnie looked around for support. No one attempted to defend her. She began to cry.

"I'm sorry, I just thought . . ."

"You weren't thinking at all," Jean snapped. "I expected everything to come out of your big trap any second."

Ronnie's eyes got big. She gasped.

"I would never . . ."

"Just keep it zipped from now on. The le[illegible] one, the better."

Jean watched Lou limp across the pa[illegible] snorted.

"Gimmie some more coffee, Hetty."

When Lou got to his car, he stopped for a minute to think. It seemed to him that a loquacious group suddenly closed the door on him. He hadn't even asked about Shelley's private life. Wouldn't people speculate on a question like that?

Maybe not. As he got into his car, he noticed the group huddling, and he wondered what they were talking about.

Maybe, he thought, I'll have better luck at the police station.

4. Seagirt's Finest

The Seagirt police housed themselves in a one-story building, with a lockup attached. Given the size of the office, the jail seemed too large. Then, Lou remembered that Seagirt was one of the spring break destinations on the Oregon coast. This led him to wonder why the police force was so small.

He opened the front door, which read "Seagirt Police Force" on the glass, and noticed the security bars on the inside of the glass. He was greeted by a smiling Gar Loober.

"Hi, Mr. Tedesco. Is that right, Tedesco?" Loober rose from his desk and extended his hand.

"Yes, sir, Officer Loober." Lou shook, and felt a strong grip.

"Call me Gar. Everyone does."

"Call me Lou."

"What can I do for you?"

"Gar, I was hoping I could get an update on the killings."

Loober went white. "Oh, I can't do that. This is an ongoing case." He shifted nervously from foot to foot, and his Adam's apple went up and down.

Then, the booming voice of Chief Lester Green roared through the pebble-glass door of his office. It sounded like, "Goddamit!"

The door flew open, almost smashing as it hit the wall. Green stood there panting, reminding Lou of a Brahma bull, hot out of the chute at a rodeo.

"What the hell do you want?"

Lou decided to go limp, figuratively speaking.

"Hello, Chief Green," he smiled, "I was just asking your deputy here for any new developments on the . . ."

"Gar," Green wheeled to face his deputy, "if you tell this parasite anything you'll be selling used cars at your Uncle Gideon's lot. You understand?"

"Now, Chief . . ." Lou began.

"Now, my ass. We have nothing to say to the press, especially your nothing little rag." His forehead wrinkled. "Uh, at this time."

"At this time? So, you . . ."

"We'll have a press conference when we've got something to say. Not before, got it?"

"Oh, yes, sir." Lou flashed a wide-eyed face.

"Keep your mouth shut, Loober. Got that?"

"Oh, yes, sir," Gar echoed Lou's tone.

Green spun around, walked back into his office and slammed the door behind him. The glass rattled, but stayed intact.

Loober waved his hand and pursed his lips. "Ooo-ee," he mimed. He walked over to Lou, and whispered, "You might want to talk to Hilda."

Lou looked perplexed.

"She's the editor of our local paper, the *North Coast Clarion*. It's two blocks down," he pointed a direction, "and left a block. Sorry about the chief."

"Hey, no problem," Lou replied. "Thanks a lot."

"And," Loober finished, "I do appreciate your help on the beach yesterday."

Lou shrugged. "Happy to do it."

They shook hands once more, and Lou walked down to

the newspaper office, passing T-shirt shops, beachwear emporiums, and dispensers of salt-water taffy. You could buy exotic seashells, among the beach property brokers, gaudy costume jewelry shops, and Tillamook ice cream parlors.

The newspaper building was a classic: the front was constructed of vertical raw-cedar boards, weather aged to a shade of gray, and the paper's name was emblazoned on the large window in gold, Western-style letters. Right out of the Hollywood idea of a small-town newspaper office.

Lou entered the office, inky dark compared to the sunny outside world. He heard, "Can I help you?"

"I need a moment for my eyes to adjust here. It's pretty bright out there since the clouds burned off."

As his eyes accustomed to the dark, he saw a woman in middle age sitting at an enormous desk with piles of paper covering it; a small green-shaded desk lamp was the only illumination. Soon, he was able to discern a printing press taking up most of the rest of the place.

"Wow. Is that press the real thing?"

"You bet," the woman arose, "and we used to print the paper on it, too."

Lou could see better now. The woman was tall, and quite casual, dressed in cut-off jeans and a tank top. Her long hair, gray going white, fell unbound past her shoulders. She wore tiny reading glasses held by a delicate chain.

"Used to?"

"Yes. The last time we printed here I was a little girl, and that was a long time ago. We got big enough to need an outside printer, but we still did the setup here. Now, we send the copy out to the printer on diskette, formatted by software for publication. All very high tech. I can't bring myself to junk the press, and schoolkids come here from miles around to look at it."

"I would sure travel to see it. Oh, sorry. I'm Lou Tedesco. I was actually sent here . . ."

"Aren't you the man who writes the music and food stuff for the *Stump*?"

"You've read my stuff?" Lou was surprised and pleased.

"Oh, yeah. Us weeklies have got to stick together. I'm Hilda Truax, editor, publisher, primary, not-to-say-only reporter, janitor, et cetera."

Lou made a mental note to start paying more attention to other weekly newspapers.

"Well, I was sent here to cover the Bijou opening and do some restaurant reviews, but against my better judgment I've become a crime reporter."

Hilda made a face. "Shelley and Larry, I guess."

Lou nodded. "What can you tell me about them? Anything?"

"Want some coffee?"

"Uh, no, but a glass of cold water wouldn't hurt, thanks."

Hilda turned and opened an old Kelvinator refrigerator, the kind with the V-shaped handle on a door that opened from both sides, and grabbed a bottle of spring water.

"Here you go. This is supposed to come from a mountain spring, but I'm betting that they fill these from the tap up in Waldorf."

"Ah, spoken like a true newspaper person. Cynical to the end."

Hilda poured herself a cup of coffee, and clinked her cup with Lou's plastic bottle. "Cheers, and right on target."

She gestured to a chair. "Take a load off."

Lou sat heavily in a creaky old swivel chair. "So," he opened, "what's your take on the murdered kids?"

She shook her head. "I can't understand it, because we don't have any experience here. My father ran this paper in the forties, fifties into the seventies, and we never had a killing, at least in my memory. And," she added, "I worked here right alongside him, from the time I could toddle around.

"Oh, sure, we've had fistfights, auto wrecks, spring break brawls, alcoholic excess, terrible accidents. A death or two resulted from some of that, but no deliberate murders. What's puzzling is why anyone would want to do it. I'm thinking it could only be random . . ." She paused a second.

"Even out here, more or less on the edge of nowhere, we could be due for the random killing, or two."

Lou was scribbling notes while she spoke, but there were a lot of question marks, each larger than the surrounding writing, and circled.

"What can you tell me about the couple, Shelley and Larry, was it?"

"Yeah," she drawled, then sipped her coffee. "Shelley was not a wild kid, really, but she made a few mistakes. Ran with some wiseass kids, slept with a few of them. She had an abortion a few years ago, and that kinda caught her up short. She began to change after that, grew up a little. Her mom was real good with her. Velma's a true saint, a real forgiving person."

"She still in town, Shelley's mom?"

"Uh-huh. Lives east of the main drag in an old house, handed down for years. I guess Shelley would have been next in line for it."

Lou shifted, and the chair creaked. "Does anyone know who the father of her baby was? That might cause some bad blood."

Hilda nodded, "Yes, it'd crossed my mind, but we don't know, for sure. Velma might. There's a lot of speculation, of course, but it's only that. No sense dignifying it by telling you."

Lou cocked an eyebrow; Hilda laughed.

"Relax. This is not an attempt to throw you off the track. I honestly don't know, and whatever guesses I have are only that. Try Velma."

"What about Larry?" Lou tipped up the water bottle and drank.

"Similar story. He was about eight or ten years older than Shelley, but this is a small town. He had a crush on her since she was in high school, and he ran with the same gang of hoodlum wannabes. Had a few small beefs with the police, juvenile delinquent stuff, nothing felonious.

"When he grew out of running around, he went to work on a salmon crew." She drank off the coffee.

"That where he lost part of his finger?"

"You noticed that? Yeah. Lots of watermen have lost body parts on the job. I saw that on lobstermen in Maine and crabbers on the Chesapeake. It's rough work: cold, icy rain, heavy nets or other equipment that get yanked around unexpectedly, even fish bites."

"I heard he bought his own boat," Lou said.

"Yes. He got smart, I guess. Some would say that the aggravation of owning your own boat isn't worth the increased income, but Larry was willing to take that chance. When he didn't piss away his money on booze and video poker, he could accumulate some cash. He took out a loan, bought a rig from an old guy, and fixed it up like new. Fishes, uh, fished, for salmon, halibut, whatever's running.

"So, he had a business, a small house, and now he wanted the girl of his dreams, never minding that she might be slightly soiled. He was no blushing virgin, himself. Besides, he was used to working on fixer-uppers, and she was good and ready."

Lou shook his head. "Jeez, you want kids like this to make it, and it breaks your heart when they die so brutally, needlessly."

"That sums up the feeling around here." Hilda nodded.

"And, I still can't get your idea of who . . ."

"Uh-uh, no." Hilda shook her head. "The more I think about it, the more I think it isn't a good idea. I'll be willing to do all I can to help. Hell, it'll be fun just to break the monotony, and none of the other media types has even bothered to come around. They're probably leaving already."

"Well, I'll be here for the foreseeable future. You can get hold of me at the Saltaire if you need me."

"That old rattrap? You can get a better room now."

Lou shrugged. "I don't mind the place. It's off the beaten track, clean . . ."

"It's off the beaten track, all right. Did Chloe soak you for the room?"

"She's charging sixty, but I may suggest that I can find other lodging now. I'll see if that brings the rate down."

"Okay, Lou. Now, scram. I got work to do."

Lou got up, and moved to the doorway.

"One more thing, Hilda. Isn't the police force a bit small even for a town of this size?"

"Not really," she mused. "The only time this place needs much policing is during spring break, when we get hundreds, maybe thousands, of drunken louts blowing off steam. Lester . . . have you met Lester?"

Lou nodded, frowning. Hilda laughed.

"By the look on your face, I can see you have. Lester hires one or two more deputies for the crowds. And, if there's any emergency, a riot, or something, there's the county and the state cops to fall back on. We have it covered.

"Oh, and there's another full-time deputy. He's out of town. Asked for time off for a family emergency in California, or something like that. So, there's two besides Lester."

"I've met Gar. He seems like there's more there than meets the eye."

"Good observation," she nodded, "I've got confidence that he'll develop into a real cop. Went to college for police work, and will someday get out from under Lester's shadow."

"Thanks, Hilda." Lou waved and exited.

"Anytime," she shouted at his back.

Lou drove back to the Saltaire. Chloe, hair still in rollers, was visible in the office, so he poked his head in. Chloe started.

"Hi, didn't mean to scare you," he flashed a friendly smile. "Mind if I come in?"

She looked at him with a wary eye. "Uh, nope."

"I'm thinking that I might look elsewhere for a room. Not that it's not nice here. Don't get me wrong, but for the same rate . . ."

Chloe made a sour face. "Thirty-five a night."

Lou smiled. "Deal. Retroactive?"

"Don't push your luck," she frowned.

"Chloe, right?"

"Right."

"It's a pleasure to do business with you. I'll see you later."

"Whatever." She glowered.

Lou went back to his room, noting the lack of cars in front of the other rooms, and singing, "All I Want is a Room, Somewhere."

He called Blanche to update her on his investigation. After a few undisturbed minutes, Blanche interrupted him.

"Hmmm," she thought aloud, "with the restrictions on salmon catches these days, a rival boat captain could have arranged this. You know, a turf battle?"

"Have to be a surf battle. Turf is on land."

"I stand corrected, wiseacre."

"No, really, it's worth looking into. I sure don't know anything about the hassles of salmon fishermen."

Lou heard a knock on the door.

"Hang on, Blanche."

Chloe stood outside with a pink message slip.

"Mr. Tadusky? Hilda wants you to call her."

"Thanks, Chloe."

"Hey," Lou said when he picked up the phone, "Hilda called. I can't escape these damn pink memo slips even out here."

"I don't know, Lou. You seem to be taking to this like you were made for it. Had I but known . . ."

"What?"

"Maybe we should have made you an investigative reporter right from the start. You know, some have greatness thrust upon them."

"Whatever I've had thrust upon me, it hardly seems like greatness. But, yeah. I'm kind of liking it."

"Later, dude," she said.

"Later, gator." Lou hung up, and dialed the number on the slip.

"Clarion," Hilda barked.

"Hilda? It's Lou. What's happening?"

"Lester called a press conference for six o'clock, at the Methodist Church. Be there, or be square." She told him how to find the church.

"Yeah, he mentioned he might have something to say. What do you think?"

"I think the District Attorney's office in Waldorf is putting some pressure on. Lester won't talk, so the media goes there, and the DA leans on Lester. This is a pretty high-profile crime for little ol' us."

"Hey, this would be front-page in Portland."

Hilda sighed. "We've arrived. Don't bother to congratulate us."

"See you later."

Lou hung up, sat down, and fretted over his notes.

SECTION TWO

What Is the Question?

1. Meet the Press

The church was straight from a calendar-art America, which Lou had never believed existed. Blinding white paint tinged with a red glow from the afternoon sun, a steeple with a belfry and a gold-colored cross resplendent against the sky, a small rose window above the door.

All this surrounded by a phalanx of newsies and their equipment: trucks, dish antennas, techs running around with skeins of cable and rolls of gaffer's tape, videographers toting cameras, and the overdressed, blow-dried, and otherwise tarted-up "talent," the pretty faces we see reporting the news.

Lou noticed especially the young Asian-American woman reporter he liked so much. She was stunning, and just like on the beach at the crime scene, she tried again in vain to keep her copy, her microphone, and her skirt under control in the strong breeze. Maybe she didn't own any slacks, he thought.

The press corps had all fled from the crime scene at the beach like a shady carnival blowing town one step ahead of the sheriff, and now they were here again. Lou stopped himself from making an unkind observation about their resemblance to flies when he realized he was there for the same reason.

He shrugged, and wove through the obstacle course of bodies and machines to the church steps. Hilda Truax stuck her head out of the church door and hissed at him.

"Psst!" She waved in Lou's direction.

Lou noticed her and hustled up the steps on his gimpy legs.

"Hello," he began. "Good to see you here."

"I wouldn't miss this for a dogfight." Hilda was dressed in a conservative business suit, but her long, silvery hair flew wild in the wind gusts.

"I heard that the DA's gonna be here," she said in a conspiratorial whisper. "Wait'll you get a load of him."

"From Waldorf? What's his name?" Lou poised his pen to take notes.

"Tom Knight, in all his glory. District Attorney of Klaskanine County, and reeking with ambition. We call him 'the Compass' here."

Lou's forehead wrinkled. "Why is that?"

"Because, wherever he is, his nose will point toward the nearest camera or microphone."

Lou laughed out loud and Hilda smiled a wicked smile.

"Why would he come down here?"

"Hey, this is a high-profile case. He's not gonna let this one get away without his name attached to it. And, legally anyway, it's his ballpark."

"Come on," she grabbed his arm, "we gotta get good seats."

They stepped from the small foyer into the church, and Lou was amazed by the amount of press and media.

"Jeez, look at all these people!"

Hilda looked around and just grunted. There were half a dozen TV cameras on tripods, and at least as many on the shoulders of roving camera people. The pews were near full of TV, radio, and print journalists and their various assistants. The church, already warm in the evening sun, was being slow-cooked from within by TV lights.

Hilda's eye never left the main chance, and she maneuvered Lou down to the second row. They were able to squeeze in on the aisle, to the consternation of a couple of NPR reporters too polite to resist.

Lou looked around. "Hilda, that's a San Francisco station, and that crew's from Vancouver, B.C. I expected Portland, and Seattle, maybe . . ."

"Yeah, and the guy in the gray suit is the local stringer for the *New York Times*. I've worked with him before on spring break stories. I wouldn't be surprised if the *L.A. Times*, maybe the *Washington* . . . Oh, here comes Lester."

At precisely six, Chief Green emerged from stage right, followed by Gar and the minister, whose face was slack-jawed and bemused. Green swaggered to the church podium, which was bristling with microphones and hung with dozens of cables.

The chief stood, arms crossed at the podium, impassive, until the hubbub died down. He reminded Lou of Yul Brynner in *The King and I*.

"If you're finished jabbering, we can start this circus," the chief drawled. Gar sweated, his eyes fixed on his boss.

"First, I'd like to thank Reverend McTeague for the use of the church." He nodded in the minister's direction. "I will make a statement of the facts, and take a few questions. There will be no calling out. Raise your hands and be recognized. You turn this into a feeding frenzy, and I'm outta here. Got it?"

The crowd rumbled with hostility.

Hilda leaned over to whisper, "Lester's happier than a pig in slop. He's got a room full of people hanging on his words." She snickered in Lou's ear, sending a thrill through him.

Lou kept staring at the tableau on the low riser that served as a stage. The arrogant chief, like Mussolini on the balcony; the minister on the verge of the vapors; and the stolid deputy, whose discomfort was evident in his bobbing Adam's apple.

Green began to speak.

"On July fourteenth, at approximately four forty-five in the morning, Shelley Korta, thirty, and Larry Narz, thirty-eight, were shot and killed by person or persons unknown. The victims were discovered about six-thirty by two people out walking their dogs. They called us immediately, and we responded by seven o'clock.

"When we discovered the bodies and established the crime scene, we determined that they had been shot by a large-caliber weapon, Shelley more than once. There were footprints and handprints in the area that may have some connection to the crime. This is being investigated.

"We have casts of the prints in question, and they have been sent to Waldorf for analysis." Lou was sure he saw Gar's eyes roll.

"At the present time, we have no suspects. Questions? And identify yourself and your media outlet."

"That's all?" called out a reporter. "We knew that yesterday." A general din erupted.

Green hitched up his belt, put his fingers to his lips, and emitted a piercing whistle. "Next one-a you gentlemen of the press yells out like that, it's over." More grumbling.

He pointed to a blonde in a short red dress. "Young lady?"

"Candy Bloomer, KWWI Radio news." Even Reverend McTeague smiled at that one. "Chief, were there any witnesses?"

"We're asking people to come forward. Next?" Green looked around, and found Lou's favorite, the pretty, mini-skirted TV reporter.

"Lana Kwan, First News Five. You said, 'person or persons.' Do you know how many were involved in the shooting?"

"No comment. Next? You there." Green pointed at another young woman, a long-haired brunette in a low-cut top.

"Carissa Stern, News Channel 7. Was it a robbery, or was there another motive?"

"No comment. Next?" Green looked around.

"Hey, how about choosing someone with a Y-chromosome, Chief?" a reporter yelled from the back.

"Yeah," another called out, "and how about some actual information?"

"Listen, you bloodsuckers," Gar cringed at the chief this time. "I won't compromise my investigation for your stinkin' little jobs."

Green took a few more questions, nearly always responding with a "No comment." Beyond that, the rest was sketchy. The crowd got restless and sarcastic, and Hilda was giggling into her hand.

Lou raised his hand on impulse, and was recognized.

"Chief, will this investigation proceed shorthanded, or will you ask for help from the county or the state?"

Green got red-faced. "Officer Loober and I can handle this just fine. We don't need help from nobody with the investigation, or with the regular police work around here."

"Follow-up, Chief," Lou went on. "The footprints had a distinctive sole pattern. Has it been identified?"

"No goddamned comment!"

A few in the crowd of reporters got to their feet and started shouting questions, when a loud crash resounded in the church. The church doors had been thrown open, and there stood a perfectly coiffed, Armani-clothed, and tanning-booth healthy man in his forties, with a small entourage huddling behind him.

"Tom Knight, in the flesh," Hilda murmured.

Knight surveyed the scene, and spoke some words to one of his minions, who scribbled madly onto a pad getting them down. Then, the DA strode toward the podium. Gar was about to swoon. Green went impassive, again.

As Knight went by him, Lou was reminded of an old movie where Richard Burton played a famous poet, and, wherever the poet went, even indoors, a breeze riffled his hair and fluttered his scarf, and a light shone on his face. The District Attorney had that same quality.

The assembled press began to yell questions as Knight moved toward the podium. Lou watched Green's face assume a tight-jawed, slitty-eyed look. Gar's Adam's apple was doing the polka. Knight raised his arms to silence the crowd, and ascended the low riser.

"Chief," he nodded at Green, as he hip-checked the cop away from the microphone. Lester made no effort to hide his contempt as he backpedaled away. Knight made a big show of greeting the minister, with a warm two-handed handshake. Knight's gaggle of followers assembled themselves in a line behind the DA.

Lou leaned over to whisper to Hilda, "They set up just like Gladys Knight and the Pips. Tom Knight and the Pups."

Hilda's guffaw was lost in the general hubbub.

Knight raised his arms again in the undiminished chaos, and spoke, calm and quiet.

"Now, we can't continue like this. Please settle down."

He spoke in such a low tone, that the crowd had to stop chattering just to hear what he was saying. Lou thought that a clever tactic, and one that Southern belles had used for years to hold attention.

The mob slowly composed itself. Knight pointed to a reporter.

"Ted, let's start with you."

"Tom, where are the victim's bodies?"

"They've been moved to Portland so that the state medical examiner can determine the cause of death, and anything else that might help us clear this case."

"Follow-up, Tom? Is the time of death sure at four forty-five? Do we know what they were doing on the beach that early? Was it a drug buy gone sour?"

"Whoa, Ted. You're conducting a personal interview, here." Knight looked at Green. "I'm pretty sure that's the estimated time, within some area of doubt, right, Chief?"

Green, grim-faced, nodded once.

"As to the rest, we won't speculate on anything like that at this point."

Knight pointed to another reporter. "Carissa? I know that if I don't get to you quickly, you become annoying and hard to get rid of. And," with a big smile, "I mean that in the nicest way."

Carissa Stern beamed. Knight was good, thought Lou. He just insulted this woman, and she liked it.

"Tom, do you have any confidence in Lester Green? This seems like it may be out of his league." She peered at Green as if he were an unsavory creature.

Chief Green looked daggers back at the reporter. Knight glanced at him, and put his hand on the chief's shoulder. Green flinched.

"Now, Carissa, there's no need to get personal. I have complete faith in these men, and the resources of the county and state are available to them for the asking.

"Bob, there in the back."

"Assuming the capture of the killers," the reporter yelled, "will you be asking for the death penalty?"

"First, you have assumed that there are more than one. We are not yet prepared to accept that as a fact. Is that right, Chief Green?"

Green grunted, and nodded his head.

"Second, this is aggravated murder. The law in Oregon calls for the death penalty in this case. Even if I wanted to, I couldn't seek a lesser sentence.

"Toni, are you all the way here from Seattle?"

"Hi, Tom," responded the venerable TV reporter, long on the crime beat and a respected newswoman. "Do we know what the weapon was?"

"It appears to be a large-caliber handgun." Knight leaned over to whisper something in Green's ear. Green's face bore an expression like he had discovered a tarantula crawling up his shirt. He responded to Knight with tight little nods or shakes of the head. Knight turned back to the podium.

"It's not been firmly established yet. Chief Green will have a follow-up conference in a few days to update you all.

I will be in touch with him on a daily basis as more information comes in. I know you've heard this before, but we can't, won't, release information that might jeopardize the investigation. All other information will be made available on a regular basis.

"Now, if you'll excuse us, I have to speak with Chief Green and Officer Loober. Thank you all for coming."

Knight waved to the assembly, and swept out, entourage in tow, smiling and ignoring the shouted questions. Green and Loober, heads hung down, followed.

Hilda nudged Lou in the ribs. "So, whaddaya think?"

"When I was a kid," Lou mused, "I saw Bobby Kennedy work a crowd. This guy has that same quality, that ability to make people listen. And," he winked, "I noticed that he managed to keep his good side to the cameras. He's slick."

"And ambitious," Hilda agreed. "He wants to ride this job into the governor's mansion, maybe the U.S. Senate. And these big cases are grist for his media mill."

"If there are media here from New York and San Francisco, this case is big news."

"So, what's next on your agenda?"

Lou thought for a second. "I guess I'll go back to the room and call my editor. Then, I don't know. A walk on the beach, some dinner."

"Well, if you want some company, give me a call." Hilda scrawled a phone number on a piece of paper torn from a reporter's notebook and handed it to Lou. "A girl doesn't get out much around here."

She slipped past him into the aisle, snapped a salute, and walked out of the church. Lou's eyes followed her out, and did not miss her trim shape or glorious mane. He wondered how old she was.

Back in the motel room, having slipped past the vigilant Chloe, Lou rang up the *Stump* and spoke with Blanche. He filled her in on the press conference.

"Dammit, Lou, you gotta file some copy on this. It's all

over the news, and you're there. The TV newsies get three or four minutes, and the *Oregonian* is sticking strictly to the facts. There probably won't be much else unless there's an arrest. Get us some human interest stuff, interviews, Pulitzer material. Don't you want a damn Pulitzer?"

"Hey, I'll settle for a decent dinner."

"Come on, Lou, work up some ambition here, if not for you then for the paper, for *me*." Blanche's voice was taking on a hysterical tone.

If you asked Lou later on, he would tell you that he felt something move here, clicking into place like the tumblers on a combination lock, and opening a chamber long shut. Only, he didn't know it at the time. He just got cranky.

"Aw, jeez . . ." Lou remembered what he owed Blanche and her father. "Yeah, sure," he answered, with as much enthusiasm as he could fake, "I'll start talking to people. I'd really like to talk with the dog walkers who found the bodies."

"That's the ticket, Lou. Who knows? You might dig it."

"Yeah, yeah. Talk to you later."

Lou fired up the ancient laptop and began to type a story. He whistled "Everything Happens To Me" as he typed.

2. On the Hunt

Velma Korta sat in her small house, watching the dark creep in. No light in the house was on, and the fire had died down to ashes. Their red glow was all that kept the gloom and chill away.

Velma had spent much time like this since her daughter's murder. Sitting and staring, her mind swinging from numbness to hyperactivity, running through Shelley's short life, or blotting it out.

Tiny and chill-prone, she was unable to stay warm even in summer. And, with her fire dying, the cold night air out on the coast made Velma uncomfortable enough to get up and stoke the ashes. She put another small log on to bring back the heat, and began to fidget. She needed some kind of activity.

Her mantlepiece held a picture of the head of Jesus, the kind making him look like a Nordic prince. Velma's church taught that Jesus was a Hebrew, who probably looked more like an Arab than a Swede, but she just liked the picture.

She went into her bedroom to get a sweater, and her eyes fell on the snapshot of Shelley on her dresser. It was her favorite photo of her daughter, taken just before her death. Shelley was healthy looking and smiling. The girl's long hair was blown straight out off her right shoulder, her eyes crinkled against the sunlight. In the lower left corner of the frame, Velma had inserted a small picture of Shelley as a little girl, in almost the same pose.

Grabbing the picture, Velma took it into the living room and set it up on the mantle. She placed the picture of Jesus alongside, and at an angle so that it faced the picture of her daughter. Then, she went to the kitchen for the emergency candles.

In a few moments, Velma had set up a kind of shrine, candles burning between the two pictures, and stood back to admire it. Falling to her knees, she began to pray for her lost daughter, and for the capture of her killer.

When the prayer was ended, Velma bundled up and went for a walk on the beach, promising herself that, this time, she would go nowhere near the scene of the crime.

It didn't take her long to break that promise.

Lou looked up and realized that the world had gone dark beyond the circle of light cast by the lamp in his room. And, he was stiff, tired, and hungry. He arose, and felt the bad knee resist. It didn't like being stuck in one position for a long time, and it had been a couple of hours at least.

"Maybe I need a walk," he said aloud, "and a sandwich, or something."

He saved the file, copied it on to a diskette for backup, and went to the motel-room door. It was cold and damp out there, and he grabbed his jacket and the baseball cap he had worn as manager of his old team. Faded and worn, it fit his head perfectly, as much an old friend as an article of clothing can be.

There was a little deli a few blocks from the motel, and Lou stopped in for a ham and cheese. The sandwich was made and served by a chubby blonde who had been lost in a teen magazine when he entered. It was prepared on a fluffy and undistinguished roll. He sighed, longing for the crusty hard rolls he remembered from before he moved west.

The ham, fortunately, was a good Westphalian, and the cheese was acceptable. Yellow mustard only, though, and no horseradish. He washed the whole thing down with a sugary fruit drink.

Lou tested the bored young girl behind the counter for information, but she was oblivious to everything that didn't directly concern the Backstreet Boys.

The evening mists were settling in and the moon was a hazy blur in the sky. He left his car in the deli parking lot and walked down to the beach. His knee ached from the damp and chill, and his limp became pronounced. But, he needed to walk.

And, much to his own surprise, he felt the need to try to absorb an impression from the site of the killings. Far from being a mystic, or trusting the indefinable, Lou was still drawn to try catching what Oregonians would call the "vibe."

If I'm not careful, he thought, I'll be dragging out the *I Ching* or casting runes before too long.

There was a nearby beach access, and he figured it was maybe half a mile down to the crime scene. Quick-marching through the soft sand, Lou sought the firmer sand near the surf to make the walk easier on himself. He set off down the beach, scrambling to avoid the occasional wave.

It felt like the first hint of autumn: rain or hints of rain in the air, sudden bursts of penetrating wind, warmth drained from his body. And, it was still July.

The strand was almost empty, except for the odd jogger or dog walker. It occurred to him that one of these might be the person who discovered the bodies, but he lacked the will to stop them to ask.

As Lou approached the area of the killings, he saw someone. The figure was small, hunched, and dressed in a bulky coat against the wind. When he got closer he saw flowers, homemade crosses, and messages left on the beach where the bodies had lain. And he heard crying.

The imprints of the two corpses were still evident in the sand, as were the dark stains from the blood. No one had walked on them, out of respect for the dead.

The scene gave Lou the creeps.

The bundled-up creature was a tiny, slender, middle-aged woman who stood and weeped, and he didn't want to scare her, so he cleared his throat. The woman startled anyway, and he held up his hands to reassure her.

"Don't be frightened," he spoke softly, "I was just passing by and I heard you crying. Are you all right?"

She sniffed and dabbed at her eyes and nose with a sodden tissue. "Oh, yes. I just can't believe she's gone."

"I'm sorry. Were you close?"

"She was my daughter."

"Oh!" Lou was nonplused. "I really am sorry. My name is Lou Tedesco."

"I'm Velma Korta." She offered a small, cold hand. Lou took it and squeezed gently without shaking it.

"I have to be honest with you. I'm a reporter, but getting the story here isn't as important as you losing your daughter, or that there are killers loose that need catching. Can I buy you a cup of coffee?"

Velma squinted up at Lou, her eyes red from weeping. She studied his face for a moment.

Acting on impulse, she replied, "Yes, I believe I can trust you." She sniffed back her tears.

"Thank you. Let's go to the Dunes."

Velma nodded, and Lou escorted her to his car.

All eyes fixed on them as they entered the Dunes Café. Phyllis and Connie were working the front, and there were a few tables occupied. Phyllis threw Connie a look and gestured them to the counter. Lou helped Velma sit down, and handed her a napkin from the holder. She dabbed her eyes and runny nose.

"Velma, honey, how're you doin'?" Phyllis reached over to pat Velma's hand. "My word, your hand is cold! Connie, get Velma some tea. Lou?"

"Got decaf?"

"Fresh made. I'll get it for you."

A few silent minutes later, Velma felt warm enough to take off her coat. She had a sweater on over jeans. Her hair was done up in a feathered, 1970s style, her face was lined, and she appeared older than she was, perhaps from her recent grief. Lou guessed that she was five feet tall, maybe ninety pounds. She clutched the hot teacup in her small hands, warming them with the heat.

"Tell me about Shelley," Lou opened.

"She was a good girl, you know?" Lou nodded at her upturned face, and her fierce green eyes.

"I know every mother says that. Charlie Manson's mother probably said that, but it was true about her." Velma hung her head. "We're religious people. When Shelley's father left, I found that Jesus was a comfort, and I joined a congregation hereabouts. I brought her up in my church, but she drifted away like the young kids do. Like I did, at her age.

"She was good in school, not a genius, but she did her homework and paid attention in class. Got mostly Bs. I expected her to go to college, maybe junior college first, then transfer to Oregon State." She sipped her tea.

"When she got to high school, she started datin'. Not many girls around here, and she was cute enough. She became boy-crazy, forgot her schoolwork, just barely graduated without havin' to go to summer school or gettin' a GED. By and by, she dated a boy from the wild crowd." She sought Lou's eyes. "A town this size, and they've got a wild crowd . . ." Her face was uncomprehending.

"Velma," Lou spoke quietly, "I played ball in more than one small town, and they all had a wild crowd, even if it was two people. The smaller the town, the more the kids seemed to need one."

"How did you resist them?"

"I didn't."

Velma smiled a knowing smile. "So, you understand?" Lou nodded.

Phyllis and Connie hovered as close as they could without being rude. Even Hetty came out when she wasn't cooking, and kept an eye on them. Lou began to squirm, a little, under their surveillance.

"How long did she hang out with these people?" he asked.

"Just long enough to make a mess out of her life. After she graduated, she got a job in a bar. I ain't necessarily against havin' a drink, although I don't indulge, myself. But, she was around it all the time, and then she started stayin' out. I finally told her that if she wasn't gonna respect my rules, she needed to be on her own. I figured she would need to save a few dollars for rent and food, and maybe not throw it all away.

"I was wrong. She moved in with a bunch of girls who shared rent, and boyfriends. All these little towns up and down the coast have kids like Shelley who find each other. Some come here, others go north or south to get away from the hometown and folks who know them. Shelley didn't go far in miles, but a long way down the wrong road." She pursed her lips. "I guess she was lucky she didn't get a *disease*." She uttered the last word with a stage-whisper hiss. Lou nodded.

"I don't know if this is true," Lou probed with delicacy, "but I heard that Shelley became pregnant." Velma's eyes grew large, then teared up. She sniffed, and nodded. Then, she began to sob. Lou apologized, and handed her another napkin. Phyllis and Connie were focused blatantly on the two of them.

"It's true," Velma went on when she collected herself. "And she . . . lost the baby. She went for an operation. You understand." It wasn't a question.

"Yes."

"It actually changed her. When God closes one door, He opens another. She straightened out, and came home. Got a job here," she gestured to indicate the café, "earned enough to tide her over, and decided to become a hairdresser. It wasn't exactly what I dreamed for her, but it's honest work, and she quit all that drinkin' and druggin' and runnin' around. It was a miracle, and I thanked God."

Lou steeled himself, and kept his face as expressionless as he could. "Velma, do you have any idea who the father was?"

He could hear the eavesdroppers gasp. He watched them as Velma responded. They were holding their collective breath.

"No, I don't." She shook her head.

Three sighs, one from Hetty, and some eye rolling. Velma seemed not to notice.

"Shelley never told me, and I never felt the need to ask her."

"Who were her friends?"

"Calvin and Troy, and their crowd."

"Are they still around, here in Seagirt?" Lou asked.

"Mostly. Calvin is a cop, one of Lester Green's deputies."

Lou jumped, almost losing his balance on the stool. "A cop?"

"Yes," she looked at Lou, "they've pretty much all grown up, like Shelley and poor Larry. Calvin Wheelock became a cop, Dub Gordon pumps gas out to the gas station on 101, Carla Higgins works at the video store. Henry Collins got the best job, he's the assistant manager up at the big market. Not exactly what you'd call careers, but they can pay the bills. Only two I ain't sure about from her old crowd . . ."

"Who?"

"Well, Phil Troy. He's Calvin's best friend, has been since they were little kids. He's still in town, but he mopes around a lot, and I can't think what he does for a livin'. And, Dunham."

"Dunham?"

"Stud Dunham. I don't even know his proper Christian name. Everybody just called him Dunham. He left town. At least I ain't seen him for a long time. Course, we don't go around in the same circles, if you know what I mean."

"I do, indeed. Would you like some more tea?"

"Oh, no, thank you so much. I feel a lot better. I shouldn't go . . . to that place on the beach. Something just pulls me there."

"Are you hungry?"

"Mr . . . ?"

"Lou, please call me Lou."

"I got to go home, Lou. I'll have something there."

She bit her lip, and got lost in thought for a moment. She looked into Lou's eyes.

"Will you promise me something?"

"Anything that's in my power."

"Will you make sure that Lester stays on this? He's good enough to keep the drunken kids from gettin' into too much trouble, but I ain't got much confidence in him for much else. Promise?"

Lou was not even sure he could keep the vow, but he felt compelled to assure her.

"I promise to do everything I can. I promise to help all I can."

"That's good enough for me. You know about sufferin'. I can see it in your eyes. You won't fail me."

Lou swallowed a lump which had appeared in his throat.

"Can I give you a ride home?"

"I'll walk. It ain't far. Good-bye, Lou."

"Good-bye, Velma."

He watched her bury herself in her clothing and walk out the café door. When he turned, three faces glared down at him: Phyllis, Connie, and Hetty. He looked back at them, trying to get into their heads. But he could not, and the moment was broken by a diner asking for a check.

More is going on here than I can figure, he thought. He paid for the drinks and left.

As soon as he was out the door, Connie leaped for the telephone.

An hour later, Velma sat in the kitchen waiting for her water to boil. A teabag sat in a cup waiting with her.

There was a knock on her door, and she arose to answer it. When she opened it, a grim-faced Jean stood before her.

"Well, twice in two days. You ain't ever visited me once before, and now it's gettin' to be a habit."

"You gonna ask me in, or what?"

Velma gestured grandly, and Jean swept in. Before she could ask her guest to sit, Jean began to wave a finger in Velma's face.

"You talked to that goddamned reporter, didn't you? I told you not to."

"Sit down, Jean. Take a load off. And, I'll ask you not to blaspheme in my house."

Jean blinked, taken aback at the blasphemy charge, but recovered.

"I can stand for the amount of time this'll take. I don't want you talking to that man."

"Now wait a minute," Velma's cool was gone, "I don't remember no one givin' you dominance over me. I talked to Lou because I believe I can trust him."

Jean jammed her hands onto her hips. "You never had any sense, and you sure haven't developed any in your old age. He doesn't care about you, or Shelley. All he wants is a damn story!"

"How do you know that? And, never mind my old age. You're ten years older'n me, if you're a day."

The teakettle began to whistle, breaking the mood, and some of the tension dissipated.

"Tea?" Velma asked.

Jean looked at the shrine on the mantelpiece, chewed her lip a bit, and relaxed.

"Yeah, sure."

Twenty minutes later, the women had arrived at a consensus. Jean found persuasion more effective than intimidation, and Velma developed doubts. They agreed that Velma should avoid Lou when possible, and be cautious when she couldn't. Jean couldn't instill actual hostility, but that was more a function of Velma's character than her lack of persuasiveness.

Jean left satisfied, and Velma was convinced that Lou might not be what he seemed. But, Velma was confused by Jean's interest. They had never been friends, and Jean didn't have any direct connection to the matter.

"I wonder what that woman's about?" she asked Shelley's picture.

Then, Velma put the kettle back on. This was at least a two-cup problem.

3. Here's Looking at You, Kid

Back at his motel room, Lou sat in the gloom for a while. The only illumination was from the parking-lot spots filtering through the sheer curtains, and they kept his room from being pitch dark. It suited his mood.

Lou wished he could read minds. He wanted to know if the women of the Dunes Café were observing his conversation with Velma because they were hungry for details, or they were afraid she would divulge something.

Every town has its little secrets, or its big ones. Sometimes, what is hidden is out of proportion to the size of the town itself.

He rubbed his damaged knee, aching in the cool and damp of the coastal night. The parts of him that really ached were harder to reach. Velma reminded him of little Patti, the *Stump*'s graphic artist and resident techno-music expert. Good, innocent, without evil thoughts, he believed. The longer he lived, the more he prized that quality, the more he felt moved to protect it. Velma was proof to him that goodness was not weakness. In a small way, it helped his own hurt to know that.

Lou thought back to the crime scene, to the women at the café, to Velma crying on the blood-stained beach. He knew a few things for sure: two people who deserved a break from life got none, something beyond his understanding lived just under the skin of the town like an infection, and he was committed to finding the truth.

Lester Green might find in himself the stuff it took to bring this case to a just end, but Lou doubted it. Green was hampered by his own limitations as a lawman, but more so as a man.

Then, Lou caught the faint light glinting off of the two bottles on the bureau. The glimpse of his own limitations brought him back to the matters at hand. Squinting, he snapped on the desk light, and grabbed the phone book.

He found the addresses of the Shoreline Foods supermarket and the Worldwide Video Rental. He already knew where the gas station was. Now, he thought, I'll get some rest and go to work in the morning.

Breakfast at the Dunes. When Lou walked in, Ronnie and Connie were standing head-to-head in a whispered conversation. Their faces showed a bit of shame when they saw Lou.

"Good morning Ronnie, Connie." Lou tipped an imaginary cap, and smiled.

"Mornin', Lou," Ronnie offered. "Girls say you were in here with Velma yesterday."

Lou decided to play it neutral, as much as he could.

"Yeah, well, I saw her on the beach, and she just seemed miserable. And cold. There's nothing to her, and that wind was freezing her to the bone. I brought her in for a cup of tea."

Ronnie seemed undecided about whether Lou was what he appeared to be. Connie was skeptical.

Ronnie nodded. "Yeah, I would've done the same. It's a good thing she's got her church. It's a comfort. I don't know what I would do if anything happened to Connie. I'm just like Velma that way; Connie's all I got in the world." She smiled at Connie. "Don't get yourself in trouble, little girl."

"Don't worry, Ma. I never did like those kids." Connie looked down, her face wrinkled with conflicting emotions.

Lou had assumed that Ronnie was Connie's mother, but this was the first time they had acknowledged it. Without another word, Connie walked into the kitchen, and the swinging door closed behind her.

Ronnie was biting her lip. She put her elbows down on the counter, and leaned toward Lou, speaking quietly.

"Lou, this is a complicated thing. We all feel real protective about Shelley, and we're worried about how this all is gonna play out, what with the papers and TV and all. Connie was never part of that bad crowd, but being good hasn't made her life wonderful. She wanted to leave town, go to Portland or Seattle, or even California, but . . . she was scared to go. This little place was safe, and she picked safe.

"Now," Ronnie sighed, "she feels stuck here. No boyfriend, no prospects, no life. She was making the best of it, and she got some hope from Shelley and Larry, from how they were gonna make their own future. After, um, it happened, she hasn't been the same. All the folks who come here have noticed. She's like a different girl. Moping, quiet . . ."

"Well, it's only a couple of days," Lou tried to ease her mind, "and she did lose a friend, and a hope."

Ronnie smiled a small, sad smile. "I know, but, there was a kind of light in her eyes, and the light went out. I don't know if I'll ever see it again."

Lou went for the brass ring.

"Ronnie, do you know who was the father of Shelley's baby?"

Ronnie's eyes closed to slits, her lips pursed.

"I . . ."

Lou could see the struggle played out on her face.

"I just don't know if there's any point."

"Here's what I think," Lou caught her eyes with his own, "I think that it's possible that the father resented the abortion, and that it festered long enough for it to cause this. There were two sets of footprints on the beach leading up to the murders, and away. I think the father and a buddy got boozed up and did it."

Ronnie thought about this for a while. "How did they know that Shelley and Larry would be on the beach at that time of morning? Answer me that."

"Good question." Lou had no answer. "Coincidence?"

"Not good enough." Ronnie's face was firm.

"Let me work on it. Can I get some breakfast?"

Ronnie straightened up to her full height. "Yes, sir. Coffee?"

After breakfast, Lou thanked Ronnie, and overtipped again. He said goodbye to Connie who had emerged from the kitchen while he ate, with a stricken look on her face. She struggled to give him an insincere smile, the best she could do.

He drove over to the Shoreline Foods market, parked the car, and went in. It was a typical small-town supermarket: a smattering of national brands, plus staples purchased from one of the corporations that services independents, locally-purchased produce and fresh fish, likely superior to the stuff in the big chains, and a friendly staff.

Lou walked up to a freckled teenage girl on a check-out line. "Hi!" He flashed a big smile.

"Hello, sir," she responded, her smile exposing a mouthful of metalwork.

"Can you tell me where I can find Henry Collins?"

"Yes, sir. Henry's the produce manager. If he isn't right around there, just ring the bell to the right of the apple bin."

"Thank you."

"Glad to help, sir."

There was something charming about the small-town ethic that Lou loved, and this cute kid personified it. He wondered why it took him so long to leave the East, then he remembered. No matter.

There was no one in evidence at the produce section, so he found the bell and rang it. He heard it ring somewhere behind the scenes. A moment later, a tall young man with a walrus mustache emerged.

"Can I help you?"

His name tag read "Henry." Dark hair curling at his collar, slender, and a bit uncomfortable in his corporate necktie, he looked more like a rock musician than a grocer.

"Are you Henry Collins?"

"Yes, sir. Something I can do for you?"

"I'm looking into the beach killings. I heard you were a friend of the victims. I'm sorry about your friends."

Henry Collins's face went pale. Lou thought Henry might pass out.

"W-what do you want, mister? I don't know nothin' about those killings." He grabbed the bins to steady himself.

"Don't worry, I'm not a cop. I only have a couple of questions."

"Look, mister, I don't wanna be rude, but I got a good job here. I can't . . ." he waved his hands in helpless circles.

"I'll cut to the chase. Do you know who was the father of Shelley Korta's baby?"

"What the hell do you need to know that for? It's ancient history, man."

Lou watched Collins's discomfort grow. "Because I think he might be the killer."

Collins's eyes popped out. "Oh, Jesus, man. Leave me alone. I don't know a damn thing, I swear."

"Come on, Henry. This is a small town. You must have known she was pregnant."

"I'm gonna call the manager. I don't have to talk to you."

Henry was starting to sweat. Lou shrugged, and attempted to play with the man's head.

"Okay, call him. Maybe he knows more than you do. I'll get him. What's his name?"

"Oh, Jesus, no. Wait, wait . . . Shelley had a boyfriend at the time, maybe it was him. I swear I don't have no idea if it ain't him."

"What was his name?"

"Oh man, I don't remember. Some dweeb. Freddie? Frankie? I don't remember."

Lou held up his hands. "Okay, relax. Thanks. Take my card, in case you remember something more."

Lou turned to leave, while Collins hyperventilated behind him.

When Lou left the store, Collins called out, "Paul!"

The assistant manager stuck his head out of the door at the back of the produce department. "Yeah, Henry?"

"Keep an eye on things for a few minutes. I got a personal errand."

"Sure, boss."

Collins tore off his apron, threw it at the produce bins, and walked to the front doors. He watched Lou get into his car, and ran out when Lou cleared the parking lot.

Back in the car, Lou decided that this might be a good time to top off his gas tank, and drove over to the Snack-n-Drive. He had been glad more than once that Oregon wouldn't allow people to pump their own gas, on cold, windy, and otherwise inclement occasions. Now, that law would allow him to initiate a conversation without causing alarm.

When he pulled in, the pump jockey came over to ask what he needed. His name patch read "Dub."

"Fill it with the cheap stuff. Uh, it may not need much. My gas gauge is shot."

"Hey, no prob," said the sandy-haired kid in the greasy coverall. "High school kids still ask for two bucks worth for a night of cruising." He opened the gas tank and inserted the hose.

Lou got out of the car, and busied himself cleaning his windshield. "Lot of excitement around here," he opened.

"Huh! Tell me about it! I musta given a hundred people directions in the last couple days. 'Where's the beach?' 'Where's the church?' If I'd sold all of 'em gas, that'd be one thing . . ."

"So, you think it was the killings?"

"Hell, yeah. I mean, after spring break we get some tourists here in the summer, and the weekends are busy, but I never saw nothin' like this."

"Shame about those kids," Lou was running the squeegee over his rear windshield. "Did you know them?"

"Are you kiddin'? I useta hang out with 'em. Larry Narz and me pounded some beers together. Shelley hung out with us, too. We were wild," he said with some pride.

"Guess there's not much to do in a small town like this?"

"You got that right. Wintertime is just dark and rainy." He lowered his voice. "All you got to do is drink and screw."

Lou laughed. "There's worse ways to kill time."

"Yeah," laughed Dub, "and I did them, too."

"I heard that one of the deputies ran with your crowd."

Dub checked the gas counter, which had stopped at just over six dollars.

"You didn't need much gas. Only six-twenty."

"Yeah, I better get that gauge fixed." Lou reached into his pocket and pulled out a ten. "Got change?"

"You bet." He flashed a roll of bills and jingled change in his coveralls. Lou handed Dub the ten and he made change, counting out the coins slowly.

"Is there a soda machine here?" Lou asked.

"Soda? You mean pop. You must be from back east."

"Yeah. Old habits die hard."

"Over there, by the air pump." Dub gestured in a vague way.

Lou pulled the car over to get it away from the pumps. He parked it, and called out, "Can I get you a drink?"

"Wouldn't mind a Coke." Lou nodded and fed coins into the machine. He walked over and handed Dub the can.

"So," Lou asked, opening his iced tea, "it's true about the deputy?"

"Oh, yeah! Calvin. Funny he became a cop. He was totally out of his mind. Born to raise hell." Dub chuckled.

"You know," Lou said between sips, "my mom grew up in a neighborhood where all the kids were tough kids. Petty thieves, fighters, real delinquents. She said half of them became cops and the other half priests."

Dub laughed out loud. "I guess Calvin ain't so unusual after all. We got to be good friends for a while. Hung out a lot."

"For a while? You guys have an argument?"

"No, uh-uh. In fact, I still talk to Calvin because the cops gas up here. We just don't hang out anymore."

"Was it a girl that got between you?"

"No, man, it was Phil."

"Phil who?" asked Lou, disingenuously.

"Phil Troy. Calvin's oldest buddy, one major weirdo, but stuck to Calvin like a tick. It got so I couldn't stand bein' around him, so I kinda drifted away. It was a package deal: you want Calvin, you gotta take Phil. If Phil was a chick, I'd say he was jealous."

Lou thought on that a moment.

"Speaking of girls, you said you knew Shelley, too?"

"Yeah, there was a bunch of girls livin' in a house on Shoreline Road, mostly town girls like Shelley, or from nearby. Calvin, poor Larry, me, a few other guys, we used to hang out, get drunk, smoke some dope," he winked, "fool around a little. Party hardy, dude!"

"I hope you guys were careful. These days, jeez, diseases left and right. Or, just knocking a girl up is enough trouble."

"Hey, I guess we were lucky. No herpes or AIDS, nothin' like that. It was just us, so nobody was exposed. Couple-a girls got pregnant, though."

"So, are you a daddy?"

"Not if I can help it," Dub laughed. "They got operations, you know?"

"Sure. It wasn't legal when I was a kid, not like now."

"What a drag!" Dub seemed sympathetic. He sipped his pop.

"I heard that a guy named Dunham used to live here. He still around?"

"Stud? He's long gone. He was a bad one. Scared the crap outta me. He . . ." Dub looked around, "he was the local dope connection. Nothin' heavy, no smack. A little coke, some pills, lotsa weed. Dope dealers never have problems getting the chicks. He got laid like a rock star." Dub looked at Lou with unease. "You ain't a cop, right?"

"No," Lou shook his head. "He ever get a girl pregnant?"

Dub shrugged. "No clue. I don't care about that stuff. None of my business."

"Where'd Stud go?"

"Lotsa stories. Some say he went to L.A. Some to Vancouver, in Canada, because they grow this great dope up there. My own personal opinion is that he hooked up with one of the biker gangs he used to do deals with. Just before he took off he got himself a restored Harley, classic bike. Beautiful machine."

"Been gone long?"

"Maybe five, six years? Not much longer."

Just long enough to be the possible father of Shelley's baby? Lou wondered to himself.

Dub drained the drink, and tossed the can in the We Recycle bin.

"It's been fun talking to you," Lou grinned at Dub. "I've been in town for a few days, and I like it here. Probably hang out for a while. Oh, just one more thing. You ever hear of a guy named Freddie, or Frankie? I heard he was Shelley's boyfriend for a while."

"Freddie the Freak? What a bozo! He used to follow Shelley around like a puppy dog. Had a crush on her all through school, but she wouldn't give him a look. After Shelley quit hangin' out, got straight, all that, they went around for a while. That's when I knew that Shelley was out of it for good."

"Why's that?"

"He was a geek, big, goony fat guy with pimples. Dorky clothes, bad hair . . . I couldn't figure why Shelley gave him the time of day. She wasn't bad-looking. I thought it was like . . . whaddaya call it when you try to make up for your sins?"

"A penance?" Lou offered.

"Yeah, that. Kinda made sense, since he was a Jesus freak." Dub looked at Lou. "Uh, you ain't religious, are you."

"Don't worry."

"Whew! No sense pissing off a customer." Dub rolled his eyes.

"So, where's Freddie these days?"

"Gone. Outta here." Dub shrugged an eloquent shrug.

"He's gone, too? Funny. Know where he is?"

"No idea. One thing I do know."

"What's that?"

"He ain't hangin' out with Stud Dunham."

Lou laughed. "Gotcha. Thanks for talking to me."

Dub gave him a hard look. "Hey, are you sure you ain't a cop? State, or something?"

"No, I'm not a cop, but I've gotta be honest with you. I am investigating the murders. I'm a reporter."

Dub's eyes opened wide. "Whoa! Cool! Am I a source? Do I get my name in the story?"

"Depends on whether your information leads to anything." Lou got cagey. "I can then either quote you by name, or as an anonymous source."

"No, no, mention my name and the gas station. I'm tryin' to buy into it, and we could use the publicity."

"You sure? It may not work out the way you think."

"I'm sure, I'm sure." Dub was very excited.

"Okay," Lou shrugged. "Here's my card. I'm at the Saltaire for the next couple of days. Call me anytime."

"Hey, and you come back any time. I owe you a pop."

"See you later." Lou drove off to the video store.

As he drove away from the station, Lou processed what Dub Gordon had told him. He was fixated on Shelley Korta's pregnancy and convinced that it was in some way the key to the whole tragic event. It could have been almost anyone in that crowd, if Dub's tales were not exaggerated. It could even have been Freddie, getting close to Shelley in a vulnerable time, and later being outraged by her decision to end the pregnancy.

Since the video store was on his list, and Chloe rented VCRs, he checked the address and drove over. He felt like seeing *Casablanca,* his favorite movie, full of sentiment, noble self-sacrifice and sappy idealism. He tried to see it at least once a year, and it was just the tonic for washing away the bad taste of murder.

Worldwide Video sat in a strip mall across from the mediocre deli. The space was small for a Worldwide, which usually occupied most of a city block, but this was not a big city. As long as they had plenty of copies of the latest star vehicle, or gross-out teen comedy, they would do fine.

Lou entered the shop, setting the bell to jangling on the door. There were two clerks, a teenage boy and a woman in her early thirties. Lou worked on an entree into more questions as he walked up and down the aisles and scanned the boxes for *Casablanca.*

He was amazed at his own ability to misrepresent himself to gain information. Perhaps he had found something else to be good at, besides starting an elegant double play, or hitting the curveball. He was getting pretty adept at throwing the curve to the people he questioned, if he had to think so himself.

He found the video, under Classics, and took it up to the front desk. The young man came over to check him out.

"Hi," he said to Lou, "did you find what you wanted?"

"You bet." Lou set the box down on the counter.

"Wow, what a great movie. What a babe that Ingrid Bergman was!"

Lou smiled. "Right, and right. About perfect, both of them, Ingrid and the flick."

"I wonder," the kid mused, "if there was ever anything like Rick's American Café?"

"Not in the real world. But, that's the beauty of the movie; it takes you to a place which *should* exist. When I was your age, I wanted the world to be worthy of Rick and his saloon."

"Can I check you out?"

"Yeah, I'm staying at a motel, the Saltaire? Is it okay for me to rent a video?"

"Heck, yeah. I'll even throw in a cleaning cassette. Chloe's machines never get any maintenance. Run the cleaner through before you play the movie. Instructions are right on the box." He reached under the counter, grabbed a yellow-cased video cleaner cassette, and set it next to *Casablanca.*

"You're all right. What's your name?"

"Danny."

"Thanks, Danny. Say, do you know a Carla Higgins? I was told to look her up."

Danny laughed. "Heck, yeah, I know her. She's my sister. Carla?" He called to the woman, who was checking inventory across the store. "Man here wants to see you."

Danny asked for a driver's license, and Lou's room number at the motel, which Lou provided. Carla came over while the business was being transacted.

She was dressed in brown slacks and a plain beige blouse, her brown hair caught back in a ribbon that matched her blue eyes. "Everything okay?" she asked.

"Hi," Lou extended his hand. "My name is Lou. A friend back in Portland told me this was a terrific video store, and told me to ask for you."

She seemed puzzled. "I wonder who that could've been. No big deal. Lots of people from Portland come through here all year. Did you find what you wanted?"

"Oh," Lou gestured toward Danny, "this young man has been extremely helpful, and he knows movies, too."

Danny beamed, and Carla smiled at him.

"In fact, he's a fan of my favorite movie . . ." Carla glanced at the video and smiled, ". . . and," Lou went on, "of Ingrid Bergman."

"Danny is a fan of every beautiful movie star there ever was. I don't think too many eighteen-year-olds know about Louise Brooks these days."

Lou whistled, and didn't have to fake being impressed.

"Another beautiful movie star, all right. Poor Ingrid went through a lot, though."

"Like what?" Danny asked.

"She had an affair with a married man, and gave birth to his child. Not the kind of thing that bothers too many fans these days, but in the forties people stopped going to her movies. It took a while for her to live that down."

"Oh, yeah," Danny brightened. "I've heard about that. Isn't Isabella Rossellini her daughter?"

"Sure enough," said Lou, "and Roberto was the man Ingrid hooked up with."

"He was a director, right?" Carla added.

"Right," Lou confirmed. "I don't know what options Ingrid had in those days, but she kept the baby, and eventually married Rossellini."

"Well, a lot of girls are keeping their babies nowadays, and they have more, um, options, like you said." Carla looked thoughtful, and wary.

"I hate to bring this up," Lou said, "but I heard that the poor girl who got killed once got into trouble with a boyfriend."

Carla reacted as if she had been slapped. "Danny," she said to her brother, "is this man checked out?"

"Uh-huh."

"Do me a favor, and straighten up the Kids movies shelf. I think some of those videos have been misfiled."

"Sure," Danny replied, and headed off.

"Mister," she turned toward Lou, spoke quietly, "please don't be offended, but I'd rather you didn't bring that up in front of Danny. It's hard enough for us grownups to deal with that. He'll hear more than he needs to from his friends."

Lou's cheeks burned.

"I really do apologize. It was crass of me to bring that up," Lou looked ashamed, reflecting his true feelings. He wondered if anyone could do this kind of probing without some personal agony.

"I knew Shelley real well. I hate to hear her memory soiled."

"Yeah, it's bad enough for me to have said that, but it's worse if you knew her. I guess you're about her age." Lou couldn't believe the words coming out of his mouth. He was like a hound on a scent.

"We hung out, went through a lot together" she said through clenched teeth.

Uh oh, back off, he thought. Hating himself, Lou tried another tack.

"You must know Calvin and Phil."

"You bet. I haven't seen them for a couple of days, but they come in here a lot."

"Really? They like classic movies, too?"

"Not really. Cop flicks and crime documentaries, mostly. Calvin says he's doing research, being a cop and all. Lately, they've been hung up on a TV miniseries of *In Cold Blood.* They rented it maybe six or eight times recently."

"The Capote book?"

"I guess," she shrugged. "I told them there was a movie that was probably better, but they like that TV series. They rent it almost as much as that X-rated stuff." She wrinkled her nose in disgust.

"Did you pay for *Casablanca* yet?"

Lou nodded

"You want a freebie? To make up for me yelling at you?"

"Thanks, but not necessary. You were absolutely right, and Danny's lucky to have a sister like you."

"Due back in three days," Carla said.

"Oh," Lou asked on a whim, "what do you know about the Bijou?"

"That old theater they just renovated? Not much. Nice work. It looks great."

"Have you met the owner?"

"Just briefly." She frowned. "I thought we might work up a mutual promotion, so I approached him, but, I guess he sees me as a competitor."

"Is he from around here?"

She shrugged. "Could be. If he lived twenty miles north or south of here, we might never run into each other. The boys knew more kids because of the sports teams. Why do you ask?"

"I don't know. I seem to be asking a lot of questions these days. Thanks."

"See you soon."

Lou left, and wanted to kick himself in the behind, but his bad knee precluded that, so he just felt miserable for a while.

Next on the agenda was a visit to the Bijou. Lou parked and locked the car in the municipal lot across the street from the theater, and went to the theater's front doors. Cupping his hands on the glass, he peered inside. He knocked. A tall, young man trotted up from somewhere and opened the doors. He was dressed in a 1940s-style double-breasted suit, and a wide floral tie.

"Lou?"

"Yup. Anthony, I presume?"

"Right." They shook hands. "That reminds me, we're showing *Stanley and Livingstone* in September." Anthony gestured Lou in.

"Spencer Tracy. 'Dr. Livingstone, I presume?' "

"Right, again," Anthony laughed. "I was just making some espresso. Want a cup?"

"You bet."

"Feel free to look around. I have to make a quick call, and then I'll get the coffee."

Fifteen minutes later, they shmoozed over a cup, and Lou got pictures of the old theater, prerenovation, and some of the new one. Anthony was charming and glib, expensively tailored and barbered. He had striking blue eyes.

"The place is beautiful," Lou indicated the theater's glitzy interior. "It reminds me of the old Paramount, only not quite so . . ."

"Enormous? Thanks. This place used to have a big pipe organ, but it's gone now."

"I love that you're opening with *To Have and Have Not*. It's a great flick."

Anthony looked shamefaced.

"We were supposed to have *Casablanca*, but the print couldn't get here in time. We'll show it later in the season."

Lou laughed. "That's very funny. I just rented it from Worldwide Video. It's my favorite of all time."

"Yeah, me too. Do you think you can make the opening on Friday? I'll comp you."

"Wow, that's really tempting. But, well, my life is a bit unsettled right now. I'm, um, involved in a few things."

"So I've heard."

"You've heard? What?"

"Hey," Anthony said, "this is a small town. The killings are the big news, you and the Bijou are tied for second. Basically, all I heard is that you're investigating. True?"

"True. Can't say I've made much headway."

"Look," Anthony said, "I'm in the middle of setting up the schedule on the computer. Is there anything else?"

"No, no. Thanks for the coffee, which, by the way, is the best in town."

Lou walked over to his car, and noticed a note trapped under his windshield wiper. He opened it and read,

KEEP YOUR NOSE OUT OF THIS TOWN.
GET OUT IF YOU KNOW WHAT'S GOOD
FOR YOU. YOU BEEN WARNED.

He looked around, but there was no one to see. The writing was a childish block lettering; the message wasn't kid stuff.

First things first, Lou thought. I've got to take this note to the police.

Chief Green was sitting in his patrol car in the police station lot reading when Lou got there. He looked up at gave an exasperated snort when they made eye contact.

"Somethin' I can do for you?" he asked with exaggerated insincerity.

Lou walked over to the car and showed Green the note. "I found this on my windshield just now, while I was parked in front of the Bijou."

The chief read it and snickered.

"You have an odd sense of humor, Chief Green. Are you amused by all threatening notes you see?"

"First of all, there ain't any overt threat. They don't say what they're gonna do. Second, how do I know you didn't write this yourself, to get some sex appeal for your damn story?"

Lou could feel the blood rising in his face. He took a deep breath, for control.

"Forgetting the insult for a second, isn't it your job to check something like this out?"

"Look at this note," the chief waved it at Lou, "it's written on paper torn off a cheap pad. You can probably buy this kind of paper in a thousand places, and that's just in Oregon. What if it came from California, or Idaho? It's possible.

"It's written in ballpoint ink, and I'll bet the rent that it's one of those cheap stick pens you buy by the dozen in any store."

"What about fingerprints?" Lou hoped he wasn't whining.

"What about them? I send this off to the state lab, maybe we get some prints. Yours, mine, the guy who wrote the note? What if his prints ain't on file?

"You stuffed this in your pocket, right? Didn't do the, *ahem*, evidence any good. You shoulda called me right away. We might've been able to collect it in a professional way. Like this," he thrust it back at Lou, "it's damn-near worthless."

Green's slitty-eyed look finished the implied sentence: a lot like you. Lou was tired of getting these kinds of looks, and recalled that this was one reason he quit doing investigative work.

Lou sighed. "Okay, if this happens again, I'll call."

"Look, Tedesco, you're gettin' in someone's face, besides mine. They just want you to mind your own business. Why don't you just let us do our job? We'll provide updates, when we can."

Green smiled. It sent Lou a chill.

"Yeah, okay, Chief. Sorry to bother you."

Green started the patrol car and drove off. He dropped the note out the car window, wiggling his fingers like something was stuck to them.

Lou collected the threatening scrap, just because.

Henry Collins was breathing heavily, panting, although he hadn't exerted himself. Not physically, at least. He could barely dial the phone.

"Hello?"

"I did it. What now?" Henry asked between gasps.

"We wait and see. It may scare him off. If not, we'll think of something."

"Do me a favor, and don't include me."

"Henry, I'm surprised at you. You told me that you wanted to be in on this."

"Yeah," the produce manager's nose developed a whistle, "but I didn't know . . ."

"What? That it would be this much fun? Aren't you having fun?"

"I'm sorry I ever got into this. I got a life, here."

"And a pathetic little life it is. Or, so you told me. Isn't your life more exciting now?"

"Any more of this kind of excitement might kill me."

"We'll see what we can do to avoid that. Do you have to get back to the store?"

"No, my shift's over." Collins had a sudden chill. "Why?"

"Well, then, enjoy your evening at home with . . . Valerie, is it?"

"Yeah, Valerie, like you needed to ask."

"The Valerie I remember was a hot, little girl who loved to drink gin, shotgun pot smoke, and screw her brains out. The Valerie I see now is a boring, overweight housewife. A lot like you, in fact. Okay, you're not overweight. I'll give you that."

Collins winced. "Hey, we all grow up. Things change." It sounded weak, but it was the best he could do.

"Tell me about it. Good-bye, Henry."

The phone clicked in Henry Collins's ear.

Lou drove back to his room, and called Blanche with an update.

"Hmmm . . . so, you must be stepping on someone's toes. Are you scared?"

"Not really," Lou fibbed. "I'm starting to think there really is a story here."

"But, everyone is clamming up on the father of the dead girl's baby?" she asked.

"It seems so."

"Do you think that this is the key to this case? Or, is it just annoying you that no one will talk about it?"

Lou thought for a bit. "A fair question. It *is* frustrating that the wall of silence is there, but this looks like a motive to me. First, the father of the baby, whoever it might be, could easily have had second thoughts about the abortion, or might have opposed it from the beginning. Because Shelley engaged in casual sex with a bunch of guys, all are potential suspects in my book."

"Lou, two days ago you were a restaurant critic. You're starting to sound like Perry Mason, here."

"Hey," Lou protested, "strictly your fault. I was content with living out my golden years complaining about underspiced Massaman curry, or overcooked pasta, and trashing Hollywood blockbusters. You're the one that resurrected my past calling. I am your Frankenstein monster, so live with it."

"Okay, you got me there," Blanche sighed. "How many guys are we talking about?"

"No clue for sure. I'm guessing five or six in the crowd, and that she didn't necessarily give it up . . ."

"Ooh, I hate that phrase." Lou could imagine her shuddering on the other end of the phone.

"I picked it up listening to the baby hipsters around the office. There is no reason to believe that she had relations with all the men in her group. Is that better?"

"Mmmph."

"Okay," he continued, "there's one guy named Dunham, the local gangster. Dope dealer, biker, tough guy. Naturally, all the guys were in awe of him, and, as we know from listening to country music . . ."

"Ladies love outlaws," Blanche sang, with an exaggerated twang.

"QED, as the logicians might say. He's been gone for a few years, but he was here when Shelley became pregnant."

"But, if he's gone, how could he do it?"

"Gone might not be long gone. Dub thinks he hooked up with a gang of bikers, and they are nothing if not mobile and nomadic."

"Yeah, but then how would he know where to find her at that very moment?"

"Another good question, and coincidence is never good enough, but not out of the question."

"I love it when you confuse me. Who else?"

"Okay, there's Freddie the Freak."

"Now, *he* sounds like a biker."

"Not unless he's undergone a complete change. He was Shelley's boyfriend for a while, and very religious. Freddie got his nickname from the wild kids, who, and I'm guessing here, disapproved of him as much as he disapproved of them. He left town, also, but I haven't found out yet why or when. Aborting his baby might have done it. And, it might have left lasting bitterness. He hasn't been seen, according to Dub, but Dub is not the kind of person Freddie would want to look up."

"What about the cops?"

"I really don't know. Tom Knight has taken an active interest in the case, and he won't let it go if his name is associated with it. That should move the progress along. Chief Green is an x-factor. I can't read the man's intentions.

Deputy Loober is a good kid, but I don't know if he can goose Green along from his lowly station as deputy."

"*There's* an attractive image. How long are you gonna be there?"

"I'll feel better about coming back when I have a few more facts. I want to know more about Freddie and Dunham, for example, and I want to see if the cops interview any of the old crowd they hung out with. If I had to guess, I would think the answer will emerge from that source. Plus," he added, "there will be a follow-up news conference when more facts are in."

"Okay. I'm willing to go with your judgment on this. Keep me posted."

"Want any restaurant reviews?"

"If you're so moved. Not a priority."

"What about the Bijou? It's a nice story, as opposed to the one I'm spending most of my time on."

"Yeah, okay, but a higher priority than the food stuff."

"Over and out," Lou signed off.

Then, he called a local pizza delivery, and rented a dented VCR from Chloe. Dutiful always, he cleaned the VCR heads, then, plugged the tape in. Here's looking at you, kid, he thought.

4. Shell Collecting

The next morning, the willies were back.

Lou rolled around on the lumpy mattress, disturbed by his dreams, his heart fluttering like a startled bird in his chest. When it seemed that he would not be getting that last hour of sleep after all, he lurched up and got out of bed.

His knee was throbbing, as it always had when he pushed himself. He headed for the bathroom to get himself ready for the day.

Showered, shaved, dressed, and starving, he planned to go out for breakfast, but not at the Dunes Café. When he opened the room door, there were two pink phone messages taped to it.

Dub Gordon had called that morning asking for Lou to call him back. Lou spun on his good heel, and headed back to his room phone.

"Snack-n-Drive," a voice answered.

"Dub there?"

"Hold the phone." The receiver clunked down. A few moments later, Dub picked it up.

"Yeah, this is Dub."

"Hi, this is Lou Tedesco. You called?"

"Yeah, wait a sec." Lou heard footsteps.

"I hadda close the door. I just remembered something. The last time I saw Troy, he told me he 'scored a nine.' Just like that."

"Phil Troy told you what?"

"He got a gun, man. A nine millimeter. He told me that."

"You're sure about this?"

"Hope to die, man. It was about a week ago, not even. At a gun show in Waldorf."

Lou ran his fingers through his hair, over and over.

"Did you ask why, or what for?"

"Hey, I don't talk to Troy unless it's necessary. I pumped his gas, end of story. He didn't say nothin' after that, either."

"Do you believe him?"

"Hard to say, he's such a little twerp. He didn't show me it, or nothin'."

"Dub, I appreciate this."

"So, am I a good source?"

"You're great, especially . . . well, let's see what happens. Stay in touch."

"Later, man."

"Later." Lou hung up, and looked at the second phone message. It was from someone named Lucy Persson. "Call me," it read, "because I can help you. I am a psychic, and have worked with the police."

"Just what I need," he said aloud, "help from the psychic BS network."

Lou limped out to his car. I need to think, he thought, and drove to the beach.

Like Velma, he found himself drawn to the site of the murders. Only, he thought, with much less reason. He sat on a driftwood log, and sulked. No fresh insights arose, and he sighed, gave up thinking about the crime, and enjoyed the beach. It was a cloudy day, not as windy as it had been, and cooler. The sun emerged from between cloud banks, and the beach warmed up quickly. He rolled up his sleeves, and took out his sunglasses.

There were a dozen scattered blankets, each with a small party of people, and a widely spaced parade of walkers and joggers along the beach.

Lou then noticed a scruffy, grizzled man dragging a Rube Goldberg apparatus through the sand, and he knew just what it was: a sand sifter.

He had made them as a kid, to comb the sand on the beaches near his house. He hadn't seen one used for years. It was a three-sided wooden frame with heavy-duty, quarter-inch screening on the bottom, and two long handles reaching up at an angle from each side, and the open end toward the back. It was made from scrap wood, old fruit crates. This one was a close copy, except the handles appeared to be fashioned from PVC pipe.

Modern materials, Lou thought.

Drag the box through the sand, and whatever is buried in it stays in the screen. Ninety-nine-point-nine percent of the stuff was garbage: cigarette butts, bottle caps, popsicle sticks. The rest ranged from loose change to lost jewelry. His friend Chowderhead had found a diamond engagement ring, returned to the owner for a $50 reward, a fortune to a kid in those days, a week's salary to many. At worst, you got money for candy or a movie. At best, it was a gold mine.

Lou watched the man dragging the sifter. He recalled the drill: Pull it for a few yards, lift and shake it, go through the gleanings, repeat until bored. An idea snaked its way into Lou's mind.

He got up, and walked over to the beachcomber.

"Hi. I haven't seen one of those since I was a kid."

The man seemed startled. He was bearded, scruffy, and overdressed for the beach. He wore a John Deere cap, sweat pants, and a sweatshirt, all soaked with sweat, and worn-out sneakers held together by duct tape.

His eyes were rheumy in his leathery face, and he squinted. His mouth worked before he spoke, as though it needed to be reminded how to form words.

"This ain't yours. I made it myself." He grabbed the handles tighter.

"Yes, of course. I just wanted to look closer. We never had that plastic pipe. The whole thing was made of crate wood. Used to steal it from the grocer's."

A grin split the man's face. "This way ain't as heavy. I'm gettin' too old."

Lou laughed. "Yeah, aren't we all? How'd you like to lend me that for a little while?"

The man gave Lou a suspicious glare. "This is my territory."

"Understood. You can sit right here and watch me use it. I'll give you ten bucks just for a few minutes."

"What if you find somethin' good?"

"It's yours. I'm looking for a specific item."

The man turned it over in his mind. "Deal," he said, a few seconds later.

Lou offered the man his seat on the log, and took the sifter. Walking over to the crime scene, now free of yellow tape, he began methodically to draw the device through the sand. He cringed as the sifter disturbed the area of the fading bloodstains.

Twenty minutes later, after the usual detritus was discarded, and the seventy-six-cent king's ransom was remitted over to his companion, Lou turned up a shell casing. He reached into his pocket and took out a tissue. He picked up the spent cartridge with care, wrapped it in the tissue, and put it back in his pocket.

Lou was well aware that people in Oregon fired weapons with impunity, often in state forests and public spaces like this beach, and that this shell was not likely to be connected to the case. But, he was aware, too, that 9 mm pistols ejected spent shells. If the killers had tried to collect them, they might have missed one in the sand, in the near-dark, and it might have been trodden under by onlookers.

In a moment, the memory of his visit to the police station faded, and the hunt was on again. He gave the sifter back to the man, and thanked him, offering him a twenty.

"Uh-uh. We made a bargain for ten. Ten it is."

Lou smiled at the man in appreciation. "I wish everyone I did business with was as scrupulous as you."

"Find what you was lookin' for?"

Lou shrugged. "Don't know, but a definite maybe."

"You ever need to rent my equipment again, you let me know. Just ask for me."

"What's your name?"

The man picked up his cap and scratched his balding head. "Jim Twitchell's my handle, but just ask for Nutty Bud. That's how they call me."

Lou shook Twitchell's hand, and walked off the beach as quickly as his bum leg would let him.

5. Contacting the Authorities

Now Lou had to think. He had a cartridge casing, which looked very new and still smelled of burnt powder, and he needed to turn it in to someone. The first choice would be the local cops, but he despaired that he would be greeted there with any enthusiasm.

Green already thought he was a flake, and, if this shell turned out to be from the killer's gun, Green might actually attempt to arrest him for interference with something or other.

Gar Loober. The name popped into his head like a light bulb in a cartoon.

The sky was threatening rain, and the wind off the ocean was chilly. Lou shivered, and trudged back to his car.

He parked a couple of blocks from the station, and skittered comically toward the building, hiding behind stores and cars as cover. He saw that Green's car was not in the lot, and walked up to the station house. Peering through the window, Lou saw Officer Loober bent over paperwork.

He let himself in, and the young cop greeted him.

"Hi, Mr. Tedesco. You're lucky: the chief is out."

"Hello, Gar. Can I call you Gar?"

A nod.

"I found this on the beach." Lou unrolled the tissue, and let the cartridge casing fall onto the desk. The cop reacted like he was stung by a bee.

He reached for blue rubber gloves, and picked up the object. "Nine millimeter. Where'd you say you found this?"

Lou told him the story. Loober found Nutty Bud's participation amusing.

"Lou, look," he sighed, "we can't use this as evidence. It was collected under, um, unideal conditions."

"Yeah, okay, but can't you get prints off it, anyway? You may not be able to use it in court, but it can point the way to go, right?"

"I can't put this into the system without going through Chief Green, and I doubt that he'll accept it coming from you."

The cop shook his head. "I wish there were some way . . ."

Lou brightened. "What if you told him you found it?"

"Whoa," Loober laughed, "then he'll have my ass on a plate for not collecting it under the chain of evidence rules. I can't risk my job for this, which may turn out to be not connected to the killings."

They both jumped as the rain exploded onto the roof and against the windows.

"Can I have it back?"

Loober dropped the shell into a baggie, and handed it to Lou.

"I have an idea," Lou said, and pocketed the baggie.

SECTION THREE

A Voyage of Discovery

1. Leaving Town

Lou came back to his room at the Saltaire. The rain was letting up, at least temporarily. He needed to sit for a while, both for his knee's sake, and for the opportunity to ruminate.

The phone rang.

"Blanche?" he asked.

"Mr. Tedesco?"

"Oh, sorry. I thought . . ."

"No problem. My name is Lucy Persson."

Lou's mind raced for a second. "Lucy . . . Oh! The psychic. Look, I . . ."

"I know, you have no need for my skills. I get that a lot."

"I don't mean to be rude, Ms. Persson, but I'm really not sure this requires your, um, skills."

"First, call me Lucy. Second, I found you, didn't I?"

Lou was nonplused. "Yes, I guess you did. Do you mind telling me how?"

She laughed.

"Actually, it wasn't that hard. I saw the story on TV, called the local cops, and a young man named, uh, Goober . . . ?"

"Loober, Gar Loober. Yes?"

"Well, he gave me your name and where to find you. So, really, no psychic energy expended."

"I don't mean to be rude . . ."

"You already said that. I understand your caution. It's nothing I haven't heard before. Here's the deal. I get images about certain things, and this story has given me some.

"Normally, I need some actual tangible things to work with: personal belongings, something from the crime scene. Here, though, it's a strong sense of a TV screen, with moving images, or maybe a movie screen. I can't say one or the other."

"I can't pay you for your information."

"None required. I give my services away when I can, and charge for them where appropriate. In this case," she sighed, "you, or anyone, can have what I can give you for free."

"It's pretty terrible, isn't it?" Lou's voice dropped, in respect.

"Yes. I've been involved in many grisly matters, but there's a heartbreaking aspect to these murders that reached me instantly."

"Thank you." Lou sensed a kind soul, whatever the value of her visions.

"Feel free to call me at any time, and thanks for keeping an open mind."

They hung up.

Lou called Blanche. She was able to detect a problem just by his tone of voice.

"Lou, is there something bothering you? You didn't call just to shoot the breeze."

He related an edited version of the morning's events, complete with a full psychological profile of his feelings. There was silence at the other end.

"Blanche, are you there?"

"Lou, I've known you since I was a little girl. I've seen you drunk and sober, in love and in misery, on a hot streak and in a slump, and I never heard you betray an iota of insight until this very minute. This assignment has turned into some kind of watershed event for you."

"If you mean 'watershed' in the sense that I'm all wet, washed up, circling the drain, and going down for the third time, bingo. I don't know about any other meaning at this point."

"Give us a break, Lou. You've run into a couple of snags. The cops put you in your place, and your reporting skills have been questioned. You want me to bench you, send in a pinch hitter?"

"If you're going to keep switching metaphors, I'm going to hang up. There's something I haven't told you . . ." Lou's voice trailed off.

"Cough up."

"I found a spent cartridge on the beach at the crime scene. It could be from the murder weapon."

There was a portentous silence on Blanche's end of the phone.

"Lou," her voice quavered, "you've messed with a crime scene. Isn't that a felony, or something? Maybe I was crazy to get you into this thing."

"Relax. The place is no longer officially a crime scene. At least the tape and stuff are gone. I can't imagine how they missed the shell."

"Are you gonna give it to the cops?"

"I tried. The deputy rejected it."

"I can't believe that. Wouldn't this help their case?"

"I'm not sure it would, anyway," Lou mused. "There's something called the chain of evidence, and there isn't one with this thing. It's not admissible in court without that. All it would be is something for them to look into."

"How do you know all this stuff?"

"Crime novels, police procedurals, cable TV shows. They're full of information about how these things are handled." Lou winced at his own "credentials."

"Well, make sure they get it, and the sooner the better. I don't want to have to bail you out on an obstruction of justice charge."

"Then you'll probably like my next idea. I'm gonna take it directly to the DA, in Waldorf."

"Yeah, okay, I guess. Let's hope he doesn't chuck your bones in the pokey."

"Yeah, what you said . . . But, still, what are our options, here? We do have the power of the press. Maybe we can create a demand for the investigation to go deeper."

Blanche laughed. "Lou, in case you hadn't noticed, we ain't the *New York Times*. I know you're frustrated, but we have limited resources, and very limited influence. Remember that thing we uncovered a few years ago about city employees sleeping on the job? We ran the story for weeks, the local NPR station picked it up for a couple days, and it went nowhere until the *Oregonian* decided to put someone on it. We're a voice crying in the wilderness, and not even the local wilderness there in Seagirt."

"Screw it, Blanche! Let's go with the story. At least I'll be able to say that we tried."

"Okay, but maybe you should talk to the DA there in Waldorf, first. You told me he was interested."

"The golden boy? Yeah, okay. I'll do it today, and then come back to Portland. I'm homesick, anyway. And when I get back I'll write up the story."

"And I'll run it by our legal department, if I can wake her up."

They rang off, and Lou began to throw his belongings into a suitcase. While disconnecting his laptop, he heard a knock on the door.

Before opening the door, he took a quick peek through the curtained window. He felt cautious about opening the door, though he couldn't think why. Then, he remembered the note. He was relieved to see that it was Velma.

"Velma, what a surprise! I was just packing to go. Do you want to come in?"

Velma appeared unsure for a second, then nodded. Lou opened the door and stood aside for her to enter. She hesitated on the threshold.

It had warmed up some that afternoon, despite the rain,

but Velma was dressed in a long-sleeve denim shirt over her jeans. Her hair was pulled back in a banana clip, and she wore no makeup. She seemed tinier than before, as though she were shrinking a bit daily. And, she looked uncomfortable.

"Is everything okay?" he asked.

"Um, yes, thanks." She didn't seem sure. She set her toe in the door like the room was cold water.

"Would you care to sit down?" Lou gestured to one of the kitchen chairs around the small table and Velma entered, walked on tiptoe, sat, and shrunk up even smaller.

"Velma, is there something wrong?"

"I . . . I never been in a hotel with a man before."

Lou gawked for a second, realizing that much of what city people take for granted doesn't apply in small towns.

"Well, please be assured that you're safe with me."

Velma nodded, but her luminous eyes darted back and forth.

"I'll leave the front door open."

She smiled, and that seemed to assure her. Lou opened the door, and a slight breeze came through it. It brightened and cleared the room's atmosphere.

"Are you goin' away?" she asked.

"For a while. I have to go see the DA in Waldorf, for one thing, and I'd like to be home for a couple of days, at least, to sort things out."

"I don't blame you for that. I don't like bein' away much."

She appeared agitated, and more uncomfortable than usual.

"Is there something wrong?" he asked.

"I can't talk to you no more, and I want you to stop stirrin' up mud. Don't be comin' to me for anything." Velma said all this while looking at the floor.

Lou was a bit stunned. "Velma, this is my job, I'm a reporter."

Lou could see Velma's internal conflict play out on her face. Her head would tilt one way, and her brow would knit.

It would tilt the other way, and her facial muscles would relax. She nodded.

"But, how do I know that you ain't in this just for your story? Why should Shelley mean anything more'n that to you? Maybe you don't care how her memory gets trashed."

Lou looked her in the eye.

"Velma, there is no way for you to know, beyond my word. Plus, I made you a promise. Remember?"

She nodded. "Yes, you made a promise. I want to believe you'll keep it. I ain't sure . . . Reporters ain't the most reliable."

Then, she sat upright. "Lester don't have anybody for the killings yet. Do you think he ever will?"

Lou sat facing her, and looked her in the eye. "Velma, I believe that Chief Green is doing the best he can. These things do take time, unless you catch someone in the act, or have witnesses, or red-handed proof.

"I'm going to see the DA so that I can be sure that he stays interested in the case."

Velma started to cry. Lou offered her a tissue from a box on the table.

"What's wrong?"

Velma dabbed at her nose. "It's a case. My little girl's life, and poor Larry's, is a case. It ain't fair that two kids' lives are a case."

Lou could only nod his assent. There was nothing for him to say. There were things for him to ask.

"I have a couple of questions, if you don't mind."

Velma stiffened. "I ain't supposed to talk to you."

Lou wondered if had gotten to her, and why, but decided not to ask, yet.

"No one knew Shelley better than you. I really am trying to help."

"If you think it'll help." She heaved a resigned sigh.

"It might," Lou shrugged, "I'm still trying to understand some things. I heard that Shelley had a boyfriend for a while, someone named Freddie?"

"Oh, yes, Fred Fleer. He was a good boy, but he went away."

"Is it possible that he was the father of Shelley's baby?"

"Oh, my, no!" she said with vehemence. "He was from my church, he wouldn't, couldn't . . ."

"I heard that he left after Shelley's uh, operation."

"Yes, sir. He left because she killed that baby."

"That's why I was wondering . . ."

"No, no, no. You don't understand." Velma became animated, and started waving her hands. "He wanted to marry Shelley. He didn't care whose the baby was. He loved my little girl. When she had that operation, he was just devastated. The church don't hold with that kind of thing. He ran away because he couldn't handle what she done. He went to Alaska, somewhere."

"So, you're certain that he couldn't have done this? You know, a couple of Alaska winters thinking about this could . . ."

"No. It was not Freddie." Velma pursed her lips, like a punctuation mark on her comment, and on the subject.

"Could it have been any of Shelley's old crowd, from the house, or the boys they knew?"

"I don't know why they would do it. We're pretty close in this little town, and I can't see no reason for them to want to do this. It must have been an outsider."

"Well, Velma, I have to get on the road. It'll take me a while to get to Waldorf, and . . ."

"Gettin' an earful, Chloe?" Velma called out.

A shame-faced Chloe showed herself behind the open door.

"I saw them curlers of yours peekin' past the door. If you're gonna sneak, you best be more careful." Velma was positively feisty.

"I was just, just cleanin' up out here. I wasn't eavesdropping." She didn't sound convincing.

"You ain't cleaned up out there in ten years, except right after spring break. If you got business with us, speak up, or go back in your hidey-hole."

"You got no right to talk to me that way, Velma."

"Get lost, nosy!" Velma shook her tiny fist, and Chloe took off for the office.

"I known her now since high school," Velma turned to Lou, "and she got her hair in those curlers every day for years, now. Nobody in *this* town has seen her hair down yet. I wonder maybe she's expectin' a prom date, or somethin'." Velma smirked what would have been an evil smirk on anyone else.

Velma made her good-byes, and Lou finished packing. The last things, as ever, were the two bottles on the dresser. He always gave special care to the vodka-and-poison. Except, all that stood on the dresser was the vodka.

Lou panicked. Wincing with pain from the effort, he moved furniture, tossed the threadbare rugs, emptied drawers, and unpacked and repacked his bags several times.

No cyanide.

It was getting late, and he needed to get on the road, if he were to make it to Waldorf before close of business. This was more disturbing than the note on his car, but he would have to think about it another time.

As he checked out, he casually asked Chloe if anyone had cleaned the room besides her, or if she had touched anything on the bureau. She was still a bit flustered from her encounter with the Mighty Mite.

"Nope. Just the bed and the bath. That's all."

He looked her in the eye, and nodded. He couldn't help smiling at Chloe's discomfiture as he paid his motel bill.

And, he couldn't help thinking, who would steal poison? Who even knew that it was there?

2. A Man of the People

It is not a long distance from Seagirt to Waldorf as the crow flies, but the crow does not have to deal with the sporadic road construction sites or the unhurried and oblivious drivers so common on Oregon highways. And, a light rain had been falling since he set out on the road. Lou realized, as he followed a poky driver whose head was not visible above the seat-back.

Finally, Lou saw the courthouse building in downtown Waldorf. Built with timber and fur fortune money, it was much grander than the modest city would be expected to boast. But, Waldorf's boom days had produced several of these anomalies, ornate buildings paid for with clear-cuts and beaver pelts. Lou resolved to come back and visit.

He parked the car at a two-hour meter and rummaged through a pocketful of change, shoving coins in the slot to get the time up to an hour and three-quarters. He limped the few blocks to the courthouse in a misty drizzle.

Voices and footsteps echoed in the vast marble vestibule of the building as Lou found Knight's office number on a directory. He took the elevator up three flights. His knee ached from the long drive and the damp weather.

Knight's office had a spacious anteroom with large, heavy, antique guest chairs, their wood cut from the old-growth forests and covered with hide from animals hunted in the woods around the city. A massive secretary's desk served as a bulwark before the DA's door. The formidable woman sitting at the desk had iron-gray hair and eyes. Lou was willing to bet she had a will to match.

Her nameplate read, 'Miss Warden'. Perfect.

"May I help you?" she asked, her tone implying that the question was mere courtesy.

Lou removed his baseball cap and cleared his throat. "Yes, ma'am," he squeaked, "I would like to see District Attorney Knight." He felt like a schoolboy in the principal's office.

Miss Warden cocked an eyebrow. "Do you have an appointment?" Her manicured hand indicated a datebook spread open on her desk. Her eyes fixed on Lou's like a cobra's.

"Uh, no I don't." Miss Warden's face assumed a cross look. "But, I attended his press conference in Seagirt, and I'd like to follow up."

"You are with the press?" Her tone indicating that the idea seemed very unlikely.

"Yes, ma'am. the *Stumptown Weekly*, in Portland."

"Is that a newspaper? I've never heard of it."

Lou considered for a moment challenging her on that point, but he felt his chances slipping toward zero, and fought the impulse.

"Well, it's been around for about ten years, and I've been with it most of that time. Is Mr. Knight available?"

"If you don't have an appointment, the best I can do is . . ."

Knight's door opened, and the man himself stuck his head out. "Mildred, can you . . ." He looked at Lou. "Weren't you at the press conference?"

The guy had an amazing memory for faces. He would go far.

"Mr. Knight, my name is Lou Tedesco."

"And he's with some newspaper I never heard of," a frosty Miss Warden said, aware that Lou would try to make an end run around her authority. "Plus, he has no appointment."

Knight stared at Lou for a few seconds. "Weren't you sitting next to Hilda Truax? Do you work for her?"

"No, sir. She's been kind enough to work with me, but I'm with the *Stump*." Lou was immediately sorry he'd used the undignified nickname.

"Are you the guy who covered the road company of that Broadway show a couple of months ago?"

Surprised, Lou answered, "Yes, sir. I do theater reviews from time to time."

"Well, you were dead right about it. It was badly acted, the singing stunk, and it was a star vehicle for that washed-up movie actress. I wish I'd taken your advice.

"You're not here to review my performance at the press conference, are you?"

Lou had to laugh. "No, sir, but I would have given you a rave. It had no second act until you showed up."

Knight smiled. "Come on in and sit down, Lou. Mildred, we don't have anything for the next hour, do we?"

Seething, Miss Warden responded, "No, sir, but Assemblyman Clutterbuck said he might drop in this afternoon."

"Let the old ward-heeler stew for a while. He just wants me to do him a favor that he'll never repay." Knight indicated that Lou should walk into his office.

Lou resisted the temptation to stick his tongue out at the miffed Mildred.

Knight's office was done in dark paneling, and the desktop was a huge slab of wood that could have done duty as a palace door. Lou sat down in one of the upholstered chairs arrayed in a semicircle facing the desk.

"Beautiful office," Lou said, as he craned his neck to take

it all in. The ceiling was some kind of parquet in different-colored woods.

"Thanks," said Knight, as he settled down in his chair. "Left over from the time when timber was king in Oregon. It'd be damn near impossible to replicate, given that some of these trees don't even exist locally any more.

"I assume," he said, looking stern, "that you're here to follow up on the press conference?"

"Yes, and no. Lester Green has not been forthcoming with information to the press. He told me there was going to be another press conference, but it wasn't scheduled yet when I left today."

"Lou, right?"

Lou nodded.

"I'm a prosecutor. I rely on local police to develop evidence that I can take to a grand jury. I find that it doesn't pay to pressure them, or second-guess them. All I can do is advise them, encourage them, and provide whatever resources they need beyond what they have on site. Are you here for additional information, or to get me to lean on Chief Green?"

Lou considered his answer before speaking.

"Mr. Knight . . ."

"Call me Tom, please."

"Tom, Green may mean well, and Gar Loober is an alert young deputy, but they may be working behind a blind spot, or refusing to see relevant evidence."

Knight's brow furrowed. "I'm not sure I like what I'm hearing, here. Do I detect a not-so-subtle accusation in your tone?"

Lou swallowed hard. The self-doubt Green had caused in him was now back, and he understood that an experienced prosecutor could see through his little games. He decided to go for it.

"That may be too strong a word. I don't impute any evil motives, just, well, being a bit closed-minded about the possibilities."

"Okay," Knight tented his fingertips, "like what?"

"I was on the beach earlier today, and I found a spent cartridge at the scene."

Lou reached into his pocket and took out the baggie. He tossed it on the desk in front of Knight.

"Goddamit, Lou!" Knight slammed his fist on the desk. "Have you screwed around with a crime scene? Don't you know that at best you may have hampered my ability to prosecute the case, and at worst you have committed a crime, yourself? There has to be an unbroken chain of evidence on anything found at the crime scene, and it has to be documented."

"No, sir. There is no crime scene there any more, to begin with. The tape is down, and if you didn't know two people had been killed there you would think it's just another stretch of beach. I didn't break any chain of evidence on this shell. I turned it up sifting the sand around the area.

"Plus, the crime scene was already badly trampled by the time I got there the morning of the murders. I'm not even sure the cops have anything from the murder weapon."

He saw Knight focus.

"I was parked in downtown Seagirt yesterday, and someone left a threatening note on the windshield of my car. When I took it to the local cops, I was thrown out. Chief Green won't even hear what I have to say."

Lou searched Knight's poker face for an indication of what the man was thinking.

"Lou, I'd like to thank you, of course, for your interest in this case. Whether as a journalist or as a citizen, I can see you're following your best instincts, here.

"However, I refuse to interfere with Chief Green's investigation. I have complete confidence in his police skills and in his ability to apprehend those responsible for this crime. And, I have complete confidence in my ability to convict the suspects at trial."

Lou's mouth opened before he could stop himself.

"So, what was that press conference in Seagirt all about? You said you had an active interest in the case. In what way? As a chance to get some face time on the six o'clock news?"

Lou could feel the temperature in the room drop. Knight gave him a look.

"Lou, I think that this interview is over." Lou expected to get a warning about getting hit with the doorknob on the way out.

Lou got up, his knee throbbing. "You can keep that cartridge case. You might need it."

He walked out as quickly as his legs would permit.

After Lou was gone, Knight stared at the baggie. He unzipped the plastic envelope. The tissue-wrapped shell slid out into his palm.

It appeared to be a 9 mm. Green told him that the murder weapon was a 9 mm, and the medical examiner had left a message confirming that. It seemed to him that competent police work would have turned it up. Instead, it was discovered by a third-rate newshound with the instincts of a beachcomber.

Knight thought about Lester Green, about his few dealings with the chief in the past. Green had not given him a feeling of confidence. In fact, he considered Green a buffoon who was in over his head throwing drunk sophomores in jail.

But, he was also loath to interfere with local law enforcement, even in a place like Seagirt. It tended to wind up in a political mess, and Tom Knight did not want one of those so close to an election. It was *always* too close to an election.

The DA pushed the bullet shell around his desk blotter with a fingernail, while he ruminated on the situation. Then, he replaced it in the envelope, reached for his phone, and dialed the Seagirt PD.

The man himself answered the phone.

"Lester? This is Tom Knight. What the hell is going on down there?"

3. The Usual Suspects

Lou stood in a funk, in dripping rain, in Waldorf, and contemplated his state of being. He decided that he might be all wet not just in the literal sense, but especially with the murders of Larry Narz and Shelley Korta.

He reached into his pocket for a coin. All he had left after feeding the meter was a penny. "Heads," he said aloud, startling a passerby, "I go back to Seagirt and cause some trouble. Tails, I go home and regroup."

He flipped the copper, and muffed the catch when it came down. The penny bounced off his hand, hit the sidewalk and rolled into the gutter. Lou hustled over to the curb. The coin lay, tails up, in a puddle.

"Home it is. And ding the fielder with an error."

He made the drive back to Portland in silence, the only sounds were from the road and the windshield wipers. He had to snap out of a deep-thought trance more than once.

Rather than go right back to his office, Lou dropped off his luggage at his apartment, took the rental car back, and walked around downtown. In contrast to the rainy coast, Portland was warm and dry, with fluffy white clouds moving across the sky. His knee began to feel better, and he window shopped for a couple of hours. He picked up a paperback mystery at a bookstore.

He also bought a copy of the daily paper, and found nothing about the murders. Yesterday's news already?

Lou got on the bus and went home. After a warm bath, and a glass of iced tea, he tried to empty his mind of Seagirt, Lester Green, and two dead youngsters in the sand. Sufficiently refreshed, Lou called Blanche.

"So," she said, after he ran through the latest developments, "Tom Knight threw you out of his office. Maybe I don't blame him."

" 'Threw out' is a bit overstated. He made it clear that my time with him was over. He seemed to be listening, then, just like that he closed up."

"I'm no expert on the law enforcement subculture, but I believe that if you prod too hard, you're bound to meet resistance. These guys have to trust and support each other, or the whole system seems suspect. They really can't have that."

"Agreed. Look, I don't know whether I'm completely off the wall, here, I just know that they aren't peeking into all the corners. I think, though . . ."

"From your vast experience watching cop shows?"

"Precisely. I think that cops sometimes zero in on a suspect, and develop blinders to any other possibilities. Okay, maybe that's understandable. They have someone they like for the crime, and they pursue him. But, they don't have anyone here."

"Do you want out of this?" Blanche asked. "I wouldn't blame you. You can go right back to reviewing beaneries and provincial theater. Same as it ever was."

Lou wasn't sure if he detected a tone of disapproval.

"Blanche, I'll sleep on it. At this point, I'm not sure I know my own mind."

"Deal. See you in the morning."

There was nothing on television, so he settled down with a mystery. The writing was clever, and the plot raced along, but Lou noticed that things happened much quicker in fiction than in real life, especially if it suited the plot.

At ten o'clock, he flipped on the tube for his favorite newscast, and his favorite reporter, Lana Kwan. She did a story on a tunnel cave-in on the coast road, a story about a drunk driver wrecking a downtown storefront, and a consumer alert on defective baby strollers.

At no time did she, nor any other reporter or anchor, mention the murders. During her stories, her e-mail address was flashed on the screen. Lou noted it down.

Sighing, he turned off the TV and went to bed. It was hours more before he got to sleep.

Lou was up with the sun, and he prepared and ate a big breakfast. After showering and shaving, he dressed and walked the few blocks to work. As usual, he was the first one there.

Like an automaton, he made coffee and ambled around the place doing what he always did. Grateful for the thoughtless efficiency of habit, he kept his focus on a story that was percolating in his mind.

Someone tapped him on the shoulder.

"Louie Louie, you're back!" Patti beamed up at him. "We missed you here."

Lou gave her a quick hug. "You missed me, Patti, and maybe Blanche. I'm not sure anyone else knew I was gone."

Patti made an exaggerated frown. "Aw, Lou. We love you."

Lou looked at her, and his mind flew back to Velma in Seagirt. He wondered how much the young Velma was like this young woman, what she would have been like if she hadn't become a wife and mother so young.

"Patti, have you ever wanted a home and family?"

She blinked with surprise, then grinned. "Louie, are you proposing to me?" She put on a shy act, digging her Doc-Martened toe into the floor. Lou laughed.

"I was just thinking about someone I met recently. You

two are not that much alike, except that you're both tiny. And, very sweet. But, you've had a different life than she's had. She was a mother at your age."

Patti looked thoughtful. "I guess I want kids. I haven't met anyone, I would, you know . . ."

"I know."

"No, I'm not a virgin." She blushed. "It's different, though, to want to make babies with someone. I haven't met that person."

Lou nodded.

"Are you interested in her?" Patti asked, cocking her head like a bird.

"No, it's, well, her daughter was murdered a few days ago."

Patti gasped. "Oh, was she . . ."

"Yes. She's Shelley Korta's mom. Her name is Velma. One way she's like you is that she's innocent. Wait, bad choice of words. Velma is good, and expects others to be, as though it was the most natural thing in the world."

"Lou," Patti said with a stern expression, hands on hips, "she just sounds naive."

Lou suppressed a laugh. "Okay, but if there's a best sense of that word, that's what I mean."

"So, do you think they'll find out who killed her daughter?"

"I hope so." Lou rubbed his chin. "I have some doubts about the local cops, but the DA seems to be interested in the case, so. . . . Let's hope so."

"Are you gonna keep in touch with her?"

Lou swallowed hard. "Uh, I sort of have to."

"What do you mean?"

"I kind of promised her I'd stay on the cops until the murders were solved." Lou's voice trailed off.

Patti smiled. "She's lucky, Lou. She asked the right person. You would never break a promise, especially an important one."

At that moment, Lou made up his mind.

"Patti, I have to get back to Seagirt this morning. I'm glad I ran into you."

"Aw, Louie, can't you stay for lunch?"

"I wish I could. Please tell Blanche that . . ."

Patti jumped up and down. "Louie, you should have seen her yesterday. She was wearing a pink vinyl minidress, white go-go boots, and pink fishnet stockings. Her hair was shoe-polish black, and she wore rhinestone cat's-eye sunglasses."

"Lou," Tubby called, "it's the boss, on line two."

Tubby was not fat. His last name was Tubman, and he claimed to be a direct descendant of Harriet Tubman. The claim would have had more validity if he weren't such a complete white boy, and if Harriet Tubman had actually given birth to any children, but no one called him on it. He was Lou's least favorite among the staff, but he was a good editor.

Lou picked up the phone.

"Blanche, Patti told me that you looked like Austin Powers's dream date yesterday."

"I'll take that as a compliment. What's up?"

"Back to Seagirt. I have promises to keep."

"And miles to go before you sleep?"

"Bingo. I'll call."

"One more thing," she said, "go see Tubby before you go."

"Okay." Lou handed Patti the phone and walked away.

Patti spoke to Blanche. "That was a way cool outfit, yesterday. Why don't you marry Lou?"

"Patti, I may dress like an idiot, but don't let that fool you."

"Okay." Patti shrugged. "Later." She hung up and went back to her work.

Lou went to see Tubby, who greeted him with something like amiability, and handed him a box. It was a brand new laptop computer.

"Here you go, Lou. Welcome to the twenty-first century."

"Okay, thanks. I suppose anything is better than the twentieth, and it ain't over yet."

"Has there ever been a good one? I'll come in later and make sure it's hooked up properly."

Lou wanted to bury his old laptop with military honors. He decided instead to take it down to the Goodwill. He went to his office and spent a few minutes copying files he needed, and made ruthless deletions of work he was keeping for sentiment only.

He opened up the new computer, and it sprang to electronic life. "Cool!" he said to his empty office.

Tubby walked in, and set the computer to work with the office network. "See," he said, "when you finish a story, save the file, click on this icon, and send the story to Editorial. Just follow the instructions."

"Thanks, Tub. Um, can I use my old word-processing program, or do I have to use the clunker that comes with the machine?"

Tubby shook his head in mock sorrow.

"Ever the holdout. Yeah, okay. Make sure Editorial has the program. Our typesetting software will handle it."

"Can I ask you a question?"

Tubby frowned. "Okay, but I might not answer it."

Lou shrugged. "Fair enough. Suppose you had a girlfriend who got pregnant . . ."

Tubby made a choking noise, and formed a cross with his fingers. "Don't even say that in jest!"

Lou chuckled, more to please Tubby than anything else.

"Look, Tub, I'm serious, here. You find out your girl is with child. She decides to get an abortion. How would you feel about that?"

"Personally? I'd buy her dinner, and pay for the abortion, besides."

"What if she was The One, the girl of your dreams?"

Tubby thought about it. "Is this a trick question?"

"In a way, maybe. I believe that most men would behave differently when it's not just some girl you're screwing."

"Okay, maybe I would think twice. Maybe I would ask her to keep it."

"What if she did it anyway, had the operation?"

"I see where this is heading. Yeah, it might piss me off. I'd feel like it wasn't just her decision."

"Last question. She's your first girlfriend, you've been gone on her since high school, you're planning to ask her to marry you. She gets pregnant."

"Yeah, I'd ask her to keep the baby."

"Even if you knew it wasn't yours?"

"I'd kill her! No, I mean . . ."

Lou held up his hands to calm Tubby down. "Thanks, Tub. I wanted that honest reaction."

"But, you understand that I wouldn't . . ."

"I understand," Lou nodded. "And I understand that your reaction was normal, and your response to your own reaction was normal. I have to think about the reaction of someone who is perhaps not so together.

"Unless," Lou said with a sigh, "we really are dealing with a random act of senseless violence."

"Do you need me for anything more?" asked an uncomfortable Tubby, who was rocking from one foot to the other like an agitated child.

"Oh, go on and go. I'll buy you a beer, sometime."

Tubby left without another word. Lou got on the paper's e-mail, and sent Lana Kwan a message.

> Dear Ms. Kwan,
>
> I was in Seagirt after the recent killings, and I noticed you were there filing reports. Not much has come out of that situation in the last few days, and I was wondering if you planned to do any follow-up. You did not mention it on last night's newscast. How do you plan to handle the story?

He signed it, "A Big Fan."

Lou installed his old word processor program on his new

computer, not without complaints from the operating system, and began a new file. He started to type.

Blood and Sand: Death in a Small, Coast Town

On July 14, before dawn, two people were shot dead on the beach at Seagirt, a town whose police blotter is full only when the spring break hordes descend upon it, and where unnatural death is rare.

Shelley Korta, 30, and Larry Narz, 38, were believed to be celebrating a big night. Folks in Seagirt were expecting that the two would be married soon. Larry might well have proposed marriage to Shelley earlier that night, and staying up all night was a way to make the magic last.

Now, their names are linked forever in Seagirt's history, but not in any way they would have wanted.

And the killer, or killers? Chief Lester Green of the Seagirt PD attributes the killing to "person, or persons, unknown," and many in the coast town are wondering aloud if the chief is up to the task.

This reporter discovered a spent cartridge casing at the crime scene, of the same caliber as the presumed murder weapon, long after the local police had given up looking for anything there and the police have been silent on any developments in the case since the initial press conference the day after the killings.

Klaskanine County District Attorney Tom Knight, who attended and spoke at the press conference, has affirmed his faith in the police work of the local PD, and it is an open question how long this unqualified support will last.

In this article, *The Stumptown Weekly* and this reporter will lay out the facts of the case as presented by the police, and will provide additional information developed through a series of interviews with local residents who knew the deceased. The reader is asked to decide whether complete faith in the Seagirt police is warranted.

• • •

Three-and-a-half hours later, Lou finished the first draft of the article. He printed it off as a draft, so he could edit the piece with a red pen in the old fashioned way. His stomach was growling, and it was a good place to break for lunch.

On a whim, he accessed his emails, and found a reply from Lana Kwan.

> Dear Mr. Fan,
>
> Thank you for your interest in our news broadcasts. My editors have decided to follow up when and if there is anything new in the case. Portland has quite enough of its own news to keep us all busy, most of the time. If there is a slow day, I may suggest I go out to Seagirt for a follow-up. I hope that this reply is satisfactory.

Lou jotted down all the reporters he remembered from the press conference and began going through the list, calling one TV station in Seattle, two in Portland, an NPR station in Waldorf, and three print reporters.

He got some variation on Kwan's response from all of them, that is: we're just waiting for something new to develop. One reporter, from the big daily, told him, "I don't care about anything but filing some copy. Lots of people die every day." Even Carissa Stern, who was notorious for hanging on despite repeated attempts to get rid of her, told him, "The story has no legs."

Lou stewed. He decided that if he ever got like that, he would take the poison he carried around with him. Check that; *used* to carry.

He ran out for a sandwich, which just soured his stomach. Popping a couple of antacids, he grabbed his red felt-tip, and worked on the article. At six-thirty, he entered the corrections into the computer file, and sent it off with a couple of mouse clicks.

"The die is cast," he proclaimed to an empty office, and went home.

The next day in the office, the article was the sole topic of conversation. Blanche was in a transport of conflicting emotions while she read it, agonized about printing it, and finally acceded to the raised voices of her staff.

"Okay," she moaned, "I'll do it!"

When the article hit the street the next day, it created a sensation. Lou got to meet Lana Kwan, as she got assigned to cover the brouhaha. Once he saw the contrived process for putting a TV news story together, he lost his illusion about the immediacy of the medium.

Tom Knight sent an angry letter, there were death threats against Lou, and the letters column was a many-factioned war zone for weeks, many of the letters coming from Seagirt residents. The *Oregonian* fulminated in editorial and op-ed pieces about the unsolved murders. The consensus seemed to be: let the cops do their job.

Then, it was off to the next frenzy, a protester who climbed up the side of a government building and ensconced himself on a window ledge to stop a timber sale in a delicate old-growth forest. The press were titillated by the pail he used for his bodily functions.

Larry and Shelley are dead again, Lou thought, killed by indifference and a slop bucket.

4. Not What They Seem

Lou called in from his flat before heading back to the beach, and got Blanche's blessing. She was tickled about the response to the article.

He threw a suit and tie in his duffel, in case he decided to attend the opening of the Bijou.

Back out to Seagirt. This time, Lou had brought moral support: CDs by Tony Bennett, Mel Torme, Connie Boswell, and a couple of show scores. He went through *Cabaret* and *Bye Bye Birdie* on the way.

Lou pulled into the parking lot at the Seagirt PD. He took a minute to compose himself as he stood before the door. He imagined he could see what Dante saw over the gates of Hell — Abandon Hope All Ye Who Enter Here.

"Showtime!" he said to himself, and walked in.

Gar Loober looked up at him with a funny expression. What now? Lou thought.

"Hi, Lou. Believe it or not, Chief Green's been expecting you. Chief?" he called out.

Green opened his door, and scowled at the sight of Lou

Tedesco in his front office. Lou couldn't put his finger on it, but something was not right.

"Look, mister," the chief began, "DA Knight says I gotta cooperate with the press, and I guess that means you. So, I won't get pissed off that you took a piece of evidence and went over my head with it, and I won't get pissed off that you think I'm incompetent. So, ask your goddamned questions."

Lou speculated for a second on what Green's definition of "cooperate" might be, then let it go.

"Chief Green, I understand that we might have gotten off on the wrong foot. I'm sorry if you think I've been sneaky or tried to undercut your authority. Let's try to . . ."

"I said, ask your goddamned questions," he growled.

"Right. Okay, do you know what caliber of gun killed those people."

"Nine millimeter."

"Were you able to get a slug that can be compared by ballistics?"

"Sorry, that's police business."

"Do you have a prime suspect?"

"Ditto."

"Ditto?"

"Ditto."

Lou soldiered on. "Do you know who was the father of Shelley Korta's baby?"

"Not relevant."

"A woman who had an abortion is killed, and the father of the baby is irrelevant?"

"Yes."

"Don't you think that you should look into the possibility that it was one of Shelley's old running buddies?"

"It's been nice interacting with the press. Now, I got police work to do." Green turned on his heel.

"Hey, wait a second," Lou was getting annoyed, "why did the conversation shut down when I brought that up?"

"You got all you're getting. I'm not gonna let you . . ."

". . . compromise the investigation. Broken record," Lou said with weary scorn.

Green walked into his office without another word. Lou shrugged, waved to Loober, and walked out.

As he was getting into his car, Lou heard a hiss. It was Gar Loober, following him out to his car.

"Sorry, Lou," the deputy said, "but Knight really ripped into him, and he's a little sensitive."

"Yeah, I'm sure that's true. He just doesn't like me, either."

"Well, he's not real happy with anyone who checks his work. Maybe it's an ego thing." The deputy spread his hands. "I don't really know."

"Thanks for apologizing, Gar. I gotta go."

"Wait. I can tell you this. We're looking at Shelley's old boyfriend, the one who dumped her, you know?"

"Freddie Fleer?"

"Yes, sir. And, Larry Narz was involved in a big hassle with another boat crew about fishing rights, and the other captain selling the catch cheap to ace out Larry's crew. This could be serious stuff. A good spot means whether you make a living or not, and losing your buyers puts you out of business. People have been killed for less."

"I've been told that Freddie was incapable of killing anyone."

Loober shrugged. "He's been away for a long time. People change. He's got what is a motive for the crime. And there's the boat crew thing. We really are looking into it."

Lou nodded. "Yes, of course. Thanks again. I'm not heading back to Portland, yet. You know where I'll be if you need to get hold of me."

"Yes, sir. Hope to see you soon."

"Gar, one more thing. Is there something going on, here? I definitely get the feeling . . ."

"No, Lou. What could be wrong?"

Lou nodded, and shook Gar's hand. For the first time, the handshake didn't seem sincere.

• • •

Lou decided a drive along the coast might clear his head. He began to think that if Narz was involved in a life-or-death struggle for his livelihood, anything was possible. And, although Velma said that Freddie was not a killer, she was incapable of thinking the worst about almost anyone.

"Okay," he said aloud, "by proxy." He slid a CD into the player, and Sinatra sang "One For My Baby."

After a few minutes of wallowing in Ol' Blue Eyes, Lou drove over to the newspaper office to see Hilda. He filled her in on the latest developments.

"So, if I have this all straight," Hilda's amused expression made Lou squirm, "you found a nine millimeter shell, talked with a psychic, visited Tom Knight, and got your wrist slapped by Lester Green. You also caused a small sensation with a critical article . . ."

"You read that?"

"I did. Nice work. Oh, and you met Nutty Bud. Pretty full schedule, if you ask me."

Lou mustered his dignity. "Scoff if you will. At least I'm trying."

"Tell me about the psychic."

Just as he was about to begin, the phone rang. Hilda held up a hand to stop the story.

"Clarion, Hilda speaking. Lester?" Her eyebrows arched. "We were just talking . . . Yeah, he's here. Don't let him leave?"

Hilda gave Lou a dark look.

"Okay," she said into the phone, and hung up.

"What was that all about?" Lou asked, feeling new anxiety.

"Lester Green is coming here. He said he's been calling around town after you."

"Did he say what for?"

Hilda shook her head. "Coffee?"

"Yeah, okay."

They sat in silence, sipping from their cups when the chief barged in.

"Lou Tedesco? I have a warrant for your arrest."

Lou jumped up, spilling coffee. "On what charge?"

"Attempted murder. You tried to poison me and Loober."

Two hours later, at the police station and after intense charges and denials, Lester Green sat down. Sweat stained his uniform at the armpits and neck.

Lou was sitting on a squeaky chair in the chief's office. Gar Loober, who had not uttered a sound during the entire interrogation, said softly, "Chief, I don't think he did it. Why would he do something like this?"

"Why do these bastards do anything?" Green wheezed, spent. He didn't sound convincing, even to himself.

"Lou," Gar asked, "can we go through this one more time?"

Lou nodded, almost as wrung out as the chief, although he hadn't expended the same energy.

"About an hour after you left the other day," the chief said, "I found an empty vial of cyanide next to the coffee machine. I recognized it from your room. Loober and me had been drinking coffee since lunch . . ."

Lou picked up his head. "And neither of you has died."

Green flashed him a look.

"Right," Loober agreed, "we are definitely alive. We called in the state cops, who rushed the bottle and the coffee to the lab in Salem. What we haven't told you is that the lab results came in a couple hours ago, just after you left here."

"And?"

"There was no cyanide in the bottle. It was distilled water with a drop of almond extract in it. Where did you get it?"

Lou could feel the blood rush to his head. "Wait a minute! You ran me through this, this, *exercise*, knowing that it wasn't poison?"

"Yeah, goddamit," Green jumped to his feet, "but you didn't know that when you tried to kill us."

Lou started to laugh, and couldn't stop for several minutes, despite Green's threats. He wiped his eyes, and got hold of himself, as the chief seethed.

"I carried that damn bottle around for years thinking I would use it to do myself in, and it was almond extract and water. Oh, that's rich."

"Like I said, you didn't know that until just now. You wanted us dead." Green was on his feet again.

"Okay, Dick Tracy, when did I poison your coffee?"

"Today, when you came in."

"Think about it. Was I ever out of your sight?"

"Nope," Gar answered. Green glowered at his deputy, but said nothing.

Lou gathered momentum. "Did I ever go near the coffee? No. Did you see me reaching into my pockets or sneaking around? No.

"That bottle went missing from my room. I asked Chloe about it when I checked out. Maybe you should ask who else had the means to get into my room, Chloe, for one."

"Why would Chloe wanna kill us?"

"Why would I?"

"Hold on," Gar said. "Let's think this over. We have nothing on Lou, and we may have nothing at all."

"Now, hold on Loober . . ."

"Sorry, chief. I know you want to get to the bottom of this, but it just doesn't add up to Lou. He wasn't in a position to pour the bottle into the coffee while he was here, and, even though he was out of town most of the time after we discovered it, he came back. Don't sound like guilty behavior."

Lou watched in fascination as the two cops argued, with Green pulling rank and Gar reasoning the facts. Finally, the discussion petered out.

"All right, Tedesco, you can go." Green's shoulders slumped. "If I get anything that nails you for this, you may never get to court."

"You threatening me, chief?" Lou rose from the chair.

"Okay, hold it." Loober stepped between them. "You don't mean that, chief. Lou, hightail it before more gets said."

Lou was out the door as fast as he could move. Gar was right behind him.

"Lou? Wait up."

"Oh, yeah. What's up, Gar?" Lou was forcing himself to be social.

"Something happened you might be interested in."

"What's that?"

"Calvin Wheelock quit."

"Calvin . . . is he the other deputy?"

"Yeah. He and his friend, Phil Troy, are staying in California. They decided they liked it better down there."

"What does Green say about this?"

Gar shrugged. "He said, 'Who don't like it better somewhere else?' "

Gar hesitated. "Uh, one more thing . . ."

"What, Gar?"

"I really shouldn't tell you this." He squirmed around in his uniform, like he was trying to escape it. "We found Larry's religious medal, some Catholic thing . . ."

"A Saint Christopher's medal?"

"Yeah, well, it was under his body, like someone had torn it off, maybe in a struggle. We sent it off to Salem, and they said there were no usable prints."

"What did you do with it?"

"We gave it to Jack Narz. It wasn't much use to us, and, well, we sorta felt like he should have it."

"Thanks, Gar. You're a good guy."

"Just don't tell the chief."

"No prob."

Gar turned, and walked back to the station house.

Too tired to do anything else, he checked back in to the Saltaire. A dubious Chloe handed him a key, and two phone messages from Lucy Persson.

The earlier one read, "Stay away from dark alleys." Good advice, Lou chuckled to himself. The second read, "Call me."

5. Crystal Ball

Two days before Lou's ordeal with the Seagirt police, Jack Narz took a little trip out to the boonies of rural Washington.

Narz peered, squinting, at the address on the mailbox illuminated by flashlight, then down at the address scrawled on the torn paper. He had to look twice, because the mailbox was in the shape of a pointed wizard's hat, and he couldn't see the number clearly.

"I guess this is it," he said aloud.

"It" was a rutted dirt driveway, about fifty miles from anything that could be called a city. Now, he had found it, and he was still unsure of what to do.

Narz sat in his old Chevy truck and lit a cigarette. The only light in the whole area was the glowing end of his smoke, although he sometimes lit his brake lights by tapping nervously on the pedal with his foot.

Do I really want to do this? he asked himself. What do I know about this stuff?

"What the hell," he said aloud, "I'm here." Grinding out the butt in his ashtray, and taking a deep breath, he started the truck and aimed it into the driveway with care.

Low-hanging branches squeaked along the top and sides of the truck. Narz cringed, but the truck's finish was mostly a memory, anyway. All attention was focused on the narrow track, and the huge trees to either side.

After a quarter of a mile, the path opened out to a gravel area. Parked there was an old VW microbus painted with stars and moons and other astronomical bodies. A house, like a house he had seen in a picture book he had read to his kids, glowed with invitation.

Narz stopped the motor, and eased his sixty-year-old bones out of the cab. Gonna have to trade Ol' Betsy in for a sedan soon, he thought, as his feet hit the ground.

He walked to the house, on a path between two small greenhouses that each housed a lush garden, and he noticed several exotic flowers he could not identify. The house itself was surrounded by multicolored shrubbery and flowered vines, all strange to him.

Gee, I wish Helen could've seen this, Narz thought, missing his late wife.

He knocked on the front door, with a heavy brass knocker shaped like a cat's head. It opened, and a plump, middle-aged woman stood there.

"Mr. Narz?" she asked in a musical voice.

"Yes, ma'am. I'm still not sure . . ."

She smiled. "Of course you're not sure. Come on in, and let's see if we can convince you."

She wore a skirt of several layers of diaphanous material, each in a different color. Above that a black, velvety top exposed deep cleavage. Her hair was long, gray-going-white, and braided. The braid swung behind her as she walked. Filigree earrings dangled from her lobes.

Narz began to sweat, although the house was cool. The place was like a magician's cave, at least like the ones he saw in those picture books. Odd and unsettling images were hung on the walls, and there were crystal balls and wands of different types on every flat surface.

"Iced tea?" she asked.

"Um, sure. Thanks," he managed to reply.

"Sit down anywhere," she called over her shoulder, on the way out of the room.

Narz sat in the most normal-looking chair, an overstuffed wing chair, careful not to hurt it. He sat straight, knees together, hands folded in his lap.

A few moments later, the woman came in with a tray holding sugar, cream, lemon slices and two large frosty glasses. She handed him one, and he sniffed it before sipping. She laughed.

"Don't worry, it's just Lipton's. I wouldn't slip you some kind of weird herbal mickey."

Narz laughed with relief.

"My house is a bit strange but, you know, most of this stuff was given to me. If it were up to me, this place would look like a dentist's waiting room. A few chairs, maybe a couch, a couple of tables with magazines . . . But, folks come here thinking I want yet another picture of Merlin, or another magic wand."

"Miss . . . ?" Narz inquired.

"Call me Lucy. It's Lucy Persson. Norwegian, on my dad's side."

"Uh, Lucy, my late wife once got a porcelain owl for a gift. Someone saw it sittin' on the shelf, and bought her another one for her birthday. Soon, she was gettin' owls from everyone. 'Jack,' she says, 'I wish folks would stop buyin' me these damn owls.' "

Lucy laughed. "I guess you know what I mean, then. Now, how can I help you, Mr. Narz?"

"Jack," he said, blushing. "I heard about you from a waitress back where I live on the Oregon coast. She told me that you can see things, that you solved a few crimes. Is that true?"

"Jack, before you go any further, I make no claims. Whatever my gift is, I have no control over it, like turning on a TV set. I either see something, or I don't. I won't make anything up just so you feel better.

"Now, I've had three people come to me who had loved ones disappear. I was able to see where they were. Two were dead, one was hospitalized with a severe head injury, and unable to communicate. The pictures that came to me were very specific, and yet it took some additional detective work to find them. But, we did find them."

Narz became very excited, almost spilling his tea.

"So, you can do it, do it for real?"

"Hold on. Three I saw. There have been at least ten, twelve, where I got nothing, zip. So, it's not a sure thing. I may see something that we can't home in on, or I may see nothing at all. Don't get your hopes up."

Narz nodded, and thought a moment.

"This ain't exactly like those cases, Lucy. I know where my boy is, he's under the ground." Narz began to sob.

Lucy found a tissue box in a drawer and handed it to Narz. She patted his shoulder while he composed himself. She sat down and urged him to begin, again.

She gasped. "Wait! You're the father of that boy. Tell me what happened, Jack."

"My boy was killed on the fourteenth, on the beach."

"I'm sorry."

Narz nodded. "He was out late with his girl, and I guess he asked her to marry him. That's what he said he'd do that night. She was a friend of his, and they started dating. Both of them had been through a lot, and they were ready to grow up and get their act together. But, someone . . ."

Narz began crying, dabbing his eyes with a tissue.

"Take your time, Jack. No hurry, here," Lucy said in her most soothing tone. She sipped tea.

A minute later, Narz resumed.

"The cops got no leads. They think maybe it was a gang of bikers who did it, but, just between you and me, they don't have one damn idea."

"What would you like me to do, Jack?"

"I brought things, Larry's things, and I brought pictures, even sand from the beach where they were killed. I didn't know what you would need. If you want more, I'll get it to you."

"Let me see it."

Narz reached into his jacket pocket, and took out a large envelope. He handed it to Lucy.

"Shall I open it?"

"Yeah, please." He gestured toward the envelope.

Lucy lifted the envelope with both hands, high above her head. She closed her eyes.

"Don't you need to open it?" Narz asked.

"Yes, but just a moment."

Lucy's hands gently palpated the contents.

"Is there something of the girl's in here, too?"

"Yeah!" Narz's face showed astonishment.

"A bracelet?"

"Yeah, yeah."

Lucy opened the envelope with a slender knife and carefully picked an object out. A gold earring.

"This is his?"

"Yup. His left ear was pierced. I don't know why guys . . ."

"No, that's fine. It was close to him." She held the earring in her fist for a moment, put it on the table, then removed a baggie of beach sand.

"That's from, uh, the place where . . ." Narz said.

"Yes. It's strong, Jack." She put down the baggie, and removed two braided strings. "What are these?"

"Shelley, that was the girl, she called them friendship bracelets. Made 'em herself."

"This one was hers?" She held one up.

"Yes."

"Good." She held it in her fist before putting it down. Then, Lucy removed two photos, and looked at them. One showed Larry and Shelley and a crowd of others holding beer bottles at a softball game. The other pictured Larry sitting in a big chair with Shelley on his lap. They were both laughing.

"These are good, Jack. These are good." Lucy removed the last object. It was Larry's St. Christopher's medal.

"I put that in," Narz explained, "because the cops think that the killer might have touched it. It was around Larry's neck when, you know . . . and it was found under the body."

Lucy rubbed it between her hands.

"Yes, maybe so. Jack, this is what I want you to do. Go home, and try to take your mind off this for a while. Do you like fishing or hunting?"

"Not much, but I like baseball."

"Go see a game, or two. Isn't the season on now?"

"Yeah, but them pro games are expensive. I, well, I don't even know if I can afford to pay you."

"Jack, I won't take any money from you for this. I do fine with readings and such from people who can afford it. If I can help, that's more than enough. Look, if I do help, that brings in business for the Tarot readings and all that. I get new customers after each time I do well at this, and they stay with me. Go watch a game."

Narz looked at her for a while. Never gifted with much insight, since his son's death he had peered into corners of his soul that he never knew he had. There was more in the world than he had ever imagined, and if anything good came from the murders, this knowledge was it. He was touched and amused by Lucy, and her being so down-to-earth.

"Lucy, I gotta say that I never met no one like you, and I don't know what I would've thought if I did. Right now, you look like an angel to me."

"Ask my ex-husband," Lucy laughed.

"I think he was damn lucky to have any time with you. Now, I guess I better go before I embarrass myself."

"I'll call you in a few days. It'll either be yes or no, so prepare yourself for either one."

"All I can say is thanks. That don't seem like a good enough word."

Lucy closed the door, and tried to call Lou again.

On the way back to Seagirt, Jack Narz smiled for the first time in a long while. And, he felt that he had done something to help. When he got home, he realized that he hadn't had a cigarette for hours.

Despite Lucy's suggestion to relax, John Narz spent the

next few hours in a state of agitation. He chain-smoked. He drank too much beer. He watched a Mariners game on TV, and he walked the beach. He wondered why cigarettes tasted different when you smoked them on the beach. Once he saw Velma Korta kneeling at the site of the killings.

He avoided talking to her, first because he did not want to intrude on her privacy, and then because he couldn't bring himself to go near the scene. When he got home, he went right to the answering machine to see if the little light was blinking.

Two days played out this way. He would call in sick, and his boss would excuse him.

Then, having heard nothing from Lucy, Narz went back to work. He didn't want to take advantage of his boss's good nature, and he needed to stop sitting around and brooding. When he came home from work he saw the little red light winking. He hoped it wasn't a wrong number as he pushed the button.

"Jack," said Lucy's voice, "call me. I have something to tell you."

Narz didn't want to get too excited, because Lucy could be telling him that it was no go.

"Hello, Lucy, I just got your message. Do you want me to come out there?"

"Hello, Jack. No, not right now. I sat down with these objects last night, and I felt something, and it's strange even to me. The sand made me cry. I got strong and unpleasant feelings. But, I also got an image I couldn't make out. The medal gave me a clear image of a volcano."

"You mean like Mount Saint Helens?"

"Not erupting, if that's what you mean. It had a snowcap, and there was black stone all around it. Then, I held the medal and the sand at the same time, and I got an image, a strong image, of a bullfighter. And a bull. He was holding that cape they use, and a sword. I feel that this has something to do with the color purple, but I can't quite see it yet."

"A bullfighter? What does that mean?"

"I don't know. We'll have to think about these things. I'll

call if there is anything else. I need to try different combinations of these objects."

"Thanks, Lucy. I guess I got something to think about."

"Jack, if it's any comfort to you, I got a strong feeling of peace when I put them all away. This usually means everything will be okay."

"I don't know what to say. Just, thank you."

"You're welcome. Call any time you like."

Narz ran back out to his truck, and spun out of his driveway, heading for the police station way too fast. Chief Green was standing at a file cabinet when Narz entered in an agitated state.

"Lester!"

"Jesus, Jack, calm down. You'll give yourself a heart attack."

"Lester, I talked to this woman who sees things, whaddaya call it, a psychic."

Green rolled his eyes. "Sit down, Jack. Want some coffee?"

"The hell with the coffee! She saw a volcano, and a bullfighter, purple something. What do you think it means?"

Lester Green's nature was such that he wanted to throw Jack Narz out, and tell him to get a grip. Internally, Green warred over his response. The better side won by a hair.

"Well, Jack, I don't know. A volcano, you say?"

"Yeah, but not like a blowing-up one. And, she saw a bullfighter and a bull."

Green made a show of taking notes. Narz described the whole story, from his going to Lucy's house, to the phone call a few minutes before. Green nodded, and scrawled things on a pad.

"So, what do we do, now?" Narz asked.

"Well, I'll talk this over with my deputy, and we'll see where it takes us."

"Thanks, Lester. This might help solve the case."

They shook hands, and a comforted John Narz headed for his truck. Then, he remembered a detail he wanted Green to know.

He got to the door, looked through the glass panel, and saw the chief laughing, and crumpling the sheet of "notes" he had taken. He felt tears burning his eyes, and he went back to his truck.

I need a drink, he thought, and drove off to The Breakers.

The Breakers Bar & Grill appealed to both locals and tourists. The locals came in for the company, and the bank of video poker machines prominent in the bar. The tourists enjoyed the seafood, especially the fresh halibut fish and chips, and the local color. But, even in the summer, it was more of a local hangout, which meant that the poker machines were all in use, the waiting list was backed up, and the place was smoky.

Narz got several greetings when he walked in, and he returned them half-heartedly. He walked up to the bar, and ordered a bourbon, beer back. The bartender, well aware of Narz's personal tragedy, nodded, and filled the order with a minimum of chat.

After two of these boilermakers, Narz was calmer, but no less in despair. He began to have thoughts of Lucy Persson, but they had nothing to do with her psychic skills. This only made him morose.

He was about to order another bourbon, when he noticed that the bartender was reading a newspaper, and the headline blared, "Scandal on the Oregon Coast: Seagirt Murders Are Still Unsolved."

"Hey, Mike, what're you readin' there?"

"Huh? Oh, that hippie paper from Portland. Got an article about . . . what happened."

"Can I see it when you're done?"

"There's a stack of 'em over by the jukebox. Take as many as you like."

Narz walked over to the jukebox and took one. Back at the bar, he sipped his beer, and read the cover piece. He decided to call this Lou Tedesco.

It took him an hour to track Lou to the Saltaire.

6. The Grand Opening

The phone rang while Lou was trying to organize his thoughts.

"Mr. Tedesco? I'm Jack Narz. It was my boy that was shot dead on the beach . . ."

Lou was nonplused. "Uh, yes, of course. What can I do for you?"

"Maybe nothin'. But, maybe you can help. I for damn-sure ain't gettin' any help from Lester Green. He was a nasty kid, and now he's a nasty man."

Narz related the story in some detail, rambling occasionally. The ramblings often centered around Lucy's many virtues. Lou stayed with every word, and was fascinated by the psychic's visions.

"Are you saying that this woman . . ."

"Lucy, Lucy Persson. You could check up on her. She ain't like those TV phonies. She got a good record."

"Actually, I've spoken with her. So, Lucy Persson took these things you brought her, and she came up with a bull-fighter and, what, a volcano?"

"Yes, sir. Not one that's going off, but an old one, I guess.

Like Mt. Hood, with snow on top. Not hot stuff like maybe from a . . . what do you call it?"

"Eruption."

"Yeah, eruption. The bullfighter, he had a cape and a sword, like he kills the bull with, and there was a bull, too."

"Jack, can you think of anything this might mean? It's pretty, uh . . ."

"Weird?"

"Good enough. Weird, it is. Do you know if any of this makes sense?"

"No, sir, I don't."

"Do you know Velma Korta?"

"Yes, I do. I see her on the beach, sometimes."

"Do me a favor, and give her a call. See if any of that means anything to her."

"Yes, I will. And, thank you."

"Can you come see me?"

"Sure, later, like after work?"

"Make it tomorrow. I need some sleep."

Lou made the appointment, and got Narz's phone number, and hung up. Then, he thought about volcanos and bullfighters. He couldn't quite recall the sequence Narz had related, but the psychic held two of the objects at the same time, sand from the crime scene, and Larry's medal, which may have been handled by the killers. And, she saw volcanos and bullfighters.

Narz believed that Lucy was the real deal, so Lou went over what she told him. Something about movies, and stay out of dark alleys.

"Okay," he said aloud, "I'll work on the movies."

There were two movie outlets in Seagirt, Lou pondered: the video rental and the new Bijou. Lucy told him that the vision, or whatever it was, might have been a movie screen, or maybe a TV screen. That pretty much covered the ground.

But, the Bijou was not opening until the next day, and, if you went with the flow, could not have affected matters. That left the video store. He tried to recall anything that he saw or heard in the place that might have some bearing on the case.

Carla Higgins, at the video store, mentioned that Calvin Wheelock, the deputy, and his friend Phil Troy had rented a miniseries of *In Cold Blood*, the story of two thrill killers who slaughtered a family in rural Kansas for no reason, then fled to Mexico.

Wheelock and Troy were in California, and Wheelock was a cop. They didn't fit the profile of random killers. Troy told Dub he had "scored" a 9 mm just before the killings, and Phil Troy was supposed to be a bit off.

Was he off enough to kill somebody? Did he have more influence on Calvin Wheelock than people gave him credit for?

"Maybe I ought to watch this miniseries," Lou said to the motel room walls.

Then, he got ready for bed.

The next day, Lou decided to lay low, organize his thoughts, and make some notes for a follow-up article. He ate at fast-food places, avoided the beach, the Dunes, and Chloe.

The one person he wanted to see, but was afraid to, called him, just as he returned from a greasy lunch.

"Hey, Lou, going to the Bijou opening tonight?"

"Hilda. Yes, I thought I would."

"Would you care to be my escort? Clearly, I'm desperate."

"Ouch. I deserve that. I would be delighted. Really."

"You sound like you're trying to convince yourself. Okay, what time? Want to have dinner first?"

"Actually, I have an appointment this evening. Can I meet you there?"

They made arrangements to meet, and hung up. Lou found a ball game on the tube, turned down the sound, and lost himself in thought.

• • •

The knock came as Lou was trying to remember how to tie a Windsor knot. He guessed that the last time he had worn a tie was at his wife's funeral.

He stuffed the fat end of the tie through the knot and yanked.

"I'll fix this later," he said half aloud, and opened the door.

A rough-looking middle-aged man stood there, with just enough menace to be scary, until Lou looked into his eyes.

They were soft with pain and regret.

"Can I help you?"

"Are you Lou?"

"Yes. Who are you?"

"I'm Jack Narz, Larry's father."

"Yes, of course. I've been expecting you."

Lou stood aside and gestured to the man, "Please come in."

Narz was dressed in working-man's clothes: faded blue chino pants, a khaki workshirt out at one elbow, with a chewed pencil sticking out of one breast pocket, and lace-up boots scuffed to holes in a few spots.

Narz held out his hand for Lou to shake, and it, too, gave evidence of strenuous labor. The grip was strong, even crushing.

"Not much place to sit," Lou pointed toward the only chair, "but I need to be standing right now, anyway."

"Thanks." Narz dropped himself into the chair, which squeaked and rattled under him.

Lou fiddled some more with the tie knot. "I got roped into going to this theater opening tonight."

Narz shrugged. "Let's see what we can get said while we got the chance."

"Okay. First," Lou started, "I'm truly sorry about Larry. From everything I've heard, he was ready to start his life all over."

Narz cleared his throat to cover a choking-up. "Already had. Shelley was the last part, gonna be."

Lou met the man's eyes.

"Yes," he nodded. "How are you doing?"

"Good days, bad days. Same when his mom died. I raised him myself, but I guess I didn't do such a good job."

Lou stopped fiddling with his clothing and sat on the bed.

"Larry turned out fine. It took me longer to get my act together. Can I ask you a question?"

"Sure."

"What do you know about Larry's beef with another boat captain over territory?"

"More than one. Fishin's dryin' up. They talk about El Niño, or whatever, but there's always been more or less fish, year to year. Problem now is that more boats took it up during the good times, and the bad years come closer and worser." He sighed.

"Can you think of any particular person Larry had trouble with?"

Narz rubbed his chin. "Larry talked about the captain of the Clatsop Queen, Murphy, I think his name is. They all had run-ins with each other from time to time, over crossed-up nets or who got where first, but Murphy was in everyone's face."

"Could Murphy have killed Larry?"

Narz reacted to the direct question, sitting upright, startled.

"Jeez, I don't know the man. Hardly seems worth killin' over, though."

Lou stood up. "Jack, right in Portland some kid killed his schoolmate over a Blazers jacket."

"Sad damn world we come to, ain't it?"

Lou looked at his watch. "Jack, I have to go. Can we get together again, soon?"

"Ya know, there's a reason I came here, and I ain't got to it yet. Can we meet later?"

"You mean Lucy Persson?"

"Yes, sir, I do."

"I don't see why not. This clam bake at the Bijou can't go on too long. Say, ten-thirty? Where at?"

Narz mentioned The Breakers, a bar Lou had passed several times in his rolling around Seagirt. "Yeah, I know where it is. See you later."

Narz shook Lou's hand again, and walked out. Lou made one last foray at his tie, made it worse, shrugged, and capitulated. He grabbed his car keys, and left.

Lou cruised the street, and scoped out the parking. It was mobbed, and cars lined the streets for blocks. He turned a corner, and parked in the alley behind the theater, both for convenience, and in hopes of being inconspicuous.

The Bijou was lit up like Oscar night in Hollywood. A couple of arc lights swept the low clouds, beams shooting through to the heavens when they found a break in the overcast.

The elite of Seagirt were in attendance: the women from the Dunes Café, with fresh hairdos and glitzy makeup; the shop owners, some in linens and silks; squads of bewildered summer people, all underdressed for the occasion; Chief Green and Officer Loober, in starched uniforms.

Lou noticed the film critics from the *Oregonian* and the Portland radio and TV stations standing in a group. He waved.

Henry Collins, produce department manager, lurked around the edges of the crowd, dressed in what looked like a rented tuxedo, with a short, squat woman, who may have been his wife, in tow. He contrived to appear that he was not interested in Lou's whereabouts. Sweat beaded on his upper lip.

The woman, tottering on her spike heels, protested with little squeaks each time he yanked her to a new position. He threw glances at Lou from each new vantage point.

Then, a vision dressed in a vintage 1940s gown of sequins and lace: Hilda Truax, hair swept up into a dazzling peak, and dripping pearls. She looked like a million bucks.

Just as Lou was about to go over and tell her, there was an audible gasp from the crowd: Chloe walked up to the theater in low-cut dress, with her hair down, out of curlers, and both decolletage and tresses looking good. This really confused the tourists, who couldn't imagine who that woman who was causing this reaction.

"There's my scoop for the evening," Hilda sidled up and whispered to Lou. " 'Chloe Lets It All Hang Out!' "

"Even I'm amazed," Lou admired her. "This is the first time since her senior prom, no?"

"That's the folklore. I was already in college, but her hair was in curlers next time I got back to town."

"By the way, you are stunning. Where did you get that dress?"

"My mother's closet, believe it or not. I can't imagine where she wore it."

Just then, Anthony John emerged from the Bijou lobby, togged up in a double-breasted, white dinner jacket, with wide lapels, and black trousers with a satin stripe at the seams. He had a gardenia pinned on his lapel. He looked like a character in a *Thin Man* movie.

His appearance caused another stir and some in the crowd applauded. Anthony shook hands, and accepted hugs, including a vehement grasp by Connie from the Dunes. She had dolled herself up for the occasion, and looked lovely. Anthony, a dashing and eligible young man, must have seemed like rescue to a drowning woman. He endured the hug with a smile.

He acknowledged Carla Higgins, and shook her hand with warmth. He worked a crowd like Tom Knight, totally in command of the moment.

Hilda said, "Hey, Lou, look at our entrepreneur. Ain't he something?"

"Sure is. I've talked with him. He knows the movies, and he sure looks good in the clothes. You could be his date, wearing that outfit. Have you done a story on him?"

Hilda affected a shocked look. "Lou, you don't read my paper?"

He reddened. "Okay, busted. But, I will definitely start now that I know you."

"Okay, nice recovery. It'll do, anyway. Just a little blurb.

But, after tonight, it's major local news, and much nicer to write about than poor Shelley and Larry."

Anthony stepped forward to greet the crowd, and raised his arms to ask for quiet. The chatter diminished and stopped.

"Ladies and gentlemen of Seagirt, and distinguished visitors and guests, my name is Anthony John." A smattering of applause, which was shyly acknowledged. "This is a great night for Seagirt, a great night for the neglected movie palaces of America, and a great night for me personally.

"In the last few years, I have examined and re-examined my life. I had all the money I could ever need from a successful software business, and I suddenly found myself bored and unfulfilled.

"More for my mental health than anything else, I started watching classic movies, first on video, then at a revival theater near me. It was a revelation. Great stories, witty dialogue, the violence was far less graphic, the sex far more romantic.

"After about six months of Jimmy Cagney and Edward G. Robinson and Jean Arthur and Spencer Tracy with Katherine Hepburn, and Fred and Ginger, well, I found my calling. Not only have I saved the Bijou from who-knows-what fate, but I will find other old movie palaces and restore them, too."

The crowd applauded with vigor, and Anthony gestured for quiet.

"And, I have started a nonprofit foundation to preserve old movies from deterioration. Movies are my life.

"Now, please come in and enjoy the movie. I promise a clean print of *Casablanca* as soon as I can locate one, and a Laurel and Hardy festival in the fall."

He swept his arm toward the theater. "Popcorn and Jujubes on the house!"

With a roar, the crowd surged to the door, and it was all Green and Loober could do to prevent mayhem.

There were local kids in usher uniforms and behind the candy counter, and real popcorn poppers, staccato pops like firecrackers as they disgorged avalanches of white popcorn. The kids shoveled and passed the snack across the counter, with Anthony keeping it all just below a feeding frenzy.

The customers, armed with movie food and drinks, quickly filled the seats. A stack of souvenir programs disappeared in seconds.

The old auditorium rang with the happy exclamations of grownups acting like kids, and kids loving to see it. Hilda and Lou got two in the center, their faces glowing.

Once they settled, the lights went down to a great cheer. The gorgeous ruffled curtain parted, and an RKO-Pathe newsreel unrolled. Bathing beauties in Brazil, President Truman and Governor Dewey chasing each other across the map trading charges, a shot of Dewey among a group of Indians, clumsy in donning a chief's war bonnet, drew a laugh, and the Berlin airlift. A history lesson in celluloid.

Next came a Bugs Bunny cartoon, to everyone's delight. Lou nudged Hilda and whispered, "Mel Blanc was born in Portland, you know."

"Everybody knows that."

Lou shrugged.

And then, the main feature. Bogart and Bacall fighting Nazis in Martinique. Adventure. Romance. Hoagy Carmichael. At some point in the evening, Hilda slipped her hand into Lou's, and he liked it.

After nearly two hours in the theater, everyone filed out with a big smile on their faces. Anthony said good night to every customer.

"Wanna come back to my place?" Hilda wiggled her eyebrows, a parody of seduction.

"Tell you what, I have to go meet Jack Narz in a bar. He needs to talk to me about something. Can we meet later?"

"A late date, huh? Well, I know the obsessive quality of a newshound on the scent. Okay, you know where I live?"

Hilda wrote directions in a reporter's notebook, and handed Lou the paper.

"See you as soon as possible," Lou turned.

"Do you need a ride to your car?"

"Thanks, no. I got a spot right behind the theater in the alley."

Lou headed for the car to keep his appointment.

The clouds had settled in for the night, and there were no street lights. He stepped with care to avoid falling. When he reached the car, he deactivated the alarm and opened the door.

Somebody grabbed and held him before he could slip in. A powerful, leather-clad arm held him in a choke hold, and he gasped for breath. Whoever it was kicked the car door closed, and the dome light went out.

"Hey, Pops," a whiskey-smelling voice hissed, "we need to talk." Judging by the height from which he was held, Lou guessed that his captor was well over six feet tall.

Lou was picked up bodily, and turned around to face another man, the typical outlaw biker, a much smaller man than the one holding him. Even in the near-dark, Lou could see light glinting off the zippers and metal studs of a motorcycle jacket, and he could smell grease and body odor, laced with booze.

"Ease up, Mojo, let the man breathe."

The choke hold was released enough for Lou to catch his wind and croak out, "What's this all about? What do you want with me?"

"Depends on you, pussycat. You been stickin' your nose in where it don't belong. It's makin' some people very unhappy."

This was beginning to sound like dialog from *Chinatown*, Lou thought, but he said, "Do you mean you? Are you the unhappy one?"

As Lou's eyes became accustomed to the dark, he could make out an eye patch over the man's left eye, and a bandana covering the bottom of his face, like a desperado's mask. Another bandana gathered his hair. Not much to memorize for an ID. The costume was completed by jeans and engineer boots.

"I'm a friendly guy, so I get unhappy when my friends are unhappy."

"Your friends wouldn't happen to include Stud Dunham, would they?"

The biker hesitated, and his brow furrowed. He looked up at his big friend and nodded, and the choke tightened. Lou was lifted off his feet, and in a few seconds, began to black out. He slumped, and was allowed to fall to the ground.

The kicking started. Lou thought he felt a rib snap.

"Hey!" Hilda's voice called out, "what the hell's going on here?"

Hilda reached into her chic evening bag, and pulled out a silver .32 pistol. It flashed a wicked glint as she brandished it.

"Quit that or I'll blow your heads off!" She fired a round into the air for emphasis.

One last kick, and his tormentors were gone, running off into the gloom.

Hilda rushed over and knelt in the dirt, heedless of her gown.

"Lou, are you all right?"

"I've been better," he groaned.

By this time, Seagirt's finest were on the scene, flashlights and guns deployed.

"What happened?" Green bellowed.

"Two of 'em, on foot. One about six-five, one maybe five-ten. They went around Bender's Snacks."

Loober took off in that direction, with Green huffing in his wake. Green was yelling into his police radio for the Emergency Squad, and falling farther behind.

"I think my rib's broken," Lou wheezed.

"I've had guys do extreme things to get out of a date with me before, but this takes the cake."

"Ow! It hurts when I laugh."

Three hours later, Lou was sitting in the police station. The EMT had taken him to the local clinic for X-rays. The rib was cracked, but not broken, and a cut on Lou's forehead needed six stitches. They gave him an elastic bandage for his ribs.

Then, they gave him a badly photocopied list of procedures to promote healing, a prescription for painkillers, and shots for pain and infection. Then, they showed him the door. Gar Loober brought him back to the station.

Loober and Green were drinking coffee, Lou was drinking bottled water, and Hilda sipped from a silver flask of brandy. All were silent after Lou and Hilda gave their statements.

"Damn!" Lou spat, making the others jump. "I was supposed to meet Jack Narz tonight."

Hilda took a nip. "I called The Breakers and talked to Jack. It's covered.

"Too bad you don't drink. This brandy has good anesthetic properties."

"Wow," Lou was impressed, "you are good. I didn't even mention where he was going to be."

"Lou," Hilda said, "in this town, the locals go to The Breakers. It wasn't exactly nuclear physics."

"Nonetheless . . ."

"Hey, you two can get acquainted on your own time," Green interjected. "Let me go over this one more time before I throw you out."

"Lester," Hilda scolded, "you've got the social skills of an ape. This man could have been killed tonight."

"Can it, Hilda. I might get the idea that you need a permit for that cannon in your purse." Hilda made a contemptuous noise, and waved him off.

"Okay, Tedesco, you went back to your car, and you got grabbed from behind. Right?"

"Yup. The guy was big, and had booze on his breath."

"You never saw him, right?"

"Right. He was wearing leather. I could feel it and smell it against my skin. And his pal called him Mojo."

"Okay, got that. His accomplice was shorter. And dressed in biker gear."

"Yeah. From what I could see, anyway. Wasn't much."

Lou sipped water. "Oh, I just thought of something."

"Shoot." Green poised his pen.

"I mentioned the name Stud Dunham, and it stopped his oration. I could only see one eye, but I was sure it caught him off guard."

Loober jumped up. "Chief, I . . ."

Green held up a hand. "Save it, Loober. Let's get this over with first.

"Okay, what next?"

Lou shrugged, then winced. "Ouch. That's about it. I got dropped on the ground, and they started booting me. Then, Hilda the Magnificent showed up, guns blazing."

Hilda bowed, and took a drink.

"You see them running away?"

"Nope. I was facing in the wrong direction, and couldn't move much."

Green spun dramatically in his swivel chair.

"Hilda?"

Hilda was unfazed. "All I could get was the relative heights. It was really dark back there. If I had to guess, I'd say biker gear, bandana on the smaller one, cowboy hat on the big one. Sounded like boots on the pavement."

"All speculation," Green groused.

"Well, not the cowboy hat part."

"Chief," Gar attempted, "this Stud Dunham thing . . ."

"Yeah," Green cut him off, "what made you bring his name up?"

"All I know about him is that he was a bad one, and that he may have gone off with a motorcycle gang. Seemed reasonable to guess . . ."

"Yeah, okay." Green settled into a funk.

"Chief, what do you know about a boat called the Clatsop Queen, and a captain named Murphy?" Lou read the silence as an opportunity.

"We checked on Murphy, because he muscles in on other boats, and had words with Larry Narz. But, he got in everyone's face out there, not just Larry, and had an alibi for the morning of the shooting."

"A solid alibi?"

"Solid enough. He was in jail for DUI that whole night."

Gar nodded from his perch on the desk.

"Have you heard from Calvin and Phil?"

Green's head snapped up. "Press conference is over, Tedesco. Loober'll take you back to the motel."

"I'll take him to my place," Hilda said. "He can't take one of Chloe's beds tonight, and he might need help."

"Fine. Loober'll drive you, too. You're too damn drunk to drive yourself. Pick up the car tomorrow."

"Agreed. See, Lester, you can protect and serve when you want to."

"Loober, get these two media giants outta here before I shoot them trying to escape."

"Okay, Chief."

The next morning, Gar called Lou at Hilda's. He got no answer, so he tried the Saltaire.

Lou had awakened, very sore, and slipped out of Hilda's house. He walked to the movie theater to get his car. On the way back to the motel, he stopped to pick up a strong coffee. The phone rang moments after he let himself into his room.

"Hi, Lou. Got some news. But, first, um . . ."

"Yes, Gar?" Lou sipped the coffee.

"That article really gave me a pain."

Lou squirmed.

"Nothing personal, Gar. I went out of my way to indicate that your presence on the Seagirt force was a good thing."

"Jeez, Lou, that made it worse. Green's on my case for sure, calling me 'traitor,' stuff like that. Plenty of people in the town felt like it was a hatchet job on the chief, and they weren't shy about using me as a sounding board."

"Gar, I regret that. An unintended consequence. I apologize."

Silence for a moment. "Yeah, okay. I'll get over it, I guess. I'm calling because Green got a hot lead from Tacoma."

"I'm listening, Gar."

"Larry Narz was known to carry one of those biker wallets, the kind with the chain? Said that it was good for workin' on a boat, so it didn't wind up in the drink. Well, there was no wallet on Larry's body. We withheld that from the press."

"What's that got to do with Tacoma?" Lou asked.

"Kid was caught using Larry Narz's credit card up there. He was tryin' to buy a Michael Jordan autographed basketball at a sports memorabilia show."

"A kid? What do you mean, 'a kid?' "

"I mean a kid. Twelve years old."

Lou felt light-headed. "Does Lester think . . ." His voice trailed off.

"He's on his way to Tacoma right now. We just heard about this."

"Gar, it's damn decent of you to call me with this information, especially since I made your life miserable with . . ."

"Hey, I told you I'd let you know if something came up. I keep my word."

"Will you keep me posted? I promise not to use this until you tell me I can."

"Listen, Lou, without you it's damn sure we never would've got those footprints, and we'll need them. I got a feeling they're gonna break the case. We have that empty shell casing here now, too. We missed that little goodie completely. So, I'm cutting you some slack here. Just between you and me, I'd be real surprised if it turned out to be a twelve-year-old who did this murder."

When they hung up, Lou thought about the case for a while. His hunch was that the Tacoma thing was a sidetrack, but it was tempting to devise strange scenarios involving a preteen killer. It would make quite a story. The idea of the thing made him shudder.

He agreed with Loober that the footprints, two pairs, both sets too big for a kid, were the key to the solution. Then, he thought about Loober being big enough to call despite the undeserved grief Lou had visited on him.

Lou elevated personal integrity to the pinnacle of goodness that had been occupied only by innocence. Then, he remembered that, here in Seagirt, he had made some promises himself.

7. The Fugitive

Lester Green pulled the police car into a visitor's spot at the Tacoma police headquarters. He looked around him in the car, making sure that he had what he needed, including a manila envelope with the photo of a shoe sole inside. Loober had insisted that he take the picture.

He got out of the car, brushed cigar ashes off his clothing and hitched up his belt, thinking it would be a good idea to lose a few. Then, he remembered the truck stop, and the scrumptious baby back ribs he had promised himself for the return trip.

He checked with the desk, and followed the instructions to the interrogation rooms. A hawk-faced detective in a short-sleeve dress shirt and out-of-style tie sat at the first desk.

"Hi," he said, startling the cop, "I'm Chief Lester Green from Seagirt, Oregon. I need to see a . . ." he sneaked a look at a piece of a scratch pad, "Paul Flynn?"

The cop gestured toward the front of his desk, peered over the pile of case folders, and realized that he had thrown his suit jacket over his nameplate.

"Oh, sorry." He grabbed the jacket and dumped it onto an empty chair. "I'm Flynn. You here to see John Dillinger?"

Green laughed. "A real menace to society, huh?"

Flynn sat back and rubbed his face with his hands. "I seen a lot of kids come through here in my time, but this choir boy takes the cake. Here, sit down."

Flynn pulled over another empty chair, and Green sat.

"What do you suspect this kid of doing?" he asked, with a skeptical tone.

"Double murder on the beach a couple days ago. Can't catch a break on it. Might as well've been Martians. And, I'm workin' shorthanded on top of everything else."

"Green, was it? Chief Green, this kid got caught usin' an unauthorized credit card, and your bulletin popped up when we traced the owner. I'll let you decide for yourself, but I don't think we got your killer, here."

Green shifted in his seat. "How'd he explain the card?"

"Told us he found it in a booth in a café on 101 in southern Oregon. He ran away from home a few weeks ago, and there was money and credit cards in the wallet, so he swiped it. Ran out of money, and used the cards."

"Did you check out the café?"

Flynn searched his desk for a folder. He found it, and withdrew an official form. "Here's the statement of a waitress at the café. She spotted the wallet, and saw the kid sitting in the booth. Next time she walked by, the wallet was not visible, and she assumed it was the kid's, and he pocketed it. I'll make copies of everything we got on this kid for you to take."

Green nodded his thanks. "Where is this place?"

"Just outside of Brookings, way the hell down near California, as you know. I hadda drive all the way down there to take the statement. Waitress remembered the kid because he didn't have any adults with him. She almost told the cops about him when they came in for their caffeine fix, but she got distracted, or something.

"Wanna see the kid?"

"Sure." Green shrugged.

Flynn took Green down the hall to series of rooms, each with a large window, that was mirrored on the other side. He jerked his thumb at one of the windows.

"That your man?"

Lester looked in. The boy was sandy-haired, and wore glasses. He was 4-foot-10, perhaps shorter. His feet didn't reach the floor, and he swung his legs from the knees as he read a comic book and sipped a soft drink.

Green took the shoe sole photo out. "His sneaker soles look like this?"

Flynn looked at the photo, and the six-inch ruler laid next to it for scale.

"Chief, this looks like maybe a size eleven to me. That kid could put both feet in it."

"What's his story?"

"Says his stepfather's a jerk, and his mom never sticks up for him. He ran away from home right after school let out. Been on the road ever since."

"Where's he from?"

"Somewhere around Fresno. Know what?"

Green shook his head. "No, what?"

"His folks never reported him missing. They're supposed to get here today. I think I'd like to talk to them. Even Dennis the Menace's folks would report it if he went missing. I also called a social worker to be here." Flynn made a face. "Maybe I don't blame the kid for running."

Green looked at the boy for a while, as he turned the pages and sipped his drink.

"Still wanna talk to him?" Flynn asked.

"Nah." Green envisioned those puny arms and tiny fists trying to fire a 9 mm.

"Sorry you had to drive all the way here for nothing."

Green waved his hand. "What the hell, I'll stop for ribs on the way home."

"Truck stop, right?"

Green smiled. "Yeah. I should lose a few, but there's gotta be some excuse for comin' up here."

"Cup of coffee before you go? It'll take a few minutes to copy the file."

"You buyin'?"

Lester Green stopped for the ribs, but did not stop back at Seagirt, continuing down the interstate. He drove the five hours down to Brookings, to speak with the waitress who made the statement.

The biker connection was foremost in his mind. That, and putting that snot-nose reporter in his place.

She was a high school girl named Ashleigh, with blue hair and a pierced nose. Green couldn't look her in the eye. All this punk stuff annoyed him.

They sat at a table, Green drinking coffee, the girl drinking Fresca.

"I already talked to the cops." She cracked gum as she spoke.

"It don't say on the police report if you saw who left the wallet."

"They didn't ask."

"I'm askin'."

"Yeah. It was two guys. One was really big."

"Can you describe them in any more detail?"

"The big one was dumb, and the little one was, like, bossing him around. They sat at the counter and ordered, like, coffee and hamburgers?"

Green was distracted by the way the girl talked. Her voice would rise at the ends of sentences, and he couldn't tell if she was asking him a question.

"Did you hear them say anything?" Green wanted to grab her by the throat. He knew now why the original statement was incomplete.

"Well, I was busy, you know? But, the little one was all, 'How did he know to say that?' and the big one was all, 'I don't know, Harry.' "

Lester perked up. "Harry? The guy called him 'Harry?' "

"Yah." She gave him an impatient look.

"Did you get the big one's name?"

She looked thoughtful. "Maybe, Hojo? Something like that?"

"That's very good." Lester hoped some praise would draw her out more. "Anything else?"

"The big one had blue eyes and brown hair? And, the little one was, like, gray? With brown eyes?"

"Gray like me?"

"Um," she looked at Lester's hair, which he was sure was grayer than when he walked in, "no. Like, more?"

"No eye patches?"

She shook her head. "Nuh-uh."

"Good. How were they dressed?"

"Like bikers, but they really weren't, like, real bikers."

"How do you know?"

"Their clothes were all, like, brand new? And, they didn't have any motorcycles."

"How do you know that?"

"Duh! No bike noise when they left? Mister, we get a lot of bikers in here, and it's like, l-l-l-loud when they leave."

"Tell me about the wallet."

"When the two guys left? They, like, stopped at the kid's booth? The wallet was on the table, when I served the kid, and like, gone when he left?

"That's all," she shrugged.

Lester dropped his card on the counter.

"Gimme a call if you think of anything else. And, thanks."

"Whatever." She shrugged again, put the card in her apron pocket, sucked out the last of the Fresca, and went to wait on tables.

A few hours after Lester Green returned from Tacoma, Hilda Truax called Lou Tedesco at the Saltaire.

"Hiya, Hilda. Good to hear from you. Thanks for the use of your guest room."

"You could pick up a phone, you know. You left without even saying goodbye." She sounded pouty.

"If you could see me, you'd know I'm blushing. I didn't want to wake you up, seeing as how you, um . . ."

"Were sleeping it off? Okay, never mind. Have you heard about the kid in Tacoma?"

"Yes. Anything happening on that?"

"Well, Lester stopped at the Dunes for coffee after he came back from Tacoma. He ran his jaws for the ladies. They gave it to me."

Hilda provided a surprisingly detailed account. Lou was amazed that Green would spill so much for the locals, but they were folks he had known all his life. Keeping it in the family, so to speak.

"So," she concluded, "The kid used up the money, then tried to use the cards. Lester said that the little bugger couldn't kill a fly with a baseball bat."

"Hey," he said, "I used to be a pretty good hitter, and I couldn't do that."

"Lester's gift for metaphor may be a bit slender. The kid was a little shrimp who was running away from home, and was nowhere near Seagirt, except to pass by it on the way to Seattle."

"Have you spoken to Green about this?"

"You know, he tolerates me just slightly more than the rest of the press. He did tell me that 'person, or persons, unknown, probably passing through town' is now the official word."

"I'm scratching my head here. What the hell does *that* mean?"

"Specifically? A gang of bikers."

"You're joking."

"Nay, nay sir. This is Lester's new bright idea."

"Does he think it has something to do with Stud Dunham?"

"Hey, didn't you already suggest that to Lester? I'll remind him. It might make me some points with him."

"No joke. He was part of that crowd that the victims hung

out with. Who knows what bad blood there might have been?"

"Who knows what evil lurks in the hearts of men?"

Lou sighed. "Why am I condemned to running into sarcastic women?"

"Well, you were either a very bad boy in your past life, or a very lucky one this time. Would you prefer someone like Chloe? I hear she's set her hair again, so she's expecting company."

"No middle ground?"

"Not at this number."

"Okay, so, is Stud Dunham a possible?"

"Could be. I was serious about telling Lester. Try to convince him he thought of it himself."

"On this case alone, what Lester Green hasn't thought of could fill books." Lou paused for a second. "By the way, what's up with Wheelock and Troy?"

"Word is that, yes, they decided to stay in California, get jobs there, start a new life, blah, blah, blah. They're staying with Calvin's relatives down there."

"Just like that? End of story?"

"Yes, sir. Calvin was not exactly police material, and no one misses Phil Troy."

"Okay, Hilda. Thanks."

"Talk to you soon. Right?"

"Right, Hilda. I'm still blushing."

Lou hung up. His thoughts free-associated for a while, then he remembered what it was like to be in a batting slump when he was an active ball player.

Some players made big changes, shaving their heads, growing beards, trying new bats, or new routes to the ball park, or eating different breakfasts. Others went the superstitious/mystical route, up to and including church services, novenas, hex candles in the locker room, burning old bats and doing weird things with the ashes, and voodoo. One Jewish guy sawed a half inch off the end of the bat.

Lou was the scientific type, watching endless videos of his at-bats to determine if the mechanics of his swing had changed, or his timing was off. He would consult other players, coaches, scouts, and even reporters. Then, he would spend hours in the batting cage attempting to fix what was wrong.

Any, and all, of these approaches "worked" at some point. If this happened, all was right with the world and life was rosy. The batter would see the hurtling ball, fix on it, and smash it. Or, the player found himself sliding down to obscurity, a job with a used-car dealership back home, and slow-pitch softball for the rest of his days.

Lou was lucky to have had few slumps, and luckier to have emerged from them with his spirit intact. Now, with these killings, he was stumped. He had no videos of his "swing," no sources for coaching on his mistakes, and no idea how to break out of it.

He knew that as the days went by, people would think of it less and less. There was, after all, a life outside Seagirt, and those not directly affected would soon forget. And, the two lovers on the beach, true to Velma's fears, were on their way to becoming statistics.

He thought a bit about Hilda Truax. She was the first woman he had any feelings for since the death of his wife. He resolved to call her.

Then, Lou turned his thoughts to the matter at hand, got out one of his reporter's notebooks and listed the possibilities.

First, Murphy, Larry's rival captain. Murphy was in the jug the night of the killings, but he had a revolving crew of about eight men. These would all have to be vetted for alibis, but that was more a police job, and he was beginning to think that Lester Green was trying to do the job, despite his hostility.

Then, there were the bikers. If they *were* bikers. The waitress told Green that she never heard motorcycles, but that didn't explain much. It was still a question.

Then, there was the absence of Wheelock and Troy. The starting a new life in California story might be true. There wasn't much keeping them in Seagirt.

Still, Troy's bragging about getting a gun the same caliber as the murder weapon needed investigation. And, this is where Green seemed oddly reluctant.

Why not clear that up? Loyalty? A deep and abiding faith in Calvin Wheelock's innocence? Lou had no answer for that, and wasn't going to get one from the chief, directly or through Gar Loober.

Person, or persons, unknown? It may yet wind up that way.

The phone rang, and Lou jumped.

"Hello?"

"Lou? It's Lucy Persson."

Lou shrugged, and thought, Well, as good as anything else at this point.

"Hello, Lucy. How are you?"

"A bit agitated, basically. I didn't sleep much last night. I'm getting strong messages, and they wake me up. That's never happened before."

"Okay, you have my attention."

"Well, you know that Jack visited me. He left me a few things that were connected with, um, the crime."

"Yeah, he told me."

Lucy described the items Narz left and sighed. "It's the sand, and the Saint Christopher's medal. The police believe that one of the killers, and I'm certain there were two, handled it. And the sand, ugh! Just thinking about it gives me the creeps."

Lou sat up straight. "You've what? Seen the murders?"

"I've seen two men. There's a tension between them I could sense. One of them might be, I don't know, disabled."

"What else?"

"Not much more about them. I did . . ."

Her voice trailed off. Lou waited, heard another deep sigh.

"I saw them do the killing. That's what kept waking me. There wasn't a lot of detail, and I can't tell if one or both did the shooting. Maybe that will come later."

"Hmmm," was all he could say.

"There's more. Remember the movie stuff?"

"Sure."

"Well, there's two distinct pictures now."

"No pun intended?"

Lucy laughed. "No, but I'll take the credit on that one.

"I see a big screen, in a big theater, and an actor's face."

Lou was getting the creeps himself.

"Do you know the actor's name?"

"Ah, gee, I knew you were going to ask that. I should know it."

"Okay, let's play twenty questions. Modern or classic actor?"

"Definitely classic, little mustache."

"Not Chaplin?"

"No, even I would know him right off. More, um, serious."

"Can you think of a movie he was in?"

Silence, then, "Yes! I just saw one on TV, *A Tale of Two Cities*. I loved that book when I was a girl, and he was just perfect for the part. He played the drunken lawyer . . ."

"Sydney Carton? Ronald Colman played him?"

"Yes! That's it. I saw his face on a big screen."

Lou was scribbling like mad: names, movies, random thoughts. He would sort it all out later.

"You said there were two pictures."

"Right. The other is definitely a TV screen. I get that very strongly when I hold the sand."

"Any more detail than that?"

"Yes, the bullfight picture, the one I told Jack about."

Lou kept scribbling. "Lucy, can I come see you?"

"Sure. Just let me know so I'll be home. I have to pop out for errands and the occasional reading. A girl's got to earn a living."

"Lucy, if any or all of this pans out, you'll have to hire help."

She laughed her musical laugh. "Maybe I'll get my own 900 number."

"Just promise me you'll never do an infomercial."

"Not even a Thighmaster?"

"Especially not. Unless, of course, you can introduce me to Suzanne Somers."

"Stay in touch, Lou."

Lou studied his scrawled notes, and ruminated for hours, jotting down ideas as they came. It was dark, and he was hungry.

He needed to speak with Anthony John, and with Carla Higgins. These seemed like solid leads to him, although he could not explain why in any rational way.

The Mexico thing was nagging at him. He recalled that the killers in Capote's story fled to Mexico after the crime. There were highly mobile bikers in the mix, as well as two local kids heading south, and they were live possibilities. Larry's wallet was found in Brookings, a short drive from California.

On a whim, he called Hilda, who invited him over for dinner. Then he called the Bijou, hoping to go right over, and Anthony invited him to come.

"Thanks for seeing me, Anthony. I know how busy you are."

"It's good to talk to you, Lou. How goes the investigation?"

Anthony, casual and elegant in linen slacks and a silk Hawaiian shirt, crossed his legs and sipped a piña colada.

"It's taken some strange turns. That's why I'm here, really."

"You sure I can't get you something to drink? A pop?"

"Yeah, okay. Club soda is good."

Anthony rose and disappeared into the kitchen. Lou spent the time going over his notes, if those scrawls could be dignified with such a term.

His host returned in a few minutes with a bottle and glass. Lou thanked him.

"Now," Anthony drawled, looking at the notebook, "what can I do for you? Am I a suspect?"

Lou chuckled. "No, even your popcorn is above suspicion."

Anthony nodded in thanks.

"Are you planning to show any Ronald Colman movies?"

Anthony's eyes narrowed in thought. Lou perked up, then realized that the man was just thinking. His suspicions were tweaked, and he had to be careful of misreading innocent body language.

"Not for the immediate future. Why, do you have a request? I would give that strong consideration."

"Hey, thanks. My favorites were always *A Tale of Two Cities* and *If I Were King.*"

Anthony smiled a wide smile, teeth gleaming. "Yes, the François Villon movie. And, the one where he goes to the guillotine for his friend. Good choices. Nothing else?"

Lou hadn't thought it beyond the two he had mentioned. "Not at this time, as they say."

"*The Third Man* is coming up, English version, rather than the inferior American cut, with the Carol Reed opening narration."

Lou smiled. "I'm giddy with delight. Since I seem to be staying in Seagirt for the time being, I may get to see it."

They exchanged small talk for a few minutes, and Anthony said, "Wanna come to tonight's show? Different cartoon and newsreel."

"Thanks, but, no. I'm having dinner with Hilda Truax."

Anthony leered. "Aha! Can I start a rumor?"

"Lordy, no! Hilda and I are just . . ."

"Good friends?"

"Actually, yes. No more than that. At this time, as they say."

"Just out of curiosity, Lou, why the interest in Ronald Colman?"

Lou felt himself blushing. "This is gonna sound crazy . . ."

"Try me."

"I got the idea from a psychic."

Anthony burst out laughing. "You didn't call one of those numbers on TV, did you?"

"Hey, give me some credit at least. No, she contacted me, and she's got an amazingly good reputation with police agencies. Anyway, she got this, what, vision? I don't know, but Ronald Colman was in it.

"Just thought I'd go to the movie capital of Seagirt, and the resident guru."

"Did you get what you want?" Anthony sucked the dregs of his drink.

"Can't say. You were very helpful, I guess. I'm just not sure what I'm looking for."

"Okay, then it's time for you to go. I have to lecture my staff on procedure before we open up tonight. The Lessons Learned thing from opening night."

"See you soon."

They shook hands, and Lou left. He was too preoccupied to notice the vehicle following him down the dark streets, headlights off.

8. Sneak Attack

The evening with Hilda went well enough, considering that she was still annoyed with Lou for his rude behavior. Lou promised to be more thoughtful in the future, despite his confusion over what social amenity he had violated. They hadn't even been in the same bed.

His limited experience with women had not left him prepared to deal with Hilda. He wondered if his wife had ever felt like her.

Lou got into the rental car and made his slow way to the road. There were few streetlights in Seagirt, and they were concentrated on and near the main road. The tree-lined side streets wound around, and visibility was often no more than a few feet.

Lou didn't see the car pull up next to him, but he did hear the gun go off, and saw the muzzle flash out of the corner of his eye. And he felt the bullet fly past his face, and the shattered glass hitting him.

He swerved into the other car, and ducked at the same time. He heard the squeal of brakes, and a crash, just as his car hit a tree.

Then, he lay there for a few seconds taking inventory of body parts. He could feel cuts on his face, and he was a bit sore in his bruised ribs from being yanked by the seat belt, but he didn't think the rib broke.

He sat up, taking care that the gunman might be outside his car. He saw an upended SUV, wheels still spinning. The vehicle had rolled over into a drainage ditch.

Lou wished he had a cell phone at times like this. He undid his seat belt, and wriggled across the seat toward the passenger door. The effort hurt his rib and caused him to cry out from the pain.

He opened the door and braced himself, then rolled out of the car and onto the ground. He groaned, but it didn't get any worse. His heart went into overdrive in his chest.

No one seemed to be getting out of the SUV. He heard a voice, coming from a small house beyond the trees.

"You have an accident? Should I call 911?"

"Yes," Lou shouted back. "There's another car out here, too. Please hurry."

Lou rose up to a crouch, and made his way over to the wrecked SUV in a duckwalk. It hurt, not the least in his knees, but he wasn't going to make too inviting a target of himself. Carefully, he stood up and peered into the car's windows.

Henry Collins lay on the padded ceiling of the overturned car, bleeding from several wounds, motionless and with his head at an angle that made Lou think that the man's neck was broken. He heard a siren in the distance.

"Tedesco, this is gettin' monotonous."

"Chief, I agree."

The interview was taking place in the clinic this time, in the lounge just off the lobby. Gar Loober was given the unhappy duty of notifying the widow, and she was coming in the door with him now.

It was the short, heavyset woman Lou saw with Collins at the Bijou opening. She was wearing rumpled sweats, and her hair was a mess. Mascara streaked down her cheeks. She threw Lou a look, somewhere between bewilderment and despair.

"Is Gar taking her to see Henry's body?"

Green kneaded his face with both hands. "Yeah. I hate this. When those college kids got run over on the beach a few years ago, it was bad enough, but we've had three of our own, now."

Lou couldn't read the emotions on the chief's face, more complex than he was used to seeing. Green snapped out of his reverie, and flipped open his notebook. He ran his finger down the pages.

"Tedesco, how do you know Collins?"

"I told you. I met him once. I went to the supermarket to ask about his relationship to the victims. He was really upset, almost panicky. He broke into a sweat. I thought that was odd."

"Why? Most people here are upset."

"Chief, Carla Higgins was, if anything, more upset. But she didn't come apart at the seams."

"No accounting for the way folks feel."

Lou shrugged. "Guess not."

A shriek made both of them jump.

"I guess Loober pulled back the sheet," Green muttered.

They were silent for a few minutes, while Lou fiddled with the magazines on the table in front of him and Green looked through his notes.

"Tedesco," Green looked toward Lou with unfocused eyes, "how come people started dyin' when you got here?"

Lou restrained himself. "Actually, chief, Shelley and Larry were dead already when I arrived. And, Collins is dead because he couldn't drive and shoot at the same time.

"I wonder who you'd be asking that question if it was me under that sheet."

Before Green could respond, a sobbing Valerie Collins was led into the lounge by Gar Loober and a male nurse. She was beside herself, and on the verge of fainting. They sat her down, and the nurse ran off for a moment, returning with a paper pill cup and a cup of water.

"Take this, ma'am, it'll calm you down."

Valerie downed the pill and chased it with the water. The nurse left, and she sat back for a moment, and then turned her gaze on Lou.

"Who the hell are you, mister? Why would my husband want to kill you?"

"I'm sorry, Mrs. Collins, about Henry. And, well, I really don't know what the problem was. I've spoken to Henry once in my life, hoping to get some insight into those two kids who were killed on the beach. I don't know . . ."

"Lester, you know what's goin' on?"

"No, Valerie, I don't. Did Henry say anything to you before he went out?"

She sighed. "Henry's been a mystery man the last few weeks. I don't even know where he got the money for that new car. When I asked him, he said he was handlin' it, and not to worry. So, I didn't worry."

"Car like that cost about thirty grand. You got no idea about how he could afford it?"

"No, sir, and he got annoyed if I asked, so I didn't ask."

"He didn't get a raise down at the market?"

"Not one where he could go out and buy that thing. Not if he wanted to pay the mortgage."

Lou cleared his throat, and asked, "Had he been going out a lot, lately?"

"Yup. I wondered if he have a girl on the side, but it didn't seem that way. Women can tell. He got a lot of phone calls, too, but it was a man. I know he wasn't seein' no man."

"How long did Henry stay out when he got these calls?"

"Different times," she shrugged. "Sometimes an hour, more or less. Mostly, just a few minutes, fifteen or twenty. He never explained where he was goin' or how long he'd be gone."

"Did you ever answer the phone when the man called?" Lou tried.

"Yes, sir, I did. He talked with a English accent."

Green and Loober both started scribbling notes. Lou went on.

"What did he say to you?"

"He was real pleasant, but he didn't waste no time with me. 'Howdy do, Mrs. Collins, and is Henry at home?' Just like that."

"Any way you could recognize the voice?"

"No, sir. I know I never heard it nowhere else."

"Had you noticed anything, any changes, in Henry's behavior lately?"

"He's been real nervous, smokin' a lot more, and takin' too many drinks. We like a drink, but . . ."

Just then, the nurse popped his head in and said, "You really ought to let her go home. That pill will be kicking in any time, now, and she's had a rough night."

Lou blushed. "Of course. I'm sorry, Mrs. Collins."

"If it helps me find out what happened to Henry, I don't mind."

"Thanks, Valerie."

Gar escorted her out the door to drive her home. Lou shook his head.

"Poor thing. Her life gets weird, and then her husband dies trying to kill a man he doesn't know. I feel sorry for her.

"By the way, chief, it wouldn't happen that the gun he used was a nine millimeter, would it?"

"Old Army Colt Forty-five. Must have been his daddy's from the war. If that slug had hit you, your head would be in the next county."

"Can we get a sample of Collins's writing? I still have that threatening note. Might help."

"Okay, Tedesco. I'll talk to 'em down at the market. I guess he had to fill out reports, and such."

"Well, chief, where do we go from here?"

Green scratched his head. "We still got some leads to run down, Murphy's crew had a couple guys with records, and they're scufflin' for alibis about now.

"Far as I know, none of 'em got no English accent."

Lou got up off the couch, and winced. Green extended him a hand.

"You okay? You been banged up enough last couple a days for a whole life."

"Gosh, chief, that's the first thoughtful comment . . ."

"Don't go buyin' me no flowers, Tedesco. I still think you're a pain in the ass, and should go back to Portland."

The receptionist peeked in.

"Is there a Mr. Tedesco here? Rental car company brought you a replacement."

"Thanks. I think I can drive. Good night, Chief Green."

Green grunted, and followed Lou with his eyes as he left the room.

9. Miniseries

Lou slept late. He awoke to a gray day of intermittent showers and cool temperatures. The TV said that Portland would have a hot, sunny day with a few clouds. Here, on the sea side of the Coast Range, the best they could hope for was some sun breaks and an end to the showers.

He felt a hundred years old. He ached in mind and body, and needed to clear his thoughts. Showered and dressed, Lou slipped yellow rain gear over his clothes, and left to take a walk on the beach. There was a note from Jack Narz on the door. He had set up a meeting with Velma Korta for later that day.

Lou walked the beach. It was hard to tell at the horizon where the sky began and the water met it, both were the same shade of gray. Wracked by more self-doubt, he tried to think of a way to make a solid connection between the murders and the two absent young men. He was more and more convinced that they had done the killings, even though that didn't account for anything that had happened in Seagirt since their leaving.

He stopped to look at the surf, high and wind driven. He

wondered whether he could see some migrating whales, or if that started later in the year. Then, he looked around at the beach, and finally at his own footprints in the sand.

Something snapped together in his mind. The left footprint was deeper, and somewhat angled in comparison to his right print. He limped on his right leg, and he supposed that accounted for it. He recalled that one set of the footprints he found at the murder scene looked like that, and that one of the killers must have limped. Now, he thought, I have one more detail, if either Troy or Wheelock limped.

He recalled Lucy Persson thinking that one of the killers was disabled. Like, with a limp? he asked himself.

He walked some more. And, he remembered something about the killers in *In Cold Blood.* One of them limped, and ate aspirin like popcorn because of the pain in his leg. Could one of these guys have assumed a limp because he identified with the killer in the story?

Then, it occurred to him how he might connect things to Wheelock and Troy. He hurried back to his car.

It's only a hunch, he said to himself, as he walked into Worldwide Video, but it's all I've got.

Lou saw Valerie Collins wandering through the video store. She was not wearing black, nor did she seem deep in mourning. Her hair and makeup were perfect, and she wore big hoop earrings. She had a couple romantic comedies in her hands.

He suspected that she was able to bear her loss with ease. Lou approached her.

"Hello, Valerie." He bowed slightly.

She started. "Oh, hi, uh . . . ?"

"Lou Tedesco. Call me Lou."

"I'm just, you know, tryin' to get my mind off, uh, things."

"Oh, I understand completely. You can't dwell on this kind of tragedy. It isn't healthy."

She brightened. "Yes, that's right."

"I'm in here looking for Carla. You know Carla."

"Oh, yeah, we go way back." She was grateful to have another topic to discuss. Lou decided to probe.

"You must have been part of that old crowd. You probably knew Dub Gordon, even Shelley and Larry."

"Not only did I know them, but Henry and me were with them on that last night. Sad about them . . ."

Lou tried to hide his excitement. "You saw Shelley and Larry that last night?"

"Oh, yeah. We were out with them for dinner and a few beers. I knew something was up with them."

"What do you mean?"

"Shelley was all, like, glowy, and Larry had that nervous thing that guys get, like when they're gonna ask a girl something? I was teasing like, 'Larry, what's bugging you?' 'Shelley, why are you blushing?' "

Lou noticed Carla moving around the edges of the video store, throwing them a look now and then.

"Henry," and here Valerie cast her eyes down, "poor Henry," she sighed, "he told me that Larry told him in the john that he was gonna propose to Shelley, even if he had to stay up all night to do it."

"Valerie, have you told this to Lester Green?"

She shrugged. "Never asked me. I didn't think it was important. Everybody in town was all, like, 'Oh, any day now, Larry's gonna do it.' Wasn't, like, a big secret."

"Thanks, Valerie. Please accept my sympathy for your loss."

She teared up. "Thanks," she sniffled, dabbing at her eyes as she went to check out her movies.

Carla Higgins walked over. "How can I help you today?"

"Hello, Carla. I apologize for the last time I was in here. I shouldn't have . . ."

"Are you the one who wrote that article in the Portland paper? We get that here."

"Yes, that was me. I have a theory, but Chief Green won't hear me out, and I need some proof. You might be able to help me."

"Me? I told you everything I knew about that, which is nothing."

"I think you can help. I believe that Calvin and Phil are the killers." Carla gasped. "And, despite what they told everyone about being in California, I think they've run off to Mexico, specifically to avoid arrest."

Carla chewed her lower lip. She was turning it over in her mind.

"Lou, I hate to say this, but it really is possible. Troy is a greasy little creep, and Calvin, well, I believe he's capable of anything. I used to know him pretty well."

"Carla, did one of them limp?"

She thought about it. "Yes, now that you bring it up. Phil limped the last couple of times I saw him. What has that got to do with anything?"

Lou related the story of the footprints on the beach, and his revelation about his own limp just earlier.

"Doesn't seem like much," she said. "He could've sprained his ankle, or got bitten by a dog, or something."

"Well, we've gotta build enough of a circumstantial case to interest the cops. This is one more puzzle piece."

"Is that all you wanted from me?"

Lou squirmed. "Um, not nearly. This is where it gets hairy."

Carla squared her shoulders. "Okay, spit it out."

"I need to trace them through their video rental card. Worldwide's cards are good anywhere there's a store, right? So, if you can access their records from here, we can trace their movements."

Carla went white. She waved her hands. "Oh, no. Not a chance. First of all, I won't do it. Second of all, it's against company policy, and I like my job. Last, it's probably illegal. Plus," her eyes narrowed, "what makes you think it would work, anyway?"

"Well, I'm thinking that, if they rented that miniseries here, they didn't stop just because they were on the road. I think it's their motivator."

Carla looked uneasy. "Uh, whether that makes sense or not, the whole thing is wrong."

"Carla, I'm not happy with this, either. If I were a cop, or a DA, I could get a warrant. All I've got is you, and your conscience. Yes, it is wrong on one level, but, if you want your friends' murders solved, this could help do it."

Lou reached into his pocket, and peeled off five twenty-dollar bills. Carla held up her hand. "No, no money. It won't make up for losing my job, and I wouldn't be doing it for that reason, anyway."

"I underestimated you, Carla, and I'm sorry for that."

"Get the heck out of here for a while. Let me do this, and be done with it." She walked over to the computer, and started rattling the keyboard.

Lou was smart enough not to say another word, and he left. Carla watched him go, and shuddered. She gathered her thoughts.

She felt angry and in pain over the murders. She knew that Calvin Wheelock had nothing but contempt for her, or for Shelley. It was Carla who had convinced Shelley to go for the abortion, and who had provided emotional support to her afterwards.

Calvin was self-centered and insecure, and he just might have held a big grudge against Shelley for ending her pregnancy. Men are funny about that, she thought. They hate it when the kid is aborted, but have no problem ignoring it after it's born.

She imagined for a moment that Calvin might return to get her as well. She went back to the keyboard, and tracked Phil Troy's video rentals. If Carla could come up with anything concrete, it would change the whole complexion of things.

In the meantime, Lou had walked over to a local espresso shop, drank half-caf lattes for an hour, and thumbed through real-estate brochures for beach property.

Finally, he stood up, and walked over to the counter.

"Do you know Carla? From the video store?" he asked the barista.

"Sure."

"Does she drink coffee?"

"Triple mocha, no whipped cream."

"Can I have one of those?"

Lou paid for everything, and walked back to the Worldwide Video. Carla was inspecting a printout.

"Triple mocha, no whipped cream," Lou said, by way of greeting, and handed her the large paper cup.

"Hey, thanks. You might be onto something."

"Was it hard?"

"If the card hadn't been issued here, I couldn't have done it. There's a way to trace to see if a lost card has been used. If the card was from another store, it would send up a red flag that I checked. I had to cancel the card, but that's fine with me. Here, look."

Lou took the computer paper, while Carla sipped at the mocha.

"Wow, the card was used in Arcata, a day after the murders, then in Los Angeles, then in Del Rio, Texas. And, twice from a Mexico City store in the last few days."

"The last time was about two hours ago. They were in Mexico City two hours ago."

"We think," Lou sighed.

"I'll bet. They sure as hell ain't in California, like they've been saying."

"And the card is issued to . . . ?"

"Phil Troy. It was always him that rented that thing."

"Carla, I will do all in my power to make sure you're never mentioned here. I can't tell you how grateful I am."

"Lou, if those bastards killed Shelley and Larry, I don't care. I just want to see them in jail."

"One more thing. Maybe I should take a look at that miniseries."

Carla nodded. "Wait here."

Carla zoomed over to the TV section of the store, and grabbed a four-tape set. She handed it to Lou.

"This one's definitely on the house," she said.

"Thanks, again."

Lou shook her hand and left. He had some TV watching to do.

Lou was hungry. He pulled into the Dunes Café parking lot. Somehow, this was the perfect place.

When he walked in, he created a wave of surprise. Hetty was at the counter, talking with Phyllis and Ronnie. Jean, the feisty older woman he had met the first day, was having coffee and sharing the news of the day. She flashed him a mean face.

The women all had looks on their faces that made Lou speculate as to how glad they were about his arrival. He had never been able to figure them out.

They discussed Henry Collins, and Lou gave them as little as he could. They were not satisfied, but they didn't pursue the matter.

"Lou," Hetty called out. "We wondered whether we'd ever see you again."

"I couldn't stay away. It's those eggs and hash browns."

"Can I fix you some?" Hetty pointed back toward the kitchen.

"Sounds good. Two over easy, side of crisp bacon, sourdough toast. And, thanks."

Hetty walked back to her work, and Lou sat down at the counter. "Phyllis, Ronnie, and Jean. Right?"

"Right as rain," Jean replied. "What brings you back, besides the grub?" Lou detected a lack of enthusiasm in her greeting.

"I want to talk to a few people around here, just to catch up."

Ronnie reached under the counter and pulled out a copy of the *Stump*, with Lou's cover article on the killings.

"Still workin' on this?" she asked.

Lou thought a moment, gave a mental shrug, and said, "Killers are still at large, as they used to say on *Gangbusters.*"

They all chuckled. "This crowd's old enough to remember that radio show, right, Ronnie?" Phyllis winked as she spoke.

Jean hadn't entered into the good humor, nor taken her eyes off Lou. Lou locked her in with his own. "I need for you all to be straight with me," he said. "Last time I was here, I felt like you were all . . . I don't know, 'hiding' seems like too strong a word. Just not telling me everything. Am I right?"

Phyllis nodded. "Yes, I guess you're right. It's not like it was a conspiracy, or anything. We've known each other for so long, it's like we can mind read each other. We just played it close to the vest. We didn't know you from the man in the moon. You turned out to be one of the good guys. I feel like maybe we should apologize or something."

"No apology necessary. In fact, it made me buckle down and dig things up. If you'd spilled everything, I would've gotten lazy."

"Whoa, cowboy," said Ronnie. "We don't even know what 'everything' is. Truth is, we couldn't have given you much more, anyway." She looked at the other women. "As for me, I was hopin' you'd dish stuff for us."

Phyllis chuckled at that. "Yeah, I guess that goes for me, too."

"Okay," Lou took a deep breath. "One thing: Who was the father of Shelley's baby?"

No one spoke for a moment. Then, Phyllis volunteered.

"Hell if we know for sure. But, we got a strong suspicion."

"Understand," Ronnie picked up, "that we always suspected it was one of that bunch she tramped around with."

"Ronnie!" Jean made a shocked noise.

"Be honest, Jeannie. Those kids did damn little except smoke pot and screw each other's eyeballs out. Maybe have a few beers in between. That's why it was so good to see them snap out of it, become honest and decent. Or, leave town."

"So, was it Stud Dunham?"

"He was on our list. So was that Freddie boy, until Velma told us how holy he was."

Lou waved his arms in exasperation. "Well? Do I need a court order?"

"Dammit, Calvin Wheelock. That's who we think." Phyllis, as exasperated as Lou, had spat it out.

Hetty came out of the kitchen, plates in hand, and found a somber group.

"Jeez, what happened here?" she asked.

"Lou gave us the third degree," Phyllis said in mock horror, "beat the truth out of us."

Hetty put the plates down. "So, that's how to get the truth from this crowd. If I'd known, I'd a done it years ago."

"Hetty, do you think Wheelock was the one who got Shelley pregnant?"

"Best guess. Even stoned, Shelley must've known that having Calvin's kid would be a losing proposition. I'm no fan of abortions, but if that kid knocked me up, I'd think about it."

"Aren't you being a bit harsh on him, Hetty?" Ronnie wanted to know.

"That kid is a loser. He's a self-centered punk, and the only reason he puts up with Phil Troy is that he looks good standing next to him. Good riddance to him. California's loss is our gain."

"So," Lou put in, "you think he and Troy are in California?"

She shrugged. "Where else? That's what they told people before they left, and there's no reason to doubt it." She fixed Lou with a look. "Is there?"

Lou decided to play it cagey for the time being.

"I don't know, Hetty. At this point, no, there's no reason to think they're anywhere else. Mind if I eat? It's getting cold."

Lou dove into the food, and the conversation wandered in a desultory way, never losing the thread of the killings completely. After he finished, and over-complimented the cook, Lou asked if there was a pay phone.

Hetty pulled the house phone out from under the counter and offered it to him. It was an aged, greasy, princess model with a dial. He mulled whether to call Jack Narz with everyone there, then he decided it made no difference, and would provide fodder for discussion after he left.

It took him a second to reorient himself to a dial. It felt odd and nostalgic. He managed to dial the number without a major age regression resulting, and it rang on the other end.

"Jack?" he asked. The women paid instant attention.

"Yes, at the Dunes."

The women held their breath when he was silent, listening to the other party, and no doubt speculating on "Jack."

"Is she there?"

The women looked at each other with questions in their eyes.

"Yeah, I'll give it a half hour, or so. Unless you want me to pick her up."

His audience was rapt.

"How do I get there? Uh-huh. Uh-huh. A left? Uh-huh. What was that number?"

Jean, who had sat stone-faced since Lou walked in, was ready to burst, wanting to know, but constrained from asking by the last shreds of her self-control.

"Okay, so, a half hour, right? See you later."

He hung up and handed the phone back to Hetty. All eyes were on him.

Savoring his little moment, he smiled at them, his face shining with feigned innocence, not saying a word. He loved watching their discomfiture, as they were consumed by the clash of curiosity and manners.

"Well," he began, twisting the knife a little more, "I guess I have time for another cup of coffee before my, um, appointment."

Ronnie, coming out of her trance, went for the coffee pot.

Jean's face was a mask of agony. Hetty twitched. Phyllis seemed to be enjoying this as much as Lou.

Ronnie poured coffee, and asked with exaggerated nonchalance, "So, Lou, where you off to?"

Phyllis burst into hysterical laughter. Soon, everyone at the counter was helpless, and with aching sides. The other customers took it all in with perplexed looks.

When he got his breath, Lou said, "Well, I guess that was a tension breaker."

Then, they laughed some more.

"You know," Phyllis said, "this town has been so uptight for days now. That was the first belly laugh I've had in a long time. Felt damn good."

"Come on Lou, give!" Phyllis's face was still crimson from the hysteria, but she kept her eyes on the prize.

"Why not? I heard from Jack Narz. He got some information that he wanted me to look at, and I wanted to talk to him and Velma at the same time."

"What kind of information?" Hetty pressed.

"I'm not sure that Jack wants it out, yet."

Groans all around.

"But, I promise you that if he doesn't mind, I'll come back and tell you."

They all decided to settle for that.

"So," Ronnie asked, "you'll be around for a few days?"

"I think so. A couple, at least. I hear Chloe's missed me."

This made everyone laugh again, and Lou drank off his lukewarm coffee.

"Got to be on my way," he said, smacking his lips. "I expect I'll see you all later?"

"If you try to get out of Seagirt without reporting in," warned Phyllis, "these girls'll hunt you down and torture the news out of you. A word to the wise." She set her hands on her hips, and winked at the others.

"You got that right," Ronnie assured Lou.

"Okay. I'm off."

When Lou got out to his car, he glanced back into the café, and chuckled at the huddle around the counter. He started the car and drove off.

"Well, we may get to the end of this thing after all," Hetty sighed.

Jean stood up, upsetting a coffee cup.

"I gotta go," Jean said, and was out the door in a second.

"I wonder what's biting her," Hetty said.

A few minutes later, Jean stormed into the police station, and threw the door open with such violence that Gar Loober jumped off his chair.

Before he could say anything, she demanded, "Is he in?"

"Uh, yeah . . ."

Then, Chief Green's door flew open, and he yelled, "What the hell? Oh, it's you, Jeannie."

Gar noticed a peculiar look on the chief's face. Jean walked over to Green, and said, "Let's go in your office."

"Uh, sure. Loober, no calls for a while."

"Okay, Chief."

Once behind closed doors, Jean pushed the chief into his chair and shook a finger in his face.

"Dammit, Lester, you gonna do anything about that Tedesco fella? I want him gone, or I'll know the reason why!"

"Relax, Jeannie, you'll give yourself a stroke."

Jean stood over the much larger man, arms akimbo, and held him cowed.

"Don't patronize me, you old walrus. What are you gonna do about him?"

"Look, I got my own reasons for wanting him gone, but my hands are tied. He's a member of the press. He can go wherever the hell he likes, and ask whatever he wants. DA Knight up in Waldorf don't want me interferin' with him, unless it affects my job."

"So," she crossed her arms above her bosom, "tell him that it does."

Green scrunched back, attempting to create some distance between them, but she stayed on him.

"It ain't as easy as that. The press got a right to ask questions. And you," he waved a finger right back, "got a right to not answer."

"Come off it, Lester. It don't make any difference what I say, it's those other bigmouths. What am I supposed to do, kill 'em?"

Green winced at the suggestion.

"Jeez, don't do that. I got enough troubles. They can't tell him nothing that will make any difference."

"Hmph!"

"Look, what are you afraid of? He won't find nothin' out. He don't even know where to look."

"He's hooked up with Hilda Truax. That nosy bitch knows things. She's gettin' to be a bigger pain than her old man was."

"She don't know everything . . ." the chief purred, with the best tone of seduction he could muster.

"Ach! You're such an idiot! I don't know why . . ."

"Because you like it. C'mere, Jeannie, come to papa."

Gar Loober wasn't sure, but he thought he heard giggling in he chief's office.

"Nah!" He shook his head and went back to work.

Lou drove according to the instructions Narz had given him. A few minutes later, he pulled up in front of a white, well-kept bungalow one house off the main road. He parked on the sandy patch at the verge of the road. There was an old Chevy truck in the driveway.

Lou could see that the garden around the house was once a showplace, but that it hadn't been maintained well for a while. He knocked on the door.

"Mr. Tedesco?"

"Lou, Jack. No formality here. Nice place." The place smelled of single man, with a rich overlay of tobacco smoke.

"Thanks," Narz answered, stepping aside so Lou could enter. "When my wife was alive, she kept it looking like a picture in a magazine. I poke around, but I ain't got her dedication."

"I lost a wife, myself. I couldn't even stay in the same house."

A silent moment passed between them.

"Can I get you a beer?"

"I don't drink alcohol, but a soft drink would be nice."

"Got some pop, will that do?"

"Perfect."

Narz offered Lou a seat in a comfortable room heavy on the chintz, and headed back into the kitchen. He came back with a beer and a bottle of a fruity soda pop.

"This okay?"

"Sure, thanks." Lou took the bottle and tipped it toward his host. "Cheers."

"Better days."

"Velma is not here yet?"

"Nah. She don't live too far away, though." Narz looked up at the ceiling for a second, or two. "Funny that Velma and me woulda been in-laws, if, you know, things had been different. I've known her a long time."

"This is a real small town. Everyone seems to know everyone else."

"That's likely so. Might change, soon, though. Word is that the state is plannin' to take over some of them old motels, and fix 'em up for poor families to live in. Not many jobs out here, except in the summer. If they're lookin' to get 'em off welfare, that seems like a bad idea."

"Jack, I've lived in big cities and small towns, and I still can't figure out how they make these decisions."

There was a knock on the door, and Lou sighed to himself, grateful that the conversation wouldn't spin off into politics.

Velma came in, dressed in late July for the kind of winter that Oregon hadn't seen since the last Ice Age, but, Lou thought, bundled for a cold that only she could feel.

"You two know each other?" Narz asked.

"Yes, sir, John. Mr. Tedesco and me have talked."

"Please, Velma, you can call me Lou. We're old friends now."

Velma smiled. "Yes, I guess you could say. John, I always loved the way Helen did this place up. Real pretty."

"Thanks, Velma. Helen always liked you. Something to drink?"

"No, thank you." Velma sat down.

Lou cleared his throat. "Jack, why don't you fill Velma in on your, um, information."

Narz blushed a bit, still not easy with his use of a psychic, but he got through the story with no interruptions.

"Velma, I know you're religious, so I hope you don't take offense at my seein' Lucy."

She shook her head. "No, sir. I know that some folks get the gift of sight, even if they don't give the credit to the Lord. And, the Lord knows what he's doin'."

Lou looked at Velma. "Does anything Lucy said make any sense to you? Bullfighters, or volcanos?"

"Not that I can think," she shook her head again. "But, I will pray on it. If that woman was given to see these things, we will know."

"Velma, what do you know about Calvin Wheelock?"

"Just what everyone does," she shrugged. Lou wondered if this were true.

"Was he close to Shelley in the old days?"

"Not when they went to school, but they got closer when she was livin' with her girlfriends in that old house. Shelley would come home from time to time, mostly to do wash or borrow money or get a good meal. She would talk about him sometimes."

"Anything specific?"

"No, not really. He paid her a lot of attention for a while."

"Was she sweet on him?"

Now, Velma's eyes narrowed. "Why do you ask?"

Lou looked at Narz before he answered. Narz was on the edge of his chair.

"Is it possible he was the father of her baby?"

Velma's face showed that pieces were falling into place in her mind, and her eyes got round.

"I never thought . . . ," her voice faded away.

"Velma," Narz said gently, "most folks around here sorta felt like that."

"Why didn't someone tell me?"

"Well, we never knew for a hundred percent, and I guess nobody thought it would do no good if you knew. It was kinda . . ." He looked at Lou.

"Irrelevant?" Lou offered.

"Yeah," Narz sighed, "irrelevant."

Velma turned to Lou. "Did you know this?"

"Not until an hour, or so, ago, and Jack's right. Nobody knows for sure," Lou said, without conviction.

Velma sighed. "Well, no help now, one way or the other. It don't really matter." She showed resignation.

"Except for one thing," Lou thought out loud. "The father of Shelley's baby had the only thing like a motive, if there was a motive for this crime. And, it doesn't work that well, because of the time element."

"What do we do now?" she asked.

"Let me think about this. You, too. I can use any reasonable suggestions, even strange ones."

Narz caught Lou's eye. "Lou, who do you think did it?"

"Okay, but this is no more than a big hunch. I have no, I mean *no,* guaranteed reason to believe that this is true."

"Yeah, and?"

"I think Wheelock and his pal Phil Troy did it. There were two sets of footprints leading up to and away from the crime scene, and no mere observer would have walked away casually after seeing that. Would you?

"So, the prints belonged to the killers. Not a gang of bikers, because there were only two sets, and they were sneakers, not boots. And, no one has seen them since that day, although they claim to be in California. I think they're in Mexico, but I have no proof of that either, except another hunch."

"They got bullfighters in Mexico," Velma whispered.

"Yes, they do. And, I think they have volcanos there, too. But, it's not all hanging together, even with what Lucy told us. Nothing you could take to court."

Velma worked up the nerve to ask, "What does Henry Collins have to do with all of this?"

"Yeah," said Jack, "that really was weird."

Lou sighed. "I wish I knew. Why would he do a thing like that? I only spoke with him once. You two have any ideas?"

"No, sir," said Velma. "He was one of Shelley's old friends, but . . ."

"Valerie Collins says they had dinner with Larry and Shelley that night. Is that true?"

Velma shook her head. "Don't know."

"Jack?"

"Hey, Larry didn't even check in with me when he was back in high school. I got no idea."

"Well," said Lou, "maybe this will all get clearer, soon. Let's hope so?"

"Where are you staying?" Narz asked.

"I'm over at Chloe's motel, the Saltaire."

Narz smiled. "Make sure you lock your door. She's dangerous when she got a single man around."

Velma laughed, then blushed. She covered her mouth with her hand, and giggled some more.

"Yeah," Lou said, "but we've got an understanding. She doesn't bother me, and I don't bring Velma around to put her in her place."

Velma giggled again. Lou got up, and they all said goodbye. Lou remembered something.

"Jack, do you want me to keep any of this secret? Is it not for publication?"

Narz rubbed his chin. "Print it if you want to. I ain't so embarrassed about seein' Lucy any more. I was nervous that people would think I was a damn nut, or somethin'. Who knows? Maybe someone can come up with a clue about bullfighters."

Lou nodded. "Velma?"

Velma shrugged. "Like John says . . ."

Lou shook hands with both, first Velma's tiny, cold little hand, then Narz's beefy paw. He walked out to the car, his mind swirling with unconnected thoughts. After collecting himself, he drove off to the Saltaire.

It took Lou almost an hour to extricate himself from Chloe's ungentle clutches. She had been worried when he didn't come back to his room, and inquired about his bandage.

She made a big show of giving him a retroactive off-season rate. She tried to wheedle information out of him, in a chilling bit of blatant seduction.

Lou used every atom of his diplomatic skills to fend Chloe off without hurting her feelings. Hanging on like a terrier, Chloe insisted on accompanying Lou to his room. At last, Lou had to fall back on a headache, backed by main force to keep her out.

Lou sat back and watched the miniseries. With the judicious use of the fast-forward, he got through it in three hours. It cemented his conviction that Troy and Wheelock were the prime suspects. And, it shook him up.

After sitting for a while to calm his nerves and refocus, he girded his loins and headed for the police station. Between Chloe and Lester Green, he was developing a new callus on his psyche. He parked his car, took a deep breath, and walked into the police station.

Gar Loober greeted him cordially. They were exchanging pleasantries when Chief Green came out of his office. Green said nothing, but stared at Lou until it became unnerving. Loober stopped in mid-sentence when he saw the look on Lou's face.

"What the hell do you want?" Green growled.

"Good morning to you, too, Chief Green." Lou said, as chipper as a talk-show host. "Gar?" Loober nodded, jaw slack.

"I want to tell you a couple of things that might be important." This sounded weak to Lou. He was reluctant to mention what he discovered at Worldwide Video, because of the repercussions for Carla. Without the rental records, he had nothing new, but he ploughed on. "I heard that Phil Troy recently acquired a nine millimeter pistol. Neither he nor

Calvin Wheelock has been seen since the murders, and I think I know where to find them." He brandished the videos.

The chief's face betrayed his inner struggle. Lou read it as: Do I kill him, or just humor him?

"What's that video, Tedesco? *How To Be A Detective in Ten Easy Lessons*?"

"No," Lou mustered his dignity, "actually, it's a TV miniseries of *In Cold Blood.* Troy and Wheelock rented this several times recently, and it's about a thrill killing done by two buddies who then flee to Mexico. Interested?"

"Take a hike," Green said without emotion.

"Come on, Chief, Troy gets a gun, maybe the same caliber as the murder weapon, and they fry their brains on this thrill kill movie. Do I have to draw a picture?"

"First, you're out of your goddamned mind. Calvin is not in Mexico. He's on leave, and I know exactly where he is. Second, it still ain't illegal to own a gun in this state, and as long as he isn't carrying concealed, I don't care if Troy has a hundred guns. Third, if they had rented X-rated videos, you think they would have screwed those kids to death?"

Gar laughed out loud, and cut it short when Green shot a look at him. Lou felt the fire leaving his gut, only to burn his cheeks.

"Listen," Green went on, "you don't know squat about police matters, you're not even a real reporter, and for sure you never even met Calvin, *or* Troy. You're accusing two people you don't know of a double homicide. Are you out of your goddamned mind?"

Lou shifted on his feet, discomfort oozing out of him.

"Okay, look, maybe I'm all wet," Lou tried, "but I think it at least—"

"I don't care what you think. Get out, before I run you in on a charge I'll think up later. You got five seconds to get your ugly butt out of this office!"

"Chief, if you don't want to talk to me, that's one thing. But, you don't have to look at me like I'm something stuck to the bottom of your shoe."

"Tedesco, there is nothing to report. That is my report. Now, you are just in the way. Loober, show the man out."

"Chief, look, someone tried to kill me. I've had threats, and one attempt. Doesn't that buy me something? Can you answer a couple of questions?"

Lou saw the chief struggle with himself. Green was very weary of having to be nice. "Yeah, but make it to the point."

"Have Wheelock and Troy returned yet?" Lou opened.

"If they have, they haven't come here."

"Gar?" Loober shrugged.

"Are you sure they're in California?"

"This is a free country. Maybe they're in Timbuktu."

"I think they're in Mexico, and I think it's to avoid arrest."

Green gave an exasperated sigh.

"What is it with Mexico? You got Mexico on the brain. They can go anywhere they like. They're not criminals."

"You don't know that for sure, do you? They should be suspects."

"Show-and-tell is over. Loober, throw him out . . ."

"Hey," Lou got indignant, "you can't . . ."

". . . and, if he comes back, read him his rights and arrest him."

"On what charge?" Lou clenched both fists at his sides.

"Interfering with a police officer in performance of his duties."

"You think you can make that stick?"

"You think you wanna spend a day or two in our jail before you get some shyster to spring you?"

"Okay, Green, I'm gone. But, I'll be back."

"Jail's empty. Come back any time."

Lou counted to ten in his head, made an awkward turn, wrenching his knee, and flung himself out the door, slamming it behind him.

"And stay the hell out!" Green bellowed through the closed door.

Gar Loober took it all in, and started thinking.

10. A Cop Calls

Gar Loober stretched his long legs out in front of him, and reached over for the TV remote. The rump-sprung couch groaned and twanged with his shifting weight. He was in the living room of his grungy, little one-bedroom apartment, as far from the beach as could be in a beach town.

Surfing around the cable channels, he settled on a bass fishing show. Then, he muted the sound.

Gar looked with slight revulsion at the half-eaten TV dinner sitting on the coffee table. The gravy was beginning to congeal, and an unhealthy sheen covered the heap of over-cooked vegetables. Although he could cook a little, he hated to use his precious time off doing anything but studying police methods, relaxing, and sleeping. Thus the frozen dinners and fast food meals eaten faster.

Sometimes he wished he still smoked. He wished he still could light a cigarette, sit back, and wait for the nicotine to kick in, calming him. He got up to throw the TV dinner away, and to grab a beer out of the refrigerator.

Gar drank the beer standing in the dark kitchen, watching

the light patterns made by the flashing TV image on the wall behind the couch. He took stock.

Gar Loober loved being a cop. It was the only thing he ever wanted to do. His father was a cop. His uncle was a cop.

Both of their marriages had failed. His mother, taken to the edge of her sanity by her husband's late nights, absences, and the two wounds he had sustained on the job, left and divorced his father. Gar, who was in high school at the time, opted to stay with his dad.

His mother began drinking, and he hadn't heard from her in years. She may have gone to live with her widowed sister in Idaho.

His uncle was a good cop, but was too easily distracted by the women who were attracted to cops like groupies were to rock stars. Gar's aunt had had enough one night, and tried to kill her husband with his service revolver. She was still in prison. His uncle's shattered arm put him on permanent desk duty, but he couldn't give up the job.

There were rumors that his uncle had been diagnosed with Hepatitis C and cirrhosis, and would not live long. No one would tell Gar, for sure. His uncle was forty-eight years old.

But, still, Gar became a cop. He had attended classes at a local community college, and some more at Oregon State, all to help him be a better cop.

Gar kept up with crime scene technique. It was a kind of hobby, besides being his job. He knew proper procedure, and was something of a stickler for it. He respected the constitution, and people's rights. When he had to run in underage, drunk, and disorderly kids at spring break, there was never a complaint about rough treatment.

One kid told him, "I been arrested four times. You're the only one who don't slap me around."

Gar wanted to be, and tried to be, a good cop. That is why he hated working for Lester Green.

Chief Green seemed to have gotten his skills from a *Police Work for Idiots* book. At least that's what Gar would say to himself from time to time, and it got a laugh every time.

Oh, Green could do the paperwork, and he knew enough to Mirandize people he arrested. Gar saw him as an overpaid clerk with a gun. He hated himself for his disloyal feelings, but he had been able to make no impact on Green's citadel of ignorance.

Whenever Gar tried, subtly, he hoped, to guide the chief in procedure, Green always came back with a variation of, "I was doing this before you were weaned." But, much cruder.

Suddenly, Gar realized that he was standing in the kitchen in the dark with an empty beer bottle. He put away the empty, opened another, walked into the living room and sat down on the couch.

His immediate frustration was centered on the beach killings. The case was going nowhere. Green was spinning his wheels, and he seemed even dumber than usual. That reporter guy was doing more solid investigation than Lester Green ever did in his life.

So, Gar Loober thought on what he should do. The TV images showed two guys in a boat, making speeches about hooks and bait. Finally, they put their lines in the water. Gar nodded.

"You can't catch nothin' if you don't put your line in the water."

He got up and grabbed his coat.

Dinner at the Dunes Café, and Lou had a rapt audience. Hetty, Ronnie and Connie, Phyllis, Jean, and several other women who had mysteriously shown up after he sat down. Lou wondered if they had a phone tree.

He recounted, as best he could remember, Jack Narz's story of his meeting with Lucy, the visions, and what they might mean. He told them that Velma had no idea, and that they wanted anyone who could come up with something to contact them.

The reactions ranged from awe to outright scoffing.

"Bah, humbug!" said Jean. "They're barking up the wrong tree. These psychics are a bunch of phonies."

"Gee," said a white-haired, bifocaled matron, "they can't all be phonies, can they?"

Ronnie was fidgeting. "I say it's worth a try. Why not? What have they got to lose? Lester Green couldn't find a football in a punch bowl."

Jean's head snapped around to face Ronnie. "Ronnie, did you tell Jack Narz to call that woman?"

Ronnie went pale. Jean rolled her eyes.

Hetty came to Ronnie's defense.

"Come on, Jean, what's the harm? If nothing else, it gives them some hope."

"*False* hope," offered a stocky blonde woman in sweats. "I'd rather take it straight than have someone play with my head."

"Bunny," Hetty replied, "this isn't like a cancer diagnosis. There's no hope for bringing those kids back, but the killer didn't disappear off the face of the earth. Anything is possible."

Phyllis, who had been taking this all in with a sour expression, spoke up. "I got an idea. Since this doesn't affect any of us in any real way, let them do what they want to do. Let 'em hire a bloodhound, if it makes 'em feel better. Meanwhile, think about bullfighters and volcanos. You never know."

Lou admired Phyllis. She was level-headed, humorous, and compassionate. And, she didn't take crap from anyone. Her remarks certainly stopped the discussion.

Lou concentrated on his *osso bucco*. It was the best meal he'd had in Seagirt, except for his breakfasts there at the café. After paying excessive compliments to Hetty's cooking, and leaving a big tip, he went back to the motel.

He surfed around cable TV for a while, drifting into a doze, when a knock came at the door.

"Lou? It's me, Gar."

Lou opened the door, and Gar stood there in uniform and rain gear. He motioned the cop inside.

"Put your raincoat over there. Can I get you something?"

"No, uh-uh. Wouldn't mind sitting down. I'm beat."

Lou brought Gar over to the table, and they sat. Gar looked off into the middle distance for a few seconds, then spoke.

"Lou, we're stuck on the killings. No leads, no prime suspects. Chief Green seems to be avoiding it. When I bring it up, he changes the subject."

"Maybe he's embarrassed."

Gar shook his head. "I don't think Lester Green knows the meaning of the word." Then, he grimaced. "I hate to talk about the chief like this, I really do."

"Gar, you must have a reason to feel this way."

Gar nodded. "Remember when you found us on the beach? The morning of the murders?"

"Sure."

"Well, Chief Green and I had just had a big fight. There were those footprints, and some handprints, right? The chief sent me back to the office to get the forensics kit. So, I come back with the kit I put together, and he pitches a fit. He wanted his plaster of paris for taking the impressions.

"Lou, nobody uses that stuff any more. I had dental stone and flour sulfur, and I know how to use both. He told me that he'd been using plaster forever, and that I didn't need to tell him his job."

"What's the difference, Gar?"

"That plaster of paris is hard to mix exactly to the right consistency, especially if you never do it, like the chief. If it's too thick, it'll crumble the sand and give you a false cast. If you mix it thin, it'll take forever to set up, and will suck the sand into itself. The dental stone is easier, quicker, and won't do as much damage to the print."

"Have you explained this to him?"

"Hell, yeah. He won't listen, and he won't let me bring it up, even. That's why I had that photographer take so many pictures of the sneaker prints. I knew that Chief Green would mess them up, too.

"And that's another thing. That crime scene photographer

is an amateur. He takes the pictures for the high school yearbook and like if you want pictures of the new baby for your mom. I had to teach him what little he knows, and out of earshot of the chief."

Lou had never seen Gar so worked up.

"What about suspects? The fishing boat idea didn't pan out?"

"We questioned everyone concerned. All of them had solid alibis. The skipper who had the hassles with Larry was visiting the county jail. When we talked to him, he was plain shocked that we could think that he'd kill someone over a fishing dispute. Seemed believable to me.

"Same with the crew. All of them were accounted for."

"What about Tom Knight? Wasn't he personally interested?"

"For a while, but, let's face it, how many votes are there in Seagirt? He has bigger fish to fry, and truly, no one outside of town seems to care. Except you."

"What is it with this place? I can't make a move without getting tracked. Radar should work so well."

"Between Chloe and the girls at the café, it's better than the newspapers. Speaking of that, do you know that your piece in your paper was the only follow-up? Nobody's been around to care about this. But hell, Lou, I care."

Lou nodded, "Yes, Gar. I know that. You've been the one who was open to considering anything I could come up with. Do you mind if I ask you some questions?"

Gar shrugged. "I'll tell you what I can. It's getting to be a cold case, and soon there'll be no investigation for you to compromise."

"What do you know about Wheelock and Troy?"

"Well, look, I didn't grow up here. I'm from eastern Oregon, and I wanted to live near the ocean. So, I was happy to find the job here. All I know is what I got from Calvin shootin' the breeze on the job. And, Phil Troy, he was just on the fringes. I saw him when he met us for beers, or a movie."

"And . . . ?" Lou prompted.

"Hey, he's like a guy in his twenties. Calvin, that is. Full of himself, a bit of a macho stud. I was a little like him a few years ago. I sure had friends like him. I know he was supposed to be a wild kid, but he was all talk in my experience."

"And Troy?"

Gar shook his head. "Strange one. I could never figure out why Calvin tolerated him. Troy was greasy, like he didn't bathe much, and annoying. Jackass laugh, always interrupting people. Couldn't hold his liquor. We'd be drinking beers, and he'd have tequila back, or scotch. A couple of rounds, and he'd be bombed.

"But, if you hung out with Calvin, you got Phil."

Lou remembered that Dub Gordon had said the same thing.

"Do you think," Lou asked with caution, "that Phil was, um . . ."

"You want to know if Phil was queer for Calvin."

Lou exhaled, and sat back. "Yes. Or, the other way around."

"Hell if I know." Gar shook his head, again. "But, it had crossed my mind, when I thought about it at all. You know, like, what's the story with these two? None of my business, though. It could've been nothing more than two kids who grew up together, did everything together . . ."

"Yes, of course."

Gar brightened. "Oh! You know what? On the sly, I called Calvin's aunt in California yesterday. Where they were supposed to be staying? She told me that the two of them had gone off to New Orleans to look for work, and she had no address or phone number for 'em. Hadn't heard from 'em."

No New Orleans video rentals, Lou thought. Gar went on.

"So, I told the Chief. He said that since they weren't suspects for anything, he didn't care if they went to the damn Sahara Desert. He said that Calvin Wheelock had come from local people, and had been his deputy, and he refused to believe that Calvin had done a murder."

Lou flashed a puzzled look at Gar.

"It's funny, Gar. Everyone here knows someone who couldn't have done it. Freddie, Wheelock, even Stud Dunham. But, nobody has any idea who might be guilty. I was raised in a big city, and I guess the neighbors would have felt the same. Even Son of Sam was considered polite and quiet by the people in his building. Police work must be tough."

"Who's Stud Dunham?" asked Gar. "His name came up, but he was before my time here. Chief Green never really filled me in."

Lou gave Gar a short talk on the wild crowd that seemed to him to be the connection for all this. Then, he asked Gar a question.

"Gar, do you know who was the father of Shelley Korta's baby?"

"Sure. Is that a secret?"

"In this town, you could learn the combination to the CIA's safe easier. Who was it?"

"Calvin. He bragged about it enough. I can't imagine why everybody doesn't know . . ." Gar scratched his head.

"If people know, they're hiding behind not being sure."

"Well, that's why Freddie dumped her."

"Velma knows that, sort of, but claims not to know the father. Was Freddie mad enough to kill her, do you think?"

"Freddie worshiped her. If he was mad enough to kill anyone, it might be Calvin."

At that moment Lou made a decision.

"Gar, let me show you something." He arose and walked to where his coat was hanging. He took the folded printout he got from Carla and gave it to Gar.

"What's this, Lou?" Gar asked as he scanned the paper.

"Those are video rentals on Phil Troy's card. Notice that the trail leads to Texas and Mexico, and nowhere near New Orleans. Wheelock and Troy are in Mexico, and I think it's to hide from the law."

"Where the hell did you get this?"

"I can't tell you, it's from an informant, but you can take that. Think it over, and look at the evidence with fresh eyes.

Talk to Dub Gordon about Troy's new gun. He loves to talk, and I bet no cop ever thought to ask him anything. It's worth a try.

"Henry Collins wouldn't talk to me, but I got the idea that he might know something. Of course, it's too late now . . ."

Gar stood up, the chair scraping the cheap linoleum.

"Yeah, Lou, thanks. I gotta think. Oh, I almost forgot. We got a handwriting sample on Collins, and it looks the same to me. I'm no expert, of course. We sent it on to Salem."

"One more question. Would it do me any good to talk to the dog walkers who found the bodies?"

"Not really. They're two old maiden ladies with a couple of those little yappy things with a lot of hair. They didn't see anything besides the victims, and they were so shook up I thought they were gonna pass out. I could give you their names, but I doubt you'd get anything, and you'd just scare 'em again."

Lou handed Gar his police raincoat. Gar slipped it on, and moved to the door. Before he left, Gar turned and asked, "What was up with that cyanide?"

Lou sighed and said it was a remnant of his drinking life, a nasty little tradition born of despair.

"So, it was, what, your final one for the road?"

"Yup. If I ever drank the vodka, I'd have chased it with the poison. I'd rather die than live again as a drunk.

"By the way, any idea who planted that stuff?"

Gar scratched his head. "Another puzzle. Damn, Lou. Does it ever get easier to figure things out?"

"Not in my life, buddy." Lou shook hands with the deputy.

Gar left, shaking his head, and Lou lay down on the bed and crashed without undressing.

11. Advice from Bud

When Lou awoke the next morning, he felt stiff in the joints and grubby in yesterday's clothes. He needed to figure out what he'd be doing in Seagirt.

He stripped off the old clothes, and staggered into the shower. A few minutes of water cascading on his body woke him sufficiently to think.

Lou headed off to walk on the beach and organize himself. He walked with his head down, partly to keep the fitful breeze from blowing spray in his face. The rain had subsided, but the wind on the surf was a passable substitute.

He avoided going near the crime scene, but couldn't have said why. The beach was littered with fresh cargoes of driftwood, commonly washed up by coastal storms. Some of these went way beyond what Lou would have thought possible: huge logs, whole sections of large trees.

He wondered whether the acre-sized log rafts that floated down Oregon's rivers to saw mills or lumber ships lost some stragglers that wound up in the ocean. Spotting a plastic tarp covering parts of two parallel tree trunks, Lou walked over to inspect. He was amazed, as he got closer, to hear humming coming from under the blue tarp. It sounded like "Hello, Dolly!"

Not sure of how to proceed, Lou just called out, "Hello in there!"

The tarp rustled, and the bearded, bemused countenance of Nutty Bud appeared from underneath. He focused his eyes on Lou's face.

"Howdy, pardner. Need my sifter?" Bud asked with a mercenary leer.

Lou laughed. "You remember? No, not this time, Bud. What the heck are you doin' out here?"

Bud emerged from the burrow between the logs, wrapped in two army blankets.

"This here's my driftwood condo. I live here."

"All year round?"

"Yes, sir, mostly. Rent's low, and it suits me."

"What do you mean, 'mostly'?"

"I ain't crazy, irregardless of what folks say. It gets too cold, or one of them storms comes up, I go to a shelter up the way. One time, a storm sent them waves up the beach, rolled these logs and nearly squished me like a bug. I can get that Loober kid to put me in jail, if I get a cup of coffee and run away without payin'. He unnerstands."

"Yeah, Gar is a good guy. So, you do a day in a warm jail, with three square meals. Sounds like an O. Henry story."

"Yeah, but this ain't Baghdad-on-the-Subway."

Lou looked at Bud with surprise, shocked that he knew O. Henry's witticism about New York. An idea occured to him.

"Bud, would you like some coffee, maybe a meal?"

Bud smiled a gapped grin. "You buyin', sport?"

"You bet. Come with me."

Lou didn't want to question Bud at the Dunes amid all the distractions. He took Bud to a Burger King on the main drag. The kids behind the counter didn't care a bit about Bud's shabby clothing.

Bud bolted a couple of hamburgers, and drank four cups

of coffee. After a polite burp, and using the men's room, he settled down for a fifth cup. Lou took the opportunity.

"You've read O. Henry?"

"Did my senior thesis on him in college."

"Did you graduate?"

"Oregon State, 1960. Bachelor's in business administration."

Lou decided that he wouldn't ask the obvious question, although Bud seemed to expect it, judging from the look on his face. But, there was a more pressing agenda.

"Can you remember July fourteenth?"

"Don't have no calendar," Bud shrugged, scratching his head.

For a moment, Bud searched Lou's face, looking for ulterior motives. Lou prodded.

"It was the night of the killings, Shelley and Larry."

Bud sighed, and spoke.

"I heard explosions. I thought they was fireworks, like left over from July fourth. I sleep light. Got to."

Lou cocked his head. "Why?"

"Man has no house around 'im, some people like to screw around with 'im."

"Anything like that ever happen to you?"

Bud nodded. "Yup. Before I came back to Seagirt, I bummed up an' down the coast. All the way from Alaska to Baja, one time or another. Seen some stuff.

"In San Diego, I was sleepin' in Balboa Park, along with my pal, Smokey. Smokey had one leg, 'cause he got shot in Vietnam. Buncha kids came up on us, kicked the crap out of us. I got away, they killed Smokey."

Lou could see that the memory still tormented him.

"I'm real alert since then. Saved my life more'n once."

"No joke," Lou said. "How do you know those explosions happened that night?"

"Same night those two kids rousted me outta my sleep. Two guys with a gun." Bud shook his head and snorted. "Busy night."

"Bud, could the explosions have been gunshots?"

Bud scratched his face and nodded. "Maybe. Coulda been."

"Do you remember what those guys looked like?"

Bud's face hardened. "Folks all look alike to me. It don't make much difference."

"Come on, Bud, you remembered me. Think."

Bud sipped coffee. "They yelled for me to get out from under my tarp. I crawled out, and they stuck a gun in the back of my neck. They wouldn't let me stand up, nor even let me look at 'em. I didn't see much." He closed his eyes.

"Did you recognize their voices?"

Bud thought this over. "Nope. Guess not."

Lou waited a second, prepared to press. Bud opened his eyes.

"Fancy sneakers. And dungarees." Bud nodded at his memory.

"Can you describe the sneakers?"

"No, but they both had the same kind. Black, with white stripes, some kind of design, maybe."

"Did they hurt you?"

"No, not much," he shook his head, "just scared me and laughed. Yelled, cursed, called me dirty names. Kicked me a couple times and walked away."

"Can you remember anything else, the gun?"

"Fancy, silver, like an automatic. Like Patton carried."

"Didn't Patton carry six-shooters?"

"Yeah, but silver. Like that."

"Okay." Lou thought he had something. The sneakers, the gun. Maybe this was leading somewhere. Then Bud held up a finger.

"One more thing."

"Yes, Bud?"

"One of 'em limped. I saw them goin' away."

Lou nodded. Bud was far from a hopeless drifter, and had potential for rehabilitation. Lou decided to talk with someone about that.

"Thanks, Bud. I appreciate your help. Can I give you a lift back to the beach?"

"No, siree. I gotta walk, clear my head. But, I got something for you to think about, pardner."

"What's that?"

"Seen that Nixon movie?"

Lou's mind reeled. "Uh, the one a couple of years ago? The Oliver Stone one?"

Bud shook his head. "Don't know that one. Two newspaper reporters after ol' Tricky Dick."

"Oh! You mean *All the President's Men*?"

"That the one with Deep Throat?"

"Yes, that's the one."

"Well, pardner, remember what Deep Throat said: Follow the money."

Before Lou could ask any more Bud turned and walked away, waving goodbye behind him. He headed straight for the beach.

Lou took stock.

He needed to figure out what Nutty Bud had meant by "follow the money." So, he went to a local place for coffee. As he drank his third cup, he thought about his agenda.

Today, he would see Velma, assuming she had the time. He could fit in Dub Gordon before or after that. Tomorrow, he would see Hilda, try to patch up her wounded feelings, and maybe take her out to dinner.

Lou couldn't understand why he felt guilty about Hilda, but he did. He decided to go with his best instincts, and find out what she wanted from him.

He assumed that Blanche would want him to check in from time to time, in case his quota of abuse needed filling. And, of course, if anything else popped up, he'd deal with that, too.

Velma's phone number was in the local book, and he called her from the coffee shop. She agreed to see him, if he gave her a few minutes to tidy up.

Lou wandered around the small Seagirt business district, most of which was in midweek mode, open for reduced hours. The rain had reappeared, diminished to a persistent mist. He was fascinated with the indoor carousel, now part of a mall that featured odd little specialty shops and snack bars.

After an hour of peering at tacky art objects, rushing through made-to-order T-shirt emporiums, and enduring the smell of frying food, Lou walked back to his car and drove to Velma's.

The street ran parallel to the beach, three blocks down from the sand. It was an old brown bungalow, small and in need of paint. Lou parked and knocked on the door.

"Hello, Lou," Velma greeted him. She was dressed in a modest blue shirtwaist, which Lou assumed to be one of her church outfits. Her hair was teased into a frothy cloud, and she might have had lipstick on.

He entered a neat, sparsely furnished parlor. It was dominated by a formidable-looking wood stove set into a fireplace, in use much of the year if he guessed right, and was comfortable and homey. The furniture was wooden, with cushions and throw pillows to provide softness. There was one overstuffed chair, and Velma guided Lou to it.

Lou smiled at Velma. "Nice little place, Velma. Have you had it for a long time?"

"Oh, yes," she said, sitting on the edge of a chair opposite Lou. "I raised my little girl here. It didn't cost much to begin with, and I sunk a bunch of my money in it after Shelley went off on her own. New plumbing, floors, the wood stove . . .

"Needs a paint job, again, though. It's hard to keep paint on a house with the salt air and all."

"Yes, I know. My grandmother owned a couple of rental places on the beach back east. The sun and the salt air faded the paint every summer. Her sons would repaint them every spring, quick and dirty. We used to joke that the wood had rotted away, and the paint was the only thing holding them up."

Velma laughed, more a girlish giggle, that Lou found charming.

"Can I get you some tea?" she asked.

"Actually, I just drank three cups of coffee. But, a glass of water would be nice."

Velma arose, and went into the kitchen. Lou looked around the room. On the mantelpiece, there was a kind of shrine: a picture of Shelley grinning in her high school graduation cap and gown, sharing a frame with her senior class picture, in black sweater and pearls, with a shy smile. There was another of the adult Shelley with her hair blowing, and a little one of her as a child in a similar pose. A few inches away was a picture of Jesus in an identical frame, and a candle burned between them. He wondered if she burned a candle every day.

Pictures of Shelley and Velma, singly or together, were scattered on tables protected by lace doilies, along with vases of dried flowers and small lamps.

Velma returned with a glass of water, and a plate of cookies. "Coconut macaroons," Velma said, as she offered the plate, "and I made 'em myself."

Lou took one out of courtesy, but wound up eating most of them by the time he left. They were good.

"Lou," Velma opened, "is there anything new?"

"One very important thing. Gar Loober is coming around. He's convinced that Chief Green is going nowhere, and is thinking about the situation. I don't know what will come of it, but he may be very valuable to us."

"How so?"

"Okay, the best case would be for him to quietly uncover any new evidence that would convince Green that there needs to be a more active investigation. Next, would be if Gar takes on the investigation himself, with or without Green's permission. This might put Gar's job on the line, so it would be risky for him."

"Would he do that?"

"I don't know," Lou shrugged. "It's obvious to me that he's a smart young guy with a lot of pride in his job. He suspects that Green is blowing off the investigation, but he can't figure out why. You have any idea?"

"What folks are saying is that Lester won't believe that anyone from around here would do a thing like that. He never did have much in the way of brains, though." She made a face.

"What about Freddie?"

Velma dismissed the idea with a wave. "That boy wouldn't hurt a fly."

"Velma, the only bad thing I ever heard you say about anybody was just now, saying Green isn't very bright. Can you be mistaken about Freddie? After all, he could be resentful about his, uh, relationship with Shelley."

"Lou, I understand that you want to be looking for every possibility, but this dog won't hunt. Fred Fleer was willing to marry Shelley, knowing it wasn't his baby. He was hurt by the . . ." Velma's face showed an inner agony. "He was hurt by the abortion. I never said that word about Shelley before."

Lou shuffled in his seat, reluctant to press. He swallowed, hard.

"Velma, that's what I mean. A couple of years can change a person . . ."

"Lou, when Freddie went to Alaska, it wasn't just to run away. He was studying to be a minister in our church. He's up there now, an assistant to an older man who's retiring. I used to hear from him every now and then, and the boy is a saved person. My church is so against killing, that I'll fight the death penalty when the murderers are caught."

"When was the last time you heard from him?"

She thought. "It's been a long while, but, you know how folks get."

Lou sat back in the chair, and nibbled a macaroon. After a moment, he said, "Yeah, okay. You ever read Sherlock Holmes?"

"No, sir," she shook her head, "I ain't read much but the Holy Bible in quite a while."

"Well, he was a great detective. He said that, when you remove everything that's not possible, whatever's left is the truth, even if it doesn't seem that way. I think I have the truth."

"You believe it was Calvin and his friend Phil?"

"I do, and I think I have some proof. I need Gar Loober to help with things only cops can do, and we'll get enough to shake up even Lester Green."

"Thank you, Lou. I had faith that you would be true to your word. I know I had my doubts . . ."

"Thank you, Velma."

"Don't mention it." She nodded.

Lou arose, brushing crumbs off his clothes. "Velma, I wish I had your faith."

Velma jumped up, ran to a drawer, and pulled out a fistful of pamphlets. She held them out to Lou.

"Take these. I would love for you to be saved."

Embarrassed to take them, but more so to refuse, Lou took the literature and thanked her. He put them in the glove compartment of the rental car, trusting Providence would see that they got into the right hands.

12. The Morgue

Later that day, Lou called on Hilda Truax, who greeted him with a mixture of warmth and derision. She was sitting at her desk, and there were lights on all over the office. It was larger than Lou remembered.

"So, having tracked all over Seagirt but here, you finally broke down. You must need something." She put her hands on her hips.

Lou raised his hands in surrender.

"Mercy. You are correct, I need your help. But," and here Lou flashed his best smile, "I wanted to see you, too."

"Okay, okay. I know I'm pushing, here, but I ain't gettin' any younger, this town is not lousy with single men, and I liked you. I was just hoping you'd call, and I guess I'm hitting it a bit too hard."

"I'll tell you what. Give me a hand, and I'll take you to dinner. Scout's honor." Lou raised his hand in the Boy Scout salute.

"Were you ever a Scout?"

"For about a week. It cut into my ball-playing time. Plus,

I couldn't get into the mass meetings and shouting things in unison. I found it a little too, um . . ."

"Fascist?"

"Overstated, but not inaccurate. Let's say it wasn't for me."

"Okay, now that we've buried the Scout hatchet, what can I do for you? Besides the Korta-Narz thing."

"Let's start with that, the once-and-future obsession. I have some definite ideas about the identity of the killers, and I'm trying to piece together a coherent case to present to . . ." Lou hesitated.

Hilda sighed in exasperation. "Lou, if you want to work with me, you'll have to trust me. I am no one's girl, in more ways than one. I want to get to the bottom of this as much as you do, and I want the exclusive if my help bags the killer. So, trust me, or this won't work."

"Yes, you're right. Except, the exclusive has to be shared with the *Stump*. You get full credit for investigation and for any writing you do. Deal?"

"Deal."

"Okay, I was visited last night by Gar Loober. He's distressed that the case is dead in the water." Lou made a face. "Poor choice of words, but you know what I mean. He has agreed to look at the evidence again with a fresh eye, no biases or preconceived notions. Just what the stuff says to him.

"Jack Narz has gone to a psychic, now don't roll your eyes, and she's seen a bullfighter, with sword and cape, and a volcano. I have some pretty good circumstantial evidence that says that Calvin Wheelock and Phil Troy are in Mexico. Since they are my prime suspects, the bullfighter thing is interesting.

"And, then there's Nutty Bud. Do you know him?"

"Sure. Everyone knows him. He drifted for a while, but he's been back in Seagirt for years."

"Back? Is he from here, originally?"

"Yes. I'm pretty sure he had a history here before he wound up a homeless beachcomber. Why is he so interesting?"

Lou recapped for Hilda the borrowed sifter, the cartridge case it turned up, the visit with Tom Knight, and his most recent conversation with Bud, including the run-in with the armed men.

"He told me to follow the money. Why do you suppose he said that?"

"Intriguing. Let's see if we can find anything in the files."

Hilda walked over to an old wooden filing cabinet of the type that held card catalogs in libraries, before everything went into the computer. She pulled out a few drawers, flicked through cards in each, and shook her head.

"There's nothing here under 'Bud' or 'Nutty Bud.' I don't recall any other name."

"Aha! The reporter's notebook sees all and tells all." Lou licked his thumb and riffled through pages. "Yes. The first time we met, he told me his name was Jim Twitchell."

"Okay." Hilda went to the 'T' drawers. "Yep. There's a card for Jim Twitchell. Write this down. 62/4, 62/5, 62/11, 63/1, 63/5, 63/6, 63/8, and 63/10."

Lou scribbled as she spoke. "What are these?"

"Microfilm, stored by year and month. We have a year's issues on each roll, so we'll need the rolls for 1962 and 1963."

"Where are they? Library?"

"Well, there is a set there, but we have them here as well. And, a viewer. Follow me."

Hilda walked to the farthest corner of the office, back behind the printing press and the print fonts. On a small desk sat a microfilm viewer, and a cabinet labeled "North Coast Clarion Morgue."

"*Voila*. Do you know how to do this?" she asked.

"I think so. Are you gonna hang around?"

"For a while. I do have a deadline, but not much is happening these days. I'll just be across the room."

Lou opened the cabinet, and ran his finger along the box labels until he found 1962 and 1963. He took the boxes, and opened the earlier one, removing the microfilm and loading it onto the reader. A few minutes later, he found the first mention of Jim Twitchell.

"Here it is." Lou scanned the article. "It says that Twitchell, owner of the dry goods and hardware store on Front Street will be running for mayor!" He looked at Hilda, who was hunched over looking at the reader screen. "Believe that? Wait, it gets better. The incumbent was a man named Arthur J. Wheelock. Any relation to Calvin?"

"I should say. He was Calvin's father."

"Was?"

Hilda shrugged. "Is. Still alive. He's not in Seagirt, in any case. Read more."

Lou went back to the article.

"Not much more, here. Location of his store, born in Seagirt, that kind of stuff. Let me go on to the next issue."

Lou wound the film slowly, scanning as he went.

"Here we go. It's Wheelock's official statement. Blah, blah, blah. He's just blowing his own horn here. Wait, it says that Wheelock has been mayor for twenty years, and that he was also the local banker. Was there only one bank in town, then?"

"It's a long time ago, and, despite how I look now, I was a kid then. But, yeah, The Bank of Seagirt. It's still in business, but it's not the only one any more. And, I think it's part of a consortium of smaller independent banks or something.

"Wheelock held the mortgage on our house for years. When my father paid it off, he burned the damn thing on the street in front of the bank. He did a little dance. I thought he was gonna moon the bank."

"Your father sounds like quite a character."

"Lou, I can honestly say that my dad was a pretty reserved guy. He had a real dry sense of humor, and he could be fun, especially after a couple of drinks, but that was in private, amongst family and friends. I was pretty shocked at this public display of insanity. And, he was stone sober."

Lou shrugged. "I guess burning the mortgage is kind of an American tradition. I've heard similar stories."

"No, you don't understand. I felt like there was something personal in it."

"Maybe there's something here that can enlighten us." Lou went back to the microfilm. The film ran squealing across the screen reels.

"Here's another piece." Lou could feel Hilda's warm breath on his neck and ear. He decided it felt good, and resisted the arousal it created.

"Wow! 'Twitchell Accuses Wheelock of Selling Out Local Business.' Let's see. It says that Twitchell had evidence that Wheelock was planning to foreclose on the businesses on Front Street, and sell the property to a developer. Um . . . Twitchell claimed that they were supposed to build high-rise apartments and bring in chains to replace the local stores. Blah, blah, blah . . . Wheelock unavailable for comment.

"Could he do that?" Lou looked up at Hilda.

Hilda made a face. "Maybe. If he was the only bank in town, he might have held the mortgages for every store and business on the street. What does the next issue say?"

Lou wheeled the film deeper into the roll. "Here we go. 'Wheelock Denies Twitchell Charge, Cites Candidate Desperation.' Okay, Wheelock calls charges reckless, asserts that he would not violate the Seagirt idea of measured growth and local control of business."

"Is that all?"

"Let's see. Uh, yup. For that issue. Next."

The reels squealed some more. "Okay. Nothing." Lou gave the crank some slow turns. After a few minutes, "Hey, check this out. '*Clarion* Learns of Wheelock Deal.' It says that the *Clarion* found an article in a California paper about how a deal to buy and redevelop a large stretch of Oregon coast property fell through because of the 'potentially negative publicity,' and the inability of the Oregon partner to acquire the land in a timely fashion. There's more . . . and, the *Clarion* called the developer to determine that the Oregon partner was Arthur J. Wheelock, who had no comment when asked to respond. How about that?"

"What's the date of the issue?"

"Uh, October fifteenth. When's the election?"

"November, just like for everything else. Go to the November issues."

Lou cranked the machine, and the copy flew across the screen. "Here we go. 'Twitchell Wins 65% of the Vote, Defeats Longtime Incumbent.' "

"Is there more?"

"Uh, not in this issue. Hold on . . . Ah! The Holiday Issue says 'Mayor Declared Local Hero by Grateful Business Owners.' There's a picture of a beardless Nutty Bud, looking sleek and prosperous. Can you see it?"

"Who knew? That old guy wasn't always a crazy drifter. Maybe it's worth a human interest story."

Lou sat back in the chair. "Yeah, but, why would Bud want us to know this? He seemed to imply that I would be interested in this, knowing I was investigating the murders."

"I dunno. Maybe he just wanted you to know he wasn't crazy." Hilda looked puzzled.

"Okay. Maybe there's something about why he, uh, dropped out."

"The card file had some more on Twitchell in 1963. Let's see what it is."

Lou rewound 1962, loaded 1963, and started scanning. "Hey, here's something right away, about Wheelock. 'Defeated Candidate Announces New Business Venture.' Uh . . . He told the *Clarion* that he had already begun work to build a new retail store in an empty space, and hadn't yet decided on what it would be. He joked that he had a lot of spare time since he left office as mayor."

"I think I know what that business is. You know that chain hardware store on Front?"

Lou shook his head. "If I saw it, it didn't register on me."

"Yeah, well, Wheelock owned it until about fifteen years ago, when he sold out to the chain. Made a bundle, I heard."

"Okay, so Bud . . . or, should we call him Jim? Anyway, the money seems to be flowing toward Arthur J. Wheelock so far. Wait, a hardware store? Didn't Twitchell own a hardware store?"

"Sure enough," Hilda answered, "and there isn't one there, now. I wonder . . ."

"Wonder no more." Lou turned the reels on the viewer. "Wheelock opened up in March. Hardware and dry goods, heavily discounted, according to the article. Oh, holy smoke!"

"What?"

"Wanna guess who the manager of Wheelock's was?"

She squinted at the screen. "Just tell me, dammit!"

"One Chester Green. Want me to guess whose daddy or older brother, or something, he is?"

"You don't have to. He was Lester's dad. So, Wheelock opens up across from Twitchell, and Chet Green is the manager. Interesting . . ."

"To say the least. Let's see what's next." Reels turned, squealing. "Nothing for the next issue, or the next . . . Okay. It's an ad: 'Chester Green Announces Customer Appreciation Sale,' and 'Twitchell's Announces Going-out-of-Business Sale.' Practically right next to each other."

"What issue is that?"

"Uh, August tenth. Maybe six months after Wheelock opened up," Lou replied.

"Okay," Hilda shifted her weight, "so Twitchell's went belly-up in six months. Maybe it had more to do with bad management, or debt service, or something like that."

"Definitely possible. Competition can make bad business practice a real liability. That's how my friend lost his minor-league team, but that's another story. Let's see what's next."

Lou scanned the microfilm. His eyes were beginning to sting from the concentration on the screen. He didn't want to move because of Hilda's close presence, which he was enjoying. She bore the faint smell of a pleasant soap, the indefinable woman scent and an aura of warmth.

"Yes, here we go. 'Mayor Resigns, Citing Business Failure, Personal Bankruptcy.' The article says . . . listen to this! 'The popular mayor has suffered trying economic reverses this year, losing his business and home to foreclosure. Wheelock's Hardware, Twitchell's major competitor, sold hardware, tools, and other home goods at such low prices, talk around town speculated on how it could make a profit. When asked, manager Chester Green said, "Volume." ' "

Lou looked at Hilda. "Lester inherited his father's gift of gab.

"Lou, look, there's more. Read the next graph."

"Uh, let's see. 'Mayor Twitchell had also been embarrassed lately by his citations for drunk driving. He resigned as much for these lapses as for his business failures.' Blah, blah . . . here. 'The town council will hold an emergency session next week to determine a course of action.'

"So, the money is leading us in a strange direction."

"Not so strange, if you know the personalities involved," Hilda mused. "It doesn't surprise me that Arthur Wheelock would try to destroy Jim Twitchell, after he humiliated him and worse, cost him a lot of money. I would bet the rent that Wheelock's Hardware lost a bunch of money putting Twitchell's store in the dumper. The old goat probably thought it was cheap at the price."

"Let's go to the next issue, and see if the town council meeting is reported. By the way," Lou quit spinning the reels and turned to look at Hilda, "I haven't noticed a byline on any of this. Do I take it that your father wrote everything?"

"Take it, and run with it. He hired a high school kid to do local sports, and occasionally a woman to cover the ladies' clubs, and sometimes even got a local to write a hunting or fishing column. The rest, he did himself. I was the last reporter he hired, and no outsider has worked here as a general interest reporter since then. I still have a local kid report the high school sports, only now it'll be a girl, more than likely. And a club woman, who doubles as a gardening columnist, and a duck hunter to write about bird murder. That's it.

"We report it, editorial 'we,' of course, and we take it in the shorts when it contains mistakes. I've actually considered taking on another reporter. The town is growing, whether we like it or not."

"What was your father's name?"

"Carroll, Carroll Truax. He hated it, 'cause it sounded like a sissy name. Went by Chuck, to one and all."

"He get into the local politics at all?"

"No more than what you're reading. Oh, he would scorch the dinner table with his opinions, but they never got into the paper. Even his rare editorials were about great issues, you know, civil rights, Vietnam, from a sort of liberal perspective. He was nominated for a Pulitzer once."

"Really?" Lou was impressed. "For what?"

"Lou, if you don't scroll to that town council report, I'll toss you off the chair and spin those reels myself."

"Yes, ma'am!" Lou snapped off a salute, and wound the microfilm. "Okay . . . jeez Louise! Look at this head: 'Unanimous Council Appoints Chester Green to Fill Resigned Mayor's Term.' "

"Well, now. Chet Green. I was still pretty young, and I sure don't remember this."

"You may have believed that your father kept out of politics, but look at this sidebar. '*Clarion* Editorial: Who's Pulling Our Strings?' Two paragraphs of fist shaking at the council, who he calls 'gutless lapdogs.' Listen to this last line: 'And how will we know what Art Wheelock is thinking? Chet Green's lips will be moving.' "

Hilda's nose was about six inches from the screen, and she was reading the news report on the council meeting.

"Wow. According to this, Wheelock wasn't even at the meeting. Maybe that's what the string-pulling reference is about. It says, '. . . absent only in body, Wheelock's presence hung over the proceedings like winter clouds.' Now, it all makes sense . . ." Hilda's voice trailed off.

"What makes sense?" Lou asked.

"Wheelock once tried to start up another paper in this town, strictly to compete with the *Clarion*. It was obvious to everyone, but he claimed that it was to achieve some balance, that the *Clarion* was left wing. Out here in Oregon, in the sixties, we were a pretty conservative state. It was Portland and Eugene that elected people like Wayne Morse, the senator that first opposed the war in Vietnam? Wheelock's paper published a drawing of Morse hanging from a tree, with a Traitor sign around his neck. Classy stuff."

Hilda sighed. "Wheelock's paper didn't last long, maybe four, five months, and he took a bath when it went under. It wasn't a newspaper, really, just a platform for Wheelock to rant from. The rest of it was also badly written and edited, like the cheap rag it was. They didn't even bother to cover local events."

Hilda flashed a big grin at Lou. "Let's just say that Art Wheelock was better at picking dry-goods clerks than newspapermen."

"I'm surprised that he didn't try to foreclose on your house, or the paper."

"I'm sure he would've, especially in light of what we just read. But, my father was never a day late on the house payments, used to hand carry them to the bank. And the newspaper, press, and building were owned outright by my great-grandfather before a Wheelock ever set foot in this town."

"Do you mind if I use this in a *Stumptown Weekly* article, full credit to you and the old man, naturally?"

"Be my guest. You'll have to get copies at the library. This reader won't do prints."

"Where's Chester Green these days? I might like to talk with him." Lou scratched his chin.

"It'll be tough, unless you have a Ouija board."

"Or, maybe I'll ask Lucy Persson."

"Very droll. Anyway, he died about ten years ago. Literally fell off a bar stool, dead before he hit the floor. He had retired from the hardware business, and I guess he never caught on as mayor, because I never knew he held the job. We tend to reelect 'em around here, unless they die or get caught with their hand in the till."

"And Arthur J. Wheelock?"

"As far as I know, the old SOB is still alive, living in bitter isolation in his egregious mansion near Waldorf. It was built in the 1880s by a lumber baron, and Art supposedly bought it for a song. The first thing he did was rebuild the security fence, and set dogs loose."

"Sounds like a prince among men. Why is he so bitter?"

"One son, the fair-haired boy, killed in the war, which he blamed on Kennedy and Johnson, although Junior was killed on Nixon's watch. A daughter married an Indian, Native American, I should say, moved to the boonies in Wyoming, and promptly got disowned."

"And Calvin?"

"*Persona non grata* at the mansion. Art considers Calvin an imbecile and petty crook. So, Art lost his favorite child, wrote off the other two. Nobody to leave his legacy to, not to mention his money. Rumor has it that Calvin is well compensated to support his lifestyle, but would have to crawl to Waldorf on his hands and knees to beg forgiveness. And, he might not get it at that.

"Meanwhile," Hilda sighed, "one of our favorite indoor sports here in scenic Seagirt, is fantasizing about what old Art will do with his money. He's no dot-com billionaire, but he'll likely leave thirty mil, or so."

"Wow," said Lou, "that's more than I made last year."

Lou looked around, surprised to see that it had gotten dark.

"Hey, where did the daylight go? What time is it?"

Hilda pointed to a big, old-fashioned wall clock, which read six forty-five.

"Hungry?" he asked Hilda.

"Famished. Here's my address. Pick me up in, say, an hour?"

"It's a date. Can we avoid the Dunes?"

"Is a fat hog heavy? I'll take you up the road to a nice place. Do you like seafood?"

"My fave. See you later."

Lou left, with complicated feelings, all of them good.

13. Business Before Pleasure

Hilda Truax took a quick shower, and did what she could with her hair. She rummaged in her medicine cabinet, then in a bathroom drawer, before she found some cosmetics.

"Oh, you hussy!" she said aloud while applying mascara and lipstick. Tarting herself up, her father called it.

She dressed in a hurry, hoping to have a few minutes to sit and relax before her date picked her up. Her date. It had been a long time between dates.

Hilda liked Lou. He was smart, had a sense of humor, and seemed to be a compassionate person. She wondered how old he was.

Sitting with care on her sofa, so as not to wrinkle her clothing, Hilda began to think about her father. What *don't* I know about the old man? she thought. Her mother, who died soon after she was born, had no influence on her beyond the genetic heritage. Hilda was a creature of Carroll Truax. She talked like him, believed a lot of what he believed, and followed him into the weekly newspaper racket.

She had returned to Seagirt after promising herself she would never come near the place again. College, two years wandering in Europe, sending stories back to her father, and getting hired by a wire service based on the reprint of one of her stories in the *Los Angeles Daily News*.

Two more years as a stringer in Boston and Washington, DC, and she went back to Seagirt to visit, never leaving the place again, despite entreaties from her editor, and the odd job offer from a big-city daily.

Her father gave her a postgraduate education in small-town journalism, as well as a set of ideals she hoped never to compromise. Her father was her mentor, guru, and role model.

And, now, she wondered if she really knew the man.

On impulse, she jumped up, ran into her home office, and began to ransack her father's files. She pulled out carbon copies of letters, newspaper stories, clippings from other papers, and letters to the editor.

One revelation led to another. There was much her father hadn't told her. "Trying to protect me," she whispered. "From what?"

She began to organize things into piles. She stopped only when she heard the doorbell, and made a vain effort to put herself back together.

Lou pulled up to the Truax home, not quite a mansion, but still a large and handsome Tudor-style house, in good repair and much too large for one person. He hadn't noticed much about it on his last visit.

A steady and heavy drizzle had begun, the mark of the northwest's autumn soaking rain. And it wasn't even August.

He hunched himself out of his car, his knees complaining. His ribs didn't hurt as much as they had. Trotting clumsily, he reached the cover of the front door and rang the bell. A moment later, Hilda answered, with a bundle of papers in her hand and an air of distraction.

"Oh, hi, Lou. Come on in out of the wet." She stood aside to let him in. He wiped his feet on the cocoa mat with care.

"Chilly and wet. Perfect beach weather for this time of year," he said as he took off his jacket.

He stopped to take her in with his eyes. She had changed clothes, put on a bit of makeup, and let her shiny silver hair hang loose, a couple of inches below her shoulders. And, she smelled good.

"Look at this." She thrust a yellowed piece of bond paper at him. It was a carbon copy of a letter, from Chuck Truax to Jim Twitchell.

"Where'd you get this?"

"After I showered and changed, I started to poke around in my father's files. He was very organized. Nowadays, I guess he'd be called obsessive-compulsive."

Lou scanned the page, absentmindedly taking off his wet baseball cap and scratching his head.

"Is this what I think it is?"

"If you think it's my father passing information to Twitchell about Wheelock's secret deal, I would say it is."

"Jeez, he lays out the whole thing. Did you know anything about this?"

"Nope. I knew my father didn't like Art Wheelock much, and I knew that he refused to run for office whenever anyone asked, and I knew that he stayed out of local politics, generally, to the extent that a newspaper editor can. I didn't know that he fed information to candidates. I wonder what else he did, in his sneaky way."

"What else is in those files?"

Hilda broke into a broad smile. "Spoken like a true newshound. Wanna look?"

Three hours later, Lou and Hilda went through the last folder in the files. They were sitting on the floor, Hilda cross-legged, and Lou with his stiff leg straight out. The file papers were spread around them, collected in piles where some connection had been made. Hilda had skittered around on her hands and knees like a schoolgirl, driven by enthusiasm and the thrill of the hunt, and as unconscious as a child of her stylish skirt which often rode up to her hips and made it hard for Lou to concentrate.

"Well," Lou exhaled, "if old Chuck Truax ever did anything else to favor a local candidate, he destroyed the evidence. Something about Arthur Wheelock really got to him."

"Yeah . . ." she began, and then her stomach growled.

They both laughed. "We never did get to dinner tonight. Should I throw something together? I've got leftovers."

"Sounds good," Lou said. "The only leftovers I see are in cardboard containers."

He got up, with effort, and held out his hand to her to help her up. Her hand was warm and soft. She brushed at her clothing to straighten it.

"Come with me." She walked toward the kitchen.

The kitchen was a blend of old and new. Large, high-ceilinged, tiled behind sinks and cooking surfaces. The floor was a kind of earthen tile, and there was a work island located near the sinks and stove. The stove was modern and stainless steel, as were the two sinks, and the appliances, but everything else was wood or tile. There was plenty of room for a massive oak table and six chairs.

"Wow, nice kitchen." Lou whistled.

"This place used to be a boarding house for loggers and fishermen. I'm told that there were secret Wobbly meetings in the front room. It had a kitchen staff, lots of pantry space, et cetera. Grandpa took out a lot of the shelving, and brought in that table. There's a formal dining room, but we took almost all our meals here.

"The stove, plumbing, refrigerator, all pretty new. We tried to keep as much of the original tile and wood as possible."

She walked over to the fridge, and peered in.

"You like curry? I've got shrimp curry, uh, salad stuff, or I could make a quick pasta."

"Curry's good. And a salad."

"I'd love to offer you a beer, or some wine . . ."

". . . but, I don't drink. Water will do."

"You're awfully easy. Here's some ice. The glasses are over the small sink."

Hilda busied herself with warming the curry and boiling a pot of fresh rice. Lou asked to make the salad, and they exchanged small talk, mostly about growing up in their respective parts of the world.

The meal was a success. Good home cooking always tastes better after aging in the refrigerator for a night or two, and Lou whipped up a salad dressing from olive oil, lemon juice, garlic, and some herbs he found wilting in the crisper.

Hilda drank white wine, and Lou watched her become animated and giggly. She glowed.

They did the dishes together; he insisted on washing, she dried. Afterward, Hilda said, "I've got some Tillamook ice cream in the freezer and some chocolate sauce. Interested?"

He was, and they retreated to the couch, eating, talking a little, and Lou could feel Hilda's eyes on him. His insides jumped at the thought. He had had no interest in women since his wife died, despite Blanche's sporadic attempts to get his attention. He felt too avuncular toward her for anything to happen, even when she succeeded in reaching the man in him.

But, Hilda was another matter. She was smart, wry, and of similar age and interests. Plus, she was attractive on several levels. Before he could give it any more thought, Hilda put down her bowl and leaned over to kiss him.

Lou never did find out what happened to his bowl.

About a mile from Hilda's love nest, Gar Loober, holding a flashlight and a warrant, kicked open the door to Calvin Wheelock's house. The smell of decaying garbage almost overwhelmed him.

He clicked on the lights, and stood in Calvin's living room. The place looked like Attila the Hun had swept through it.

"Jeez," Gar said aloud, "I'm gonna clean my place up, if this is what happens when you let it go."

There were mounds of nasty stuff everywhere: dirty clothes, fast-food containers in varying states of emptiness, magazines, heavy on the hot-rod and naked woman varieties, unopened mail, and mysterious middens not open to quick analysis. Gar thought he saw mice or rats scurrying around the corners of the room.

"Yuck." Gar practically tiptoed through the room, thankful for the rubber crime scene gloves. He held a trash bag, and had several smaller plastic zipper bags in his pockets; he searched for anything that might be evidence.

Nothing significant made itself obvious on his first sweep of the living room, so he went on to the hallway, and stopped at the kitchen. It was worse than the first room, smelled like the main source of decay, and the rats didn't even scatter when the lights went on.

Gar's hair stood up, and he shuddered. Rats were not his favorite creatures. He decided to save the kitchen for last.

The bathroom light had been left on, and the bulb had burned out. Gar's flashlight showed an almost-empty medicine cabinet, toiletries scattered everywhere. He took an old toothbrush and the gummy bathroom glass for DNA samples, and secured them in bags.

Next stop was the two back rooms. The one on the left had apparently functioned as a guest room. Someone's clothing, Gar guessed it was Phil Troy's, was everywhere. He collected a couple of dirty socks and a pair of briefs, at arm's length, and placed them in separate plastic bags.

He inspected the closets, and the dresser drawers, but they were empty of anything of interest. Nothing else looked likely, so he moved on to Calvin's lair, the bedroom on the right.

It presented the same kind of mess. Gar wondered if this was typical disorder, or if it had been enhanced as the side effects of a hasty getaway.

The deputy gave the room a once-over, checked out the dresser drawers, and went on to the closet. The light in the room was too dim to see well enough into the closet, so he snapped on the flashlight, and peered into the corners.

Something on the closet floor caught his eye. He shined the beam on it.

"Well," he said, and tipped back his cap, "boy, howdy!"

• • •

Lou awoke before dawn, panicked for a second by the strange surroundings. Then, he remembered where he was, and with whom.

The light of the moon, which had found a break in the clouds to peek through, caught Hilda's silvery hair coming through a window. Lou brushed her cheek with a gentle touch.

"Mmmm. . . ." she smiled, and stretched. "Hiya," she said, even before opening her eyes.

"Hiya. I've gotta ask. Should I go before morning, or do you want me to stay?"

Hilda looked at Lou, and rubbed sleep from her eyes. "Good question." She sat up, unashamed as the cover slipped from her naked torso. "I want you to stay, but it might not be the best idea. It would look better if the relationship seemed purely professional."

"I agree, for now. But, I owe you a homemade breakfast."

"Kiss me before you go. I'm going back to sleep."

She was asleep before her head hit the pillow. Lou adjusted the covers over her, and stepped out of the bed. A few minutes later he leaned over to kiss her forehead, then left.

He wished he had called her sooner.

Lou pulled up to the Saltaire, hoping that the relentless Chloe was still asleep. He turned the TV on to the Weather Channel, muted the sound, and watched the weather geeks point to the electronic images. TV as lava lamp. He let his mind take a pleasant drift through the previous evening.

About seven o'clock, he hauled himself out of bed, turned on a morning news program, and showered. As he finished dressing, he heard a knock on the door. It was Gar Loober.

"Hi, Lou. Did I wake you up?"

"No, Gar, I've been up for a while, thinking. Come on in."

Lou noticed that Gar's slicker was dry. He took the deputy's coat and threw it on a chair.

"What's going on?"

Gar cleared his throat, and Lou thought he detected a slight smile on the man's face.

"I got some news for you." Now, he grinned. "I sent a fax to the DA in Waldorf with the photo of the shoe treads we took from the beach. Chief Green didn't know. Actually, he's been away for a day fishin' for halibut."

"He get anything?"

"No, but I did. The shoes had a pretty unique sole pattern. In fact, they're real expensive, what they call skateboarding shoes, Skaters brand. Only about a dozen stores in Oregon handle them, mostly high-end kinds of places. I asked the DA to check on how many have been sold lately, and he did."

"Well?" Lou was tight with anxiety.

"Well, DA Knight turned up a credit card purchase of two pairs up in Waldorf, five days before the killings, on Calvin Wheelock's credit card."

"Yes!" Lou thrust his fist at the ceiling.

"There's more. Based on the shoes, I got a search warrant for Wheelock's house. I found a shoe box for one pair of the shoes, and a receipt for a Glock nine millimeter pistol purchased at the gun show."

"Is there a name on the receipt?"

"Yeah, but it's no one I know. Do you know a Rufus T. Firefly?"

Lou laughed. "Yeah, it's the name of a Groucho Marx character. Did you find the gun?"

"No, but I found a box of bullets of the same brand as the shell found on the beach, with seven missing."

"Can we match the shells with that very box?"

Gar nodded. "Yes, I think they can."

Lou let out a whoop, and began to leap around the room. Gar laughed, as Lou kangaroo-jumped and yelled.

"Careful, Lou. Your legs."

Lou stopped leaping, but not whooping.

They heard a knock on the door. "Mr. Tadusky? You okay in there?"

"Yes, Chloe," Lou yelled at the door, "better than I've been in years. But, thanks for asking."

Gar stood there smiling, as Lou caught his breath.

"What do we do, now, Gar?"

"Well, I been thinking that Chief Green needs to be caught up on the investigation."

"He doesn't know? Oh, this is just too good to be true." Lou shuddered with delight. "Can I go with you?"

Gar looked dubious. "Uh, gee, Lou, I don't know . . ."

"Oh, come on. I'll follow you by about ten minutes. He'll never connect us. Just make sure that he doesn't take you into his office. I wanna see this."

Gar's Adam's apple went up and down; the deputy was nervous.

"Okay, I guess you deserve the satisfaction. But, don't let on that I've been workin' with you. He can still fire my skinny butt."

"Promise." Lou made a big show of crossing his heart.

Gar left, shaking his head. Lou got into his car, and went to buy coffee. He hung around the coffee shop for a couple of minutes, decided it was time enough, and headed off to the police station. Gar's cruiser was parked near the entrance, next to the chief's car.

When Lou entered, he saw a tableau: Gar standing with his hands in his back pockets and leaning back just a bit, Green with his fists clenched at his sides, face red.

Green looked at Lou, and his eyes rolled.

"Just what I goddamn needed!" Green bellowed. "What do *you* want?"

Lou raised his hand in a peace gesture. "Did I come at a bad time?" he asked ingenuously.

"There ain't no good time to see you."

"I was just here to check up on . . ."

"Ain't that swell? Deputy Loober here's got all kinds of news, don't ya?"

"Hello, Lou. I was telling Chief Green that we have some new leads." Gar went through the story, enduring Green's fitful expressions of rage. Lou made the proper responses of amazement, as though he were hearing it for the first time.

When Gar finished, there was silence. Lou dared break it.

"Well, this is great! I assume you're going to check with Wheelock's California relatives to determine . . ."

"Determine nothing! Calvin had nothin' to do with this."

Green blustered, but he was shaken. He was pale and broke a sweat, even in the chill of the office.

Gar Loober looked at him with undisguised disdain. "You've got to be kidding! What the hell do you want, a signed confession? There's enough evidence here for an arrest warrant."

Now, it was Gar's turn to get red in the face. He wagged a finger under Green's nose.

"You've been walkin' around this case with a blindfold on for too long, now. Wake up, dammit. If Calvin Wheelock ain't guilty, let's find out!"

Green puffed himself up. "Don't you yell at me, you pissant. I was doin' police work when you was still messin' your pants. I don't care if I'm the only damn cop for a hundred miles. You open your mouth to me like that once more, and you're through!"

Lou, the knight in shining armor, leaped into the fray.

"Green, what's your problem? I found out that your father was a lapdog for Wheelock's father. Arthur Wheelock gave him a job in his store, and then installed him as mayor after he took Twitchell down. Is this payback? Are you giving Calvin a pass because old man Wheelock owned your father?"

"I'll kill you, goddamnit!" Lester Green leaped at Lou, and got his fingers around Lou's windpipe. Loober pulled the chief off, but not until Lou started to black out.

Loober threw the chief into a chair, and pinned his arms behind him. Green struggled, but Loober was younger and stronger.

Lou coughed and choked, and stars swam before his eyes. He tried to say something, but was unable.

Green continued to strain against Loober's grip, and

spouted a string of obscenities. He was in a state, and it took him a few minutes to calm down enough for Loober to relax a bit.

"Chief," Gar asked, "you about ready to quit assaulting this man?"

"Yes, goddamit. Lemme go!"

"I tell you, if I have to restrain you again, I'll use the cuffs."

Lou watched all this while fighting against fainting. His throat was bruised, but now he could breathe without choking. His heart was still pounding in his chest.

"Now, Chief, you go home and think this all over. I'll try to talk Mr. Tedesco out of suing the city and the police department, or filing an assault charge."

Green's face looked drawn, as though his outburst had depleted him of his substance. The chief slumped, and Loober released his grip, then grabbed the chief's shoulders again, so he wouldn't slide to the floor.

"Really, why don't you go home? Can you get home without help?"

Green nodded, stood up, and almost lost his feet. He stumbled to the door, and walked out.

"What now?" Lou asked.

"Let's call DA Knight."

Gar spoke with Tom Knight for almost half an hour, in large part about Lester Green's recent behavior. He transmitted the gist of the conversation to Lou by means of gestures and facial expressions. Knight put Gar in charge of the investigation at that end, and promised to come down to evaluate Green's status.

After dealing with Green, Knight said, "Deputy, based on the shoe box, the ammo box, and the trail of video rentals, good work on that, by the way," Gar smiled and gave Lou a thumbs-up, "I will issue an arrest warrant, and notify the FBI in Portland that two murder suspects are presumed to be somewhere in Mexico. Unless I misunderstand how this is done, the Bureau will notify the Mexican police, Interpol, and the U.S. Customs Service."

"What then, sir?" Gar asked.

"All that's left is to wait. If you come up with any more information, call me ASAP." He pronounced it A-sap. "And, real good work on this, Deputy. I see a big future for you in law enforcement."

Gar winked at Lou. "Thank you, sir, but a lot of this came from work done by Lou Tedesco. I consider him an asset on this case."

"Yeah, well, if I didn't make it a policy never to apologize to a reporter, I might thank him. I gotta go. I called a press conference today at eleven o'clock on another matter, and I'll be happy to add this news. It's a feather in your cap, officer."

"Thanks again, sir." They hung up.

Gar Loober was grinning with justifiable pride. He looked so satisfied with himself that Lou had to laugh.

"So, DA Knight gave you an 'atta-boy?' "

"Lou, I haven't heard anything like that since I made the winning basket in the state basketball finals. Knight said that you deserved credit, too, but it wouldn't come from him."

"I don't want a medal, I just want those two in custody. And, we are no closer to that now than we were a month ago."

"Hey, are you kiddin'? Knight's gonna bring in the FBI, Interpol . . . I don't know what all. We'll get 'em!"

"Mexico's a big place. They could be on a beach in Baja, or in the jungles in Yucatán. We don't have a clue. In truth," Lou made a sour face, "they might be in Brazil. Who knows if they stopped in Mexico? We can't trace them any more, because the video card's been canceled. We need a break here."

Gar crossed his arms. "I'm not gonna let you bring me down, Lou. I wanna let this moment roll around in my head for a while. Then," he sighed, "I'll admit you're right."

"What's gonna be with Lester?"

"Your guess is as good as mine. I hope he's come to his senses."

Lou laughed. “I hope he’s come to someone else’s, someone smarter and more reasonable.”

“I got a bunch of routine paperwork to get rid of. Why’nt you find something to amuse yourself, like catching Knight’s eleven o’clock press conference, and I’ll talk to you later?”

“Deal.” Lou rose and shook hands with the young cop. Then, he got up and left.

14. Postcards from the Edge

Lou's gut reminded him that he hadn't had breakfast. He felt like going to the Dunes.

"Lou!" Hetty Conrad called out from behind the counter. "Something must be happening, or you wouldn't be here." Ronnie and Connie stood nearby, arms akimbo.

"You got a TV handy?" he asked.

Connie pointed up, and Lou saw a small television on a high shelf. "We put it on when the men want to watch football."

"Yeah," Hetty drawled, "and when you wanna watch the soaps."

Ronnie laughed and blushed. "Guilty as charged."

"Why do you need a TV?" Hetty asked.

"DA Knight is having a press conference at eleven." He checked his watch. "About forty minutes. Fix me a big breakfast, and then you can be amazed."

Phyllis walked out from the kitchen. "Why, will Knight fail to flash his best side to the camera?"

"Hi, Phyllis. Nope. He would never neglect that. But, he will be saying something amazing."

"Come on, Lou," Ronnie whined, "give us a clue."

"Hey, if you guys had a clue you would lose all your charm. Hetty, how about corned-beef hash and eggs? Fry the hash crisp, and poach the eggs soft. Potatoes, and a side of whole wheat toast, ought to round it out."

"Round you out, too, if you eat like that all the time," Hetty said. "Coming up. Ronnie, pour Lou some coffee."

Lou sat at the counter, and bantered with the women. Phyllis's wise cracks were pointed and funny, as usual, and the food was first rate.

He sat back, and drank off the rest of his coffee.

"You know," he said, "I really don't come here for the grub. It's the floor show I like. Speaking of which . . ." he looked at his watch, "Tom Knight should be running his sculptured jaw any time now. You get the Waldorf stations, right?"

"Oh, yeah, and the Portland ones. Let me see . . ." Hetty played with a remote, and the little set blinked to life. A blow-dried anchor man made inane chatter with a big-haired blonde half his age. Then, they threw it to a live remote from the courthouse. A few moments later, the magnificent Tom Knight strode to a podium, his entourage trailing him like a dust plume.

Hetty cranked up the sound, and caught Knight in the middle of his opening sentence.

". . . you all here today. I was going to talk about the ongoing investigation of the eco-vandals who stole all those genetically modified chickens, and I will get to that.

"But first, I am very happy to announce a development in the tragic murders of those two young people on Seagirt beach this summer. The investigation had, frankly, stalled. The local police had run out of suspects, with nothing new on the horizon.

"However, the persistence of a young officer, Deputy Gar Loober of the Seagirt PD, under the guidance of Chief Lester Green . . . ,"

"Ha!" Lou yelled.

". . . has paid off in a break in the case. I have obtained

arrest warrants today for Phillip Troy and Calvin Wheelock of Seagirt, both of whom were known to the victims."

All the women, and the other customers whose attention had been captured by the TV, gasped as one.

"In a cruel irony," Knight continued, "Wheelock was an occasional Seagirt police deputy, who had worked with officer Loober and Chief Green during spring break festivities, and whenever else he was needed. Part of the problem was the natural reluctance of the two permanent police officers to believe that a colleague could be capable of so vicious a crime."

Damn, Lou thought, this guy is really smooth. He's turned all the negatives into sad stories.

"I'm not at liberty to discuss all the details of the case, but I can tell you that apprehension of Wheelock and Troy will require the assistance of the Federal Bureau of Investigation and Interpol. We have a strong circumstantial case against the suspects, and I am confident that the combined resources of the local and state police, with the power and reach of the national and international police agencies, will result in a quick capture and a speedy trial. Questions?"

Reporters leaped up, and Hetty shut off the TV.

"Lou," Connie asked, astonishment on her face, "did you do that?"

"No," Lou demurred, "Gar did it, but I helped him to know what to look for."

"What's he not telling us?" asked Phyllis, yanking her thumb at the TV set.

Lou's worst instincts got to him. "He's not telling you that Lester Green did everything he could to keep me, and Gar, from investigating Calvin Wheelock. He's not telling you that Lester's father and Calvin's father had a business and personal relationship that affected Green's behavior."

Lou realized that he was running his mouth indiscriminately, and should shut up.

"Hey," said Phyllis, "Chet Green worked in Art Wheelock's store, managed it, right? Then, Art made him mayor.

I haven't thought about that in years. Is that what you mean?"

"I've already said too much. I don't want to make any more trouble than I have." Lou looked ashamed.

"No, you're right," Hetty put in. "Chet Green was a terrible mayor, completely incompetent. We voted him out after one term. Charlie Castle beat him."

"Another thing," Phyllis added, "we never voted for him in the first place. It was the council who appointed him after Jim Twitchell quit."

"I wonder whatever happened to poor Jim?" Hetty asked.

Lou couldn't resist. "He's living on the beach, under a plastic tarp."

"You don't mean Nutty Bud?" Connie asked, astonished once more.

"One and the same. He helped break the case. I thought everyone in town knew that Bud was Jim Twitchell."

"After all these years, I guess I just forgot . . ." Connie's voice trailed off.

"I guess we all did," Hetty agreed.

The group, now including every customer in the place, buzzed about this for several minutes, until people started to run home to spread the choice gossip.

Phyllis got a devilish look on her face.

"Um, Lou, did I see your car parked over to Hilda's house late last night?"

Lou blushed a deep red. "Oh, hey, Hilda's been helping me with, uh . . ." He waved his arms helplessly.

The women laughed.

"Forget it, Lou. Whatever you say, your red face says more."

"Hey, I'm outta here. Can I pay for breakfast?"

"It's on the house, Lou." Hetty waved him off. "You've provided us more entertainment in one morning than we've had in a dog's age."

Lou said a hasty goodbye, and left.

• • •

After a few moments thought, Lou decided to go see Carla Higgins at the video store. He wanted to congratulate her on her decision to help, and to ask about Gar's subsequent investigation.

"Hi, Carla."

"Hello, Lou. It's good to see you."

"Did you see the press conference?"

"No, but my mom called and told me about it. I guess I'm glad I decided to help, although I'll never feel really comfortable about it."

"That says good things about you. You have a real conscience . . ."

"Oh, wait! I knew there was something I had to tell you. I stopped for gas this morning at the Snack-n-Drive. You might want to talk with Dub Gordon."

"What's this about?"

"He got a postcard from Mexico."

Lou was out of the video shop and on his way at once. When Lou pulled up to the pump, driving a different rental car this time, Dub stuck his head into the car window and asked, "Help you? Hey, Lou. Lou, right?"

"Uh, right. Hi, Dub. Wanna check the oil on this bomb? I'm not sure it's full."

"Sure, but we gotta wait a few minutes. Engine's still too warm for a good level."

"Okay."

Dub busied himself with stacking cans and wiping down the pumps with a rag. Soon, he came back to the car. He wagged his finger at Lou with a knowing look on his face.

"Hey, you still interested in the murder case here?"

"Sure, you know I am."

"I knew them. Remember?"

" 'Them?' The victims?" Lou played dumb.

"The killers, too. Calvin and Phil."

"They found the killers?"

"Uh-uh," he shook his head, "they're hidin' out in Mexico."

"Now, how do you know that?"

Dub looked around, and lowered his voice. "I got a post-card from Phil. Wanna see it?"

"Sure."

Dub wiped his hands with a clean paper towel, and reached under his coverall. He extracted an envelope.

"I put it in this here envelope 'cause it's evidence. Here," he handed it to Lou, "take a look."

"Aren't you gonna take this to the cops?"

"Maybe." He grinned. "Unless you want some, what-do-you-call, memorabilia? You're a newspaper guy, right? Give you a scoop."

Lou used his fingernails to withdraw the card from the envelope. It read:

> Hey, Dub. Sure hate this place. Food sucks, music sucks, air's dirty. Wish I was back in Oregon, even in crummy Seagirt. Even to look at your ugly mug. See you.
> Phil.

Lou turned the card over. On the picture side was an ad for a bar called El Torero. It was like the cheesy bullfight posters on people's walls years ago. A snorting bull, and a bullfighter dressed in purple, wielding a cape and a sword dripping blood.

Lou got light-headed.

"How much do you want for this, uh, memorabilia?"

Dub looked around some more. "Fifty?"

Lou took some bills out of his pocket, handed them to Dub, and started his car.

"What about your oil?"

"Later for that. Thanks."

Lou sped off for his motel room.

Hands shaking, he called Blanche, gave her a quick review of the latest, and told her what he held in his hand.

"Didn't that psychic mention a bullfighter?" she asked.

"Damn right, she did, and the color purple. And, what the heck, these things have been known to pan out. She's been right about other things, I figured this case had as much chance as any. I asked people to think about it."

"So, are you gonna take that to the deputy?"

"Well, yes. But, I don't know . . . I think I want to meet Ms. Lucy first."

"I've never known you to believe in this stuff."

"Blanche, the bullfighter on the postcard is in a purple outfit, and volcanos are mountains."

"Okay, whatever. Keep me posted."

"Thanks. I'll be back in Portland as soon as I can. I have to see a fortune teller."

He checked out, and told Chloe he might be back. She promised to keep his room just as he left it.

After a quick stop at a baseball card collector's shop, he headed out for the boonies of Washington state.

15. Woo-Woo

Lou looked around before he knocked on the door. No trolls, elves, or fairies, and the house seemed normal enough. The exotic growth around the cottage was a perfect setting. He imagined that the misty, rainy atmosphere in the winter and all the tall trees lent it even spookier ambience.

"Mr. Tedesco?" a handsome woman opened the door, dressed in blue sweats. Her long hair was caught in a braid.

"Yes. Ms. Persson?"

"Come on in, call me Lucy, and I'll call you Lou. After all, we're old friends on the phone at least."

"Sounds like a good idea."

Lou entered the warm, homey front room and sat on the couch. A fire burned in the hearth, radiating fragrant heat. Lou guessed that the logs were western cedar.

"I've just made some iced tea. Want a glass? Or, would you prefer hot? It's chilly enough out there"

"Iced is fine, thanks. You have a pleasant house."

"Thanks. Do you know Jack Narz?"

"Yes. He's very taken with you. I can see why."

"You're making me blush. I'll be right back."

Lou noticed the trappings of the trade lying around the room, but figured that you have clocks around a watchmaker's shop. Just then, Lucy came back with a tea tray.

"I loved what you wrote in the *Stumptown Weekly*," she said, as she served tea.

"Yes. In fact, that's why I'm here. You've supplied me with valuable leads. Are you always this good?"

"I wish." Lucy sat next to Lou on the couch. "I felt what I call emanations about the case, right from the first. It's a kind of precondition to getting the mental pictures I sometimes get. If I don't get the emanations, I see nothing."

"How did Jack Narz find you?"

"Now, that amazed even me. He told me that a waitress told him about me, someone I don't know. She read about me, or saw that awful TV thing they did. It made me look like a weirdo. Anyway, I'm not sure exactly how."

"Given how this worked out, it's quite a coincidence."

Lucy smiled. "Lou, some people I know don't put any faith in the idea of a coincidence. They would say that it was foreordained, or good magic."

Lou smiled back. "I've never been much of a believer in . . ."

"This woo-woo stuff?"

"Forgive me, but, yes. However, I saw no harm in Jack and Velma finding hope in your visions. Now, well, I'm not sure about anything."

"And, why is that?"

Lou put his tea down on the tray.

"Lucy, please go over what you told Jack, and have you seen anything since then?"

"Well, you probably know what I saw, the bullfighter and the volcano. Since then, nothing, I'm afraid."

"Tell me about the volcano. As I understand it, it was not an erupting volcano. True?"

Lucy sipped tea. "Yes. I was here when Saint Helens erupted. It was nothing like that."

"What did you see?"

She looked up at the ceiling and closed her eyes.

"A snowcapped mountain against a bright blue sky. Quite a beautiful picture, really. Like a postcard."

"Where does the volcano part come in?"

Lucy scrunched her eyes tighter. "I'm using my mind's eye . . ." She was quiet for a minute. "You know, I just know it. It's like the Cascade Mountains. They all used to be volcanoes, and they have a different, uh . . ."

"Emanation?"

"Okay," she opened her eyes and looked at Lou. "That works. I grew up in Colorado, the Rockies. Those mountains *feel* different than the Cascades. The mountain in my vision felt like the Cascades."

"Did you recognize it?" Lou asked. "Could it have been Mount Rainier, or Mount Hood, or . . ."

"Uh-uh." She shook her head. "I'm fairly familiar with those."

"I'm going to show you something. You must handle it carefully, because it might have fingerprints, or other forensic evidence on it. But, you should see it."

Lou took the postcard, which he had secured in a plastic sleeve used for baseball cards, and handed it to her. Lucy took a look at it, gasped, and fainted. Her tea splashed to the floor.

Nonplused, Lou didn't know whether to pick up the glass and mop the spilled tea, or revive Lucy. He ran to the kitchen, moistened a towel, and dabbed at Lucy's face. She came out of it in a few seconds.

"Oh, my heavens, Lou. Can I see that again?"

She examined the picture. "This is exactly what I saw. The picture is very much like the old bullfight posters we put up on our walls years ago. I recall a vivid impression of the color purple."

"Yes," Lou nodded, "the poster thing occurred to me, too. All my bohemian friends had them on their dorm walls."

"I didn't connect it until now. Out of context, I guess. Where does this come from?"

"Turn it over and read it."

Lucy read the message.

"Is this Phil person involved?"

"We believe that he is one of the killers."

"Lou, can I touch the card?"

"Sure, but be careful."

With painstaking care, Lucy slid the postcard out of the sleeve, holding it by the edge, and took it between both hands, palms to the edges. Her face took on a stricken, agonized look.

"Oh! I see a snow-capped mountain, a field of trees, sparse evergreens growing up among black stones like large cinders."

She started to twitch, made alarming noises, and breathed deeply through her nose. She groaned.

Then she shrieked and passed out again.

A few minutes later, drinking a sip of water from a glass Lou was holding, Lucy began to regain her color. He hovered over her, after laying her on the couch, and raising her feet above her head with a pillow.

Lou had secured the postcard back in its sleeve, but it was in sight on the table. Lucy asked, "Can I see the card again?"

"Uh, I'm not sure that's a good idea."

"It'll be all right," she said, sitting up slowly.

"Okay." He handed it to her.

"Lou, I saw something more, before I blacked out. By the mountain, and the black stones. I saw a tree, split by lightning, and a gray box buried under it."

"Lucy, you're sure this is the same mountain?"

"Oh, yes! It's like a Polaroid photo, where the image develops more detail as you watch it. First, I saw the peak and the sky, then, the scattered trees, then the black stones, then the split tree. Not one of the evergreens. It was more like, maybe an oak or something like that. I'm not much of a naturalist."

"With a garden like yours?"

She shrugged, as if in apology. Lou had started scribbling notes in his reporter's notebook.

"Oh, Lou, a lake! I saw a lake behind the split tree, and the mountain was reflected in the lake."

"Were there leaves on the tree?"

"Yes, but, also . . . snow! There was snow on the ground, in patches, like it had mostly melted, but there were patches left. Oh, I can't believe how much more I can recall with someone probing my memory."

"Well, I'm happy to be of service. Anything else? Can you see a cabin, or a road, or any animals or birds?"

"I don't know . . ."

"Close your eyes again. Look down, like you were looking at your feet."

"A road. I see a road. Blacktop, with gravel at the shoulders."

"Look left."

"Uh, the road goes up and to my left, and disappears between the trees. More trees like the split one. The road is lined with these trees."

"Look right."

Lucy's head did a slow swivel right.

"Oh, this is wonderful! The mountain, the tree, the lake, the road goes down and a gate! Lou, there's a gate there, a distance down the road. I can just see it. And, one of those booths like in state parks, where rangers sell admission."

Lou was trying to keep up, his pen scratching the paper.

"Lucy, look up."

Her head tilted back on her neck. "Blue sky. A puffy cloud, or two."

Lou thought for a second.

"The gray box, Lucy. Can you tell me where it's buried?"

"Wait, the box seems to be materializing, no the ground is becoming transparent. The box is . . . at the base of the split tree, on the side away from the road, and toward the lake."

"Can you turn around, look behind you?"

"I'll try. Oh, Lou—the picture is fading. I'm losing it."

She opened her eyes, rubbed them with the heels of her hands. "Sorry. It's gone."

"Lucy, this is very complete. If we can identify the location, it may be extremely important."

"Oh, my head." She put her fingers up to her temples. "I have a headache."

"Can I get you anything?"

"I'll be all right."

He stowed the reporter's pad, and reached into his pocket.

"Can I pay you for your time?"

"Not a chance. I can't take any money for this."

Lou arose. "Well, if you're sure . . . If you can think of anything else, please call me." He handed Lucy a card. "Are you sure you're okay? I'm a little worried, with the fainting and all."

"I'll be fine. I'm tired, and I think a nap is in order."

Lou walked to the door.

"Thanks again, Lucy. If your information about this place is as accurate as your sight of the bullfighter, we may be able to close this case."

"What about Ronald Colman?"

"Nothing on that, yet. The video store thing panned out, though. It caused a major break in the case."

She extended her hand. "I'm glad. And, I'm glad to have met you.

"Come again, Lou. I work well with you."

Lou drove back toward Portland in silence. He ran the vision in his mind. There was something familiar about the scene Lucy had described. He felt like he might have been there.

He squinted, keeping at least a part of his attention on the road, while the scene played in his imagination.

He added his own details to the scene: the trees swaying in the breeze, the only sounds were birdsong and leaves rustling, a smell of fresh air and a distant wood fire, a fish jumping in the lake. . . .

In a second, he knew where the scene was. It was Mount

Lassen in northern California. He knew the lake Lucy had described, and could find the tree from her description.

He pulled over at his first opportunity to gas up and buy a cup of coffee and a bad plastic-wrapped sandwich, soggy, and awash in mayonnaise. He bought a road map, even though he was sure he didn't need it.

After using the men's room, he drove straight to the I-5, and headed south to California.

SECTION FOUR

I Have Been to the Mountaintop . . .

1. A Quick Trip to the Park

On the way to the interstate, Lou stopped, called Gar and arranged to send him the Mexican postcard by messenger from Coos Bay, Oregon. Gar grumbled about Lou running around with important evidence, but decided to let it go.

"Damn, Lou. When all this is over, I'm sending you for a basic criminology course over to the community college."

"Don't do it. You'll ruin my native instincts."

"I'll ruin *you* if that gets lost. Why can't you bring it back here yourself?"

"Let's just say that I'm taking a little R&R in a scenic state park."

Gar made a noise. "Okay, I guess I know better than to try to get a straight answer out of you. Call me when you get back."

Lou smiled. If there was any of this that he was doing according to regulations, it was by accident. He bought a large cup of black coffee, and got back in the car.

Lou calculated that it would take six or seven hours of driving from where he was. He girded himself and resolved to pull over and nap if he felt tired, to buy coffee and a snack, and to relieve himself. He was not going to stop otherwise, until he got to Lassen Peak.

Even at that time of year, the I-5 might be slick with ice. He had heard of horror stories about eighteen-wheelers jackknifing on the snaky Siskiyou Mountain section straddling southern Oregon and northern California.

Thankful for a glove compartment full of CDs so he could sing along at the top of his lungs, he thought back to his first view of the mountain, as his car plunged south. Some stretches of the road were so dark, it was hard to discern the world beyond the verge.

When Lou was young and single, he had played for Visalia in the California League. Single-A baseball in the vast agricultural Central Valley. It didn't pay much and there wasn't much to do after a game.

The young men on his team quickly tired of butting heads with the local studs for the favor of the local girls. They expanded their circle of exploration as time allowed. Eventually, they reached the limits in all directions.

"What's it gonna be, boys," someone would ask, flipping a coin, "the road to Fresno or the road to Bakersfield?" Then, everyone would groan.

After his last season with the team, Lou got into his old junker and took off without an agenda. He chose north because he wanted to say good-bye to a girl in Fresno, and just kept going, with a vague idea that he would end up in Seattle.

The girl thing didn't pan out, and Lou decided to do a Kerouac. On the road!

He stopped for a beer in a roadhouse bar near Redding, entering only because he didn't hear country music coming from the jukebox.

He was astounded to see a bunch of aging hippies sitting around a table drinking shots and beers, and rolling fat joints.

"Hey, dude," a red-eyed, grizzle-bearded, broken-nosed man called out, "pull yourself a beer and come on over." Lou did just that.

After several more trips behind the bar for refills, and a few circulated joints, Lou was one of the gang. They loved that he was a ballplayer, and each of them admitted a secret childhood desire to play for the Dodgers or the Giants or the Athletics.

When it came time for him to leave, one of them asked, "Where ya headin', dude?"

Lou shrugged. "Just lookin'. See what I can see."

"Hey, you gotta go up to Shasta," said a longhaired biker with an earring. "It's holy ground, man. The Indians say so."

"Shasta's okay," allowed another, wearing a suede shirt with embroidered marijuana leaves, "but Lassen's nicer, and you're under no pressure to have a mystical experience."

"Hey," Lou said, "I'll hit 'em both. I am in no hurry to do nothin'."

He liked Lassen better, and came as close to a mystical experience as he ever had, before he met Lucy. It was the supernatural quiet, the smell of mountain air, and the triumph of life over the devastation of the last series of eruptions, the worst being in 1915. He had camped there for days before going on to Mount Shasta. And now, he was on his way there again.

There were still patches of snow on the ground, but the road to Lassen Peak was clear, and the sun was shining. Lou was exhausted, but he had made it, stopping only once to nap for a couple of hours.

When he got to the gate it was open, and no park employee was on duty. A hand-lettered sign read, "Road Closed 5 miles (8 km) Ahead—Road Conditions." He drove through the gate, and started up the mountain road toward the lake, in his memory a short distance away.

Before too long, a park ranger's SUV came down the road from the other direction. Lou waved him down.

"Help you, sir?" The ranger was young, skinny, and wore glasses. His uniform looked too big on him. The name tag on his coat read Hagedorn.

"Hi, I'm looking for a tree split by lightning."

Lou read a brief look on the ranger's face as: another loony.

"We have a bunch of those, and most of them are up in the closed part of the road. We're repairing winter damage. Can't you come back another time?"

Lou cleared his throat, and told the ranger as much of the story as he needed to before the man understood what the mission was. He omitted everything about Lucy. The look of skepticism on Hagedorn's face was already making Lou uncomfortable.

The ranger waited to speak, the effort for him like attempting to digest a knot of something hard.

"Do I understand you to say that there might be a piece of evidence from an unsolved murder case buried under a tree, in this park?"

"Yes, Officer Hagedorn. I have no official status in the case, which is in Oregon anyway. But, if you call Deputy Gar Loober of the Seagirt police, he'll vouch for me. My name is Lou Tedesco."

"Look, I don't know what you think you're doing, but even my dim understanding of the criminal law tells me that there's no chain of evidence here."

"Should we call the state cops?" Lou chafed inside at the idea of giving the box over to the California police.

The ranger shuffled his feet, wrinkled his brow. An impulse seized him. "You know what? I'm a police officer," he grinned with the realization. "Let's work something out."

He told Lou to park his car by the road, and to go back to the ranger station with him in the SUV. The station was basic but homey. They went into the cramped office.

Lou gave him Gar's phone number in Seagirt, and Gar answered. They talked back and forth for a while, and Lou fidgeted. The ranger hung up.

"Okay, here's what I'm going to do. I will accompany you to the site, with a video camera, and document the process of you looking for this . . . ?"

"Gray box."

"Gray box," he said, doubt in his voice. "When, and if, you find it, I will place it into a paper sack. Will it fit into a paper sack?"

Lou shrugged, and prayed that the ranger didn't ask him how he knew it was there.

"I guess . . ."

"Hmmm. Okay, I'll bring a really big one, just in case. I'll seal it with tape, sign the seal, and write out an affidavit to the effect that I was with you when you found the object, and I sealed it. Then, we'll go down to the general store, and old Bernie can witness it. How's that?"

"Officer, it sounds good to me."

"Let's do it."

Hagedorn rummaged around and came up with a brown-paper lawn and leaf bag, a roll of one-inch masking tape, an official evidence bag which Hagedorn had discovered squirreled away in the ranger station, and a video camera. He secured it in the back of his vehicle, and said to Lou, "Let's roll."

Just like the cop shows, Lou thought.

When the lake came into view, a country mile away, Hagedorn slowed down.

"You say you're looking for a tree split by lightning?"

"Yes, officer."

"Okay, there's two on the lake on this road. One's real old, the other happened this past summer."

Lou thought for a second.

"Is there one both close to the lake, and close to the road?"

He nodded. "That would be the older one. It's not far."

Moments later, Hagedorn slid the SUV over to the side of the road and stopped the engine. Lou peered out the window, and saw the tree, sundered like a wishbone, but holding its parts together at the roots. Snow had collected in the deep wound, its pristine whiteness stood out against the ebony scorch of the lightning scar.

"This look like it?"

Lou caught himself before Lucy's name slipped out. But, he knew that this was the tree.

"Sure does."

"Let's go."

They walked over to the tree, Hagedorn lugging the video camera. Lou sized up the lay of the land. The tree was right on the water, roots exposed before they submerged in the lake. He looked out at the glassy surface of the lake, Lassen Peak rising up into a blue sky, its reflection diving into the blue water.

Very auspicious place, Lou thought.

"Officer Hagedorn, I'm sure that this is it. I'd like you to start taping, and I'll provide a commentary. Please feel free to ask leading questions."

The ranger lifted the camera to his eye. "Okay, rolling."

"My name is Lou Tedesco. I am here, at Lassen Peak in California, based on information from an, uh, informant. I am looking for a gray box of as-yet-indeterminate size, which is supposed to be buried at the base of this tree."

"Lou, give the date and time."

Lou, tired and a bit disoriented, looked helpless. The ranger said, "I am park ranger Kurt Hagedorn, accompanying Lou Tedesco, and videotaping this event for evidentiary purposes."

Hagedorn gave the date and time, and the approximate location within the park.

"Go on, Lou."

"Thanks, Officer Hagedorn. There is no obvious place to dig, so I'm going to probe the ground with a stick to determine if there is soft ground here. This may indicate recently dug-up soil."

Lou picked up a twig, which promptly broke when he tried to poke it in the ground. He smiled a sheepish smile, thinking that he probably looked like Elmer Fudd, and found a stouter probe.

"The informant said it was buried on the lake side, so I will begin there."

Lou walked around to the back side of the tree, and began poking the ground. He kept this up for a minute, until he lost his balance, and began to slide down the slope toward the lake.

"Goddamit!" he yelled. This was followed by a string of obscenities enriched by a life in minor-league baseball. Lou clutched for a rock as he fell, but the rock came loose, and a shower of rocks followed him down the few feet to the water.

Momentarily stunned, Hagedorn sprang into action and raced to the lake. "You okay?" he yelled, swinging the video camera as he ran. Lou stood up in the thigh-high water, and began to shiver.

"I'm not hurt, but it's cold as a well digger's ass in here. Help me out."

The ranger squatted down and gave Lou his hand. Lou took hold, and pulled himself out of the lake, grabbing at tree roots for support. As he hit dry land, something caught his eye.

"Hey, there it is!"

Lou pointed at the roots of the tree. The rocks had been covering a dirty, caved-in shoebox wrapped in duct tape.

"Stand right there, Lou. I'm going to get you a blanket from the vehicle, and some latex gloves." He handed Lou the video camera, and Lou videoed the trail of rocks down to the lake, and the corner of the shoebox protruding from the hole at the roots of the tree, controlling his shaking as much as possible. Even in high summer, the air was chilly, and the water was frigid. He described what he was shooting as the tape ran.

Hagedorn returned with an army blanket, which he draped around Lou's shoulders.

"Lou, turn the camera to me." Lou swung the camera and focused on the ranger.

"I'm Ranger Hagedorn. I am now putting latex gloves on, to avoid contaminating the evidence. Follow me with the camera, Lou."

Hagedorn walked to the tree.

"The box was uncovered by Lou Tedesco when he slipped into the lake. I will now retrieve it from its place. Stay with me, here."

Lou followed the ranger's movements as he kneeled and worked the box loose from among the roots, the image going in and out of focus in the great tradition of amateur video. Hagedorn then placed the box on the ground. He looked up at the camera.

"It appears to be a shoebox from something called Skaters. It's wrapped around with duct tape, and appears to have spent very little time in the ground, because it has not decomposed much. I'll leave it to the lab boys for a definitive answer, and I will include dirt samples from the hole."

He reached into his pocket and pulled out a plastic sandwich bag. He scooped a handful of earth from the hole, and put it in the bag.

"This will be included in the sealed bag with the box and its contents. Now . . ." he took a sheath knife from his belt, and slowly slit the tape along one side of the box, then another, then the third. "I've left one side of the tape uncut to preserve it. And now, I will carefully open the box."

Lou watched fascinated through the eyepiece of the camera, as Hagedorn's gloved hands worked the weathered lid of the box. It opened, and Lou's breath caught at the back of his throat. Even Hagedorn couldn't help gasping.

In the box, wrapped in several layers of bubble wrap, was an object with the rough shape of a handgun. Hagedorn lifted it, almost daintily.

"This appears to be a handgun, just visible through the bubble wrap. It is also sealed with one, two pieces of duct tape. Should I open it?"

"No, no!" Lou called out. "Let the lab guys do it."

"Sure," Hagedorn nodded. "I'm placing the object back in the shoebox, closing the lid, and putting the box and the bag of dirt into this," he held up the evidence bag, "paper sack."

He did that, and looked up at the camera.

"I will now wrap this in masking tape, and sign the tape in several places. Get this, Lou. Zoom in."

In a few minutes, the task was accomplished, including placing the package in the official evidence bag. Then, Hagedorn looked into the camera and gave an extemporaneous statement about the veracity of the tape, and promising a written statement to accompany it. He took the camera from Lou, videoed Lou giving a similar statement, and turned off the camera.

"Let's go back to the station. I'll make you some hot coffee, and give you dry clothes."

"Ranger Hagedorn," said a shivering Lou, "I appreciate everything you've done. I could hardly imagine that you would have believed me in the first place."

"Lou, call me Kurt. I haven't had this much fun in a long time. I don't get to play cop very often. I just hope that this holds up in court. Get in the car."

They drove off, heater blasting away, back to the ranger station.

2. Disorder at the Border

At the same time Lou Tedesco left Lassen Peak, with the evidence bag, the samples, a signed videotape, and an affidavit from Ranger Kurt Hagedorn, and started on the long return trip to Waldorf, Oregon, a disheveled young man appeared at the U.S.-Mexico border at Matamoros.

He was dirty, and he looked like he hadn't slept in days. He carried a bundle fashioned from a bedsheet. His sneakers were worn and his toes were visible through holes in the uppers.

The Mexican police gave him a cursory frisk, and made it clear that they were happy to see him go.

"Adios," he saluted them.

As the young man crossed into the United States, Customs Officer Jerry Ramirez gave him an expert look, and decided that they should speak. Ramirez stepped into the young man's path, causing a quick stop in the shuffling gait. The officer would later mention, offhandedly, that "the kid looked more relieved than anything."

Ramirez took the young man into the office, where it was a little less stifling than it was outside.

"Want some cold water? There's a bottle in the cooler over there." The officer gestured at an ice chest in the corner.

"Thanks," the young man replied, barely audible.

After a few moments, Ramirez asked, "Do you have some ID? Just routine."

The young man reached into his pocket and took out a new, tooled-leather wallet of a kind commonly sold in Mexico. He extracted a driver's license, and handed it to the officer.

Ramirez sat at the computer, and punched in the man's name and information. A moment later, he said, "Mr. Troy, there are some folks up in Oregon who want to speak with you."

The young man began to weep, the tears making muddy tracks on his dusty face.

Later that same day, in the company of a federal marshal, Phil Troy was on a plane to Portland.

3. Keeping Promises

Looking more than a bit disheveled himself, Lou Tedesco showed up in Waldorf the next morning. He had been on the road for the better part of two days, round trip, and had slept fitfully in his car on the shoulder of the freeway.

He parked in an illegal space and dragged himself up to Tom Knight's office, dressed in a motley assortment of his clothes, Kurt Hagedorn's castoffs, and a clean T-shirt purchased on the road somewhere between Redding and Medford. When he got to the office door, two security guards were on his heels believing that he was an insane guy with some beef.

Lou would have admitted that it was much too close to the truth.

He strode into Knight's anteroom, and dropped the evidence bag and videotape on the desk of the horrified Miss Warden. The security guards were right behind him, and laid hands on him, suspecting that he was about to do her harm.

"Tell Knight he's got to see me, right now!"

Miss Warden was struck speechless by this unprecedented assault on her domain. Her mouth moved but nothing came out.

"I've been to California and back, and I have the murder weapon in the Seagirt murder case. Now, call Knight, and I don't mean later."

The security guards began to drag Lou away, and he yelled in objection, when Knight's office door flew open. The DA stood there in shirt sleeves, a bewildered look on his face.

"What the hell is going on out here?"

"Knight, tell these rent-a-goons to get their damn hands off me. I've got the Seagirt murder weapon in that bag." He indicated the evidence bag with a nod of the head, as his arms were pinioned at his sides.

Knight took in the situation, looked down at the packages, and said, "Yes, okay, let him go."

"Are you sure, sir? This guy is nuts!" one of the guards insisted.

Knight nodded. "Yes. I'm sure."

The guards let Lou go, and he shook himself free. Knight gestured for the guards to go.

"Mr. Tedesco, bring your packages in here, and let's talk."

The look on Miss Warden's face, and the outraged noises she uttered, made it clear that she thought her boss had gone nuts, himself, and was allowing the Hun through the gate.

Lou brought the bag and videotape in and placed them on Knight's desk. He drew up a chair, and sat back with his arms folded. Knight took his seat.

"Okay, what's this?"

Lou launched into his story. At one point, Knight stopped him and began taking notes. Lou relaxed, and told the rest in a measured, coherent way.

Knight continued to write for a few moments after Lou stopped talking.

"So, what you're telling me is that the evidence bag contains the shoebox, right? And, there's what looks like a gun in there? And the video includes a statement by a park ranger who accompanied you. Right?"

"Right. And, there's a written affidavit supporting the tape, just in case."

"Mr. Tedesco, do you have any idea how stupid it was for you to recover this item yourself? How you may have poisoned the chain of evidence so that it will be inadmissable in court?"

"Look, sir, the ranger did everything by the book. It's a good find, it was in a shallow hole covered by a few stones, in the open in a public place, and the whole thing was documented. Just watch the tape."

Knight wrote some more. "Okay, I'm going to call for one of the officers working the case, so he can be here when I open it. And, then we'll decide what to do."

He picked up the phone and buzzed Miss Warden.

"Yes, I'm fine. Call Detective Klein and tell him to come up to my office, ASAP. Thanks." He put down the phone.

"I don't think she'll ever be the same," Knight frowned. "But," he brightened, "it might be an improvement."

Lou laughed at the DA's sly smile.

"Mr. Tedesco . . ."

"Please, call me Lou."

"Lou, I don't know whether to throw you in jail or give you a medal. I might do both."

"I would plead insanity. Even you couldn't beat me on that one."

"Damn right. What possessed you? You seem like a rational sort, if a bit obsessed. I don't understand."

Lou took a deep breath. "I promised Velma Korta that I would do everything I could to find Shelley's killers. Lester Green wasn't doing the job, and you didn't see that. I was compelled by my oath to Velma."

"Well, I can't say I'm sorry . . ."

There was a knock on the door. "Come in!"

A wiry cop in a wrinkled suit came in.

"Detective Dave Klein, this is Lou Tedesco. He's brought us something, and I wanted you to be here when I opened it.

And, yes, I've already read him the riot act about evidence handling."

Lou shook the cop's hand, recoiling from the stench of tobacco smoke coming off him. Klein hovered over Knight's desk, peering at the package.

"Whadda we got?"

"Let's see," replied Knight, and opened the evidence bag. He removed the paper bag. Then, he rummaged in his desk drawer, took out a letter opener, and began to work on the tape.

"Should we be videotaping this?" Lou asked.

"Good question, but not necessary." Knight slit the masking tape, trying to preserve the ranger's signatures. When the tape was cut enough to allow the bag to open, Knight unfolded the heavy brown paper, and reached inside the bag.

"First, here is the affidavit. Right, Lou?"

"Yes, sir. The envelope is signed as well. And, Hagedorn will be happy to testify, if need be."

"And this . . ." Knight's voice strained as he withdrew the shoebox, "is the box that you found under the tree, right?"

"Yes, sir. Buried in a hole under some rocks. It's all on the video."

Klein picked up the video and held it up to the light, as though it would help him see what was on it.

"Klein, do you have some gloves?"

The cop snapped out of it, and handed the DA a pair of rubber gloves. Knight put them on and opened the shoebox.

"What does that look like to you, detective?"

"Bubble wrap in the general shape of a gun. Looks silver, the gun."

"Right. Should I slit the plastic, or try to open the tape?"

Klein rubbed his chin. "Slit it. The lab might find something under the tape. And, be careful. There may be something under the bubble wrap."

"You know what? I'm going to leave this as is. The lab techs will kill us if we screw up."

Klein grunted. "Good idea."

"Care to guess what kind of weapon it is?"

"Semi-auto from the shape. Could be a Glock. Need to look closer." Klein had the tight, clipped cop argot down perfectly. Lou wondered what came first: *Dragnet*, or the style.

Knight looked at Lou.

"Lou, once again, if anything you did poisons the evidence, you're in deep doo-doo. But, there's one way we can use this that won't taint it as evidence."

He turned to the cop.

"Klein, what do you say we show this to Troy?"

Lou jumped like he had sat on a hornet. "Troy? How the hell are you gonna do that?"

Klein nodded. "I like it."

"Are you talking about Phil Troy?" Lou's eyes were bugging out.

"Yes, Lou. He's right downstairs in a holding cell. He crossed the border into Texas yesterday, got pinched by the border patrol, and was flown in last night."

"Well, has he confessed?"

"Nope," Klein frowned.

"He says he knows nothing about it. All we have on him is that he and Wheelock bought overpriced sneakers, and rented videos all the way to Mexico. Let's see what this item does for him."

"Can I come?"

Knight looked at Klein. Klein shrugged. "Okay, but stay the hell out of the way, and don't say anything. If this works, I'll give you a free pass on evidence tampering."

The three took the elevator to a subbasement, and over to the holding cells. Lou couldn't wait to get a look at Phil Troy.

He was not impressed. Dub Gordon's descriptions were close, but that was before Troy's ordeals in Mexico. A weasely punk at his best, he was now scruffy and sleep-deprived.

Troy was dressed in an orange jumpsuit, which hung from his skinny shoulders like a blanket. His eyes were sunken into dark pits, his greasy hair hung lank over his forehead, and a smoking cigarette dangled from his knobby fingers. He was sitting on a bench, talking to a rumpled, middle-aged man.

"Counselor," Knight acknowledged the man. "We have something to show your client." The DA held the shoebox behind his back like a surprise present. "Any objection?"

The lawyer's face, drawn into a permanent frown, registered weary resignation. He looked at his client, who shook his head once.

"No. What do you have?"

"Recognize this, Phil?"

Knight whipped the box around with a look of malign glee. Lou expected him to sing "Happy Birthday." The object inside slid, making a noise.

"Oh, Jesus," Troy hissed, and began to sob. The lawyer whispered something in Troy's ear, then said to Knight, "Can I have a minute with him?"

"Sure," a magnanimous Knight said. He led Klein and Lou a few yards down the hall. Angry hisses and muffled conversation, punctuated by yells of, "No!" were audible for the next few minutes.

Klein lit a smoke. Knight frowned, but said nothing.

"So," Klein said, smoke streaming from his mouth, "looks like sonny boy recognized the box. Whaddaya think's goin' on in there?"

Knight sniffed. "Unless I'm very much mistaken, the public defender is asking what's in the box. Troy will tell him, and once the idea sinks in, that it's the murder weapon covered with fingerprints, they will ask for a deal."

"You don't think they wiped it clean?" Lou asked.

"I don't think they ever expected to see it again. You want to tell me who clued you in on this?"

Lou smiled. "An anonymous informant. You might say it was like a vision."

Klein snorted. Knight said, "*You* might say that, being a reporter."

"Whatever. Watch the video. It'll explain everything you need to know."

"Lou, Deputy Loober called me about the postcard. He told me that it was you who turfed up the evidence and that much of the case was developed by your efforts. I'm cutting you a lot of slack in recognition of your persistence and your success. But you can't keep this up. You're going to get in over your head sometime, somewhere, and you'll be sorry."

"Well, so far it's only been up to my thighs."

Klein and Knight said, "Huh?" at the same time.

"Watch the video. And, I do appreciate your concern."

"Mr. Knight?" came a voice from the cell. The public defender stuck his head out and gestured.

They walked back to the cell.

"Okay," Knight opened, "what have you got?"

"First," said the lawyer, "the death penalty is out."

"Even a PD lawyer knows that aggravated murder calls for the death penalty. It's in the penal code. Check it out sometime."

"Look, Tom, never mind the tough DA talk. The kid doesn't go to the death house."

"I ask again: What have you got?"

"We'll give you a complete confession, soup to nuts, chapter and verse."

"Not good enough," Knight shook his head. "We want Wheelock."

"Calvin had nothin' to do with it! It was me!" Phil Troy threw himself against the bars.

With a weary voice, the lawyer said, "Sit down, Phil. Let me handle this."

Troy flopped down on the bench. He banged his fists against the wall, and began to cry.

"Before my client here breaks the walls, if we give you Wheelock, you'll eighty-six the death penalty?"

Knight hesitated, for drama's sake, then nodded. "Done."

The lawyer whispered in Troy's ear, an angry hiss audible.

"No, no!" Troy bawled.

More whispering, then more crying. Then, Troy nodded his head.

"Calvin Wheelock is in Mexico City. He works at a bar called El Torero. He's a bartender, and," the lawyer smirked, "a male stripper."

"Residence?"

"Phil says he crashes at people's apartments. No fixed address, besides the bar."

Troy hissed, and gestured to the lawyer, who leaned down to hear what his client had to say.

"Mr. Troy insists that Calvin Wheelock had nothing to do with the crime."

"Noted. Okay, don't ask for bail. He's a flight risk."

"I gotta make the effort. By the way, who's this guy?" The lawyer jerked a thumb at Lou.

Knight grinned. "He's your client's worst nightmare. Let's go. We've got papers to draw up."

Knight marched off, followed by his small entourage.

Back in his office, after enduring a disapproving look from Miss Warden, Knight phoned Interpol and arranged for Calvin Wheelock to be apprehended. Klein shook both men's hands, and went back to file a report.

"What now?" asked Lou.

Knight spread his arms in an expansive gesture. "We just wait for the call from Mexico, and then arrange extradition. Meanwhile, we give Troy a chance to compose himself, then take a statement. We'll want a complete confession, and a chronological account of the crime."

"I want an exclusive on the story."

Knight thought for a moment. "I'll do what I can. Word is already out about Troy being here. Maybe I can squelch the details."

"Thanks. I'm curious about one aspect of the crime. These guys watched a miniseries of *In Cold Blood* numerous times. It's mostly what they rented from the video stores. I want you to ask them what role it played in their decision to commit the crime and the aftermath. Will do?"

"Sure. I can use it to establish state of mind. It does seem obsessive. So, what's next for you?"

"Well," Lou stretched, "I'm gonna drive back to Portland, take a bath and a long nap, and then start writing. Please call me when Wheelock is here."

"You bet. Thanks again, Lou, and I'm sorry if I was rough on you."

Lou cocked his head at the DA. "I thought you made it a policy never to apologize to a reporter, or thank one."

Knight looked around. "You see anybody else in this room? I wouldn't do it in the presence of another human being."

"You're welcome, then."

Lou shook Knight's hand and left.

4. Home, Again

Lou drove back to Portland running on adrenaline fumes. He returned the rental car and took a cab home. The cabbie was reluctant to pick Lou up because of his disreputable appearance and then had to wake him once they got to his loft.

He called Blanche while he soaked in the tub. It was the late afternoon, prime time for the *Stumptown Weekly.*

"Hello, stranger. I thought I was going to have to file a missing persons report to find you. Your dialing finger break?"

"Slash away. I'm impervious, not to mention brain dead."

"I always suspected that you were brain-dead."

"I told you not to mention that."

"Okay, never mind the old Soupy Sales routines. What have you got?"

"You mean besides terminal exhaustion and incipient pneumonia? Tear out the front page! I always wanted to say that."

"Lou, have you been hit on the head by a Ben Hecht novel? Talk English."

"Okay, how's this for a headline? 'Intrepid Reporter

Risks Life to Solve Beach Murders; DA Uses Reporter's Evidence to Extract Confession.' Like it?"

"It's overripe, but it scans. Is it true?"

"Well, 'Risks Life' is a bit overstated. 'Risks Sanity' is more like it. All else is gospel."

"When can you have it written up?"

"Blanche, if Raquel Welch walked in the door now stark naked, I would still have to sleep for an undetermined amount of time before I could take care of business."

"Raquel Welch? Isn't she somebody's grandmother now? You need to get out more. Can you have it by tomorrow night?"

"Um, okay. Do I get the cover?"

"If you deliver the kind of story I'm hoping for, you can have the back cover, too."

"Well, then. See you tomorrow night."

"Lou?" There was a change in Blanche's voice. "I was worried about you. I'm glad to hear that you're okay."

"Nothing some shut-eye won't cure."

They rang off. Lou finished his bath, put on a fresh pair of pajamas, and dreamed of Raquel Welch.

The next evening, the dutiful Lou Tedesco delivered the story to the *Stumptown Weekly*. When he entered the loft office, he got a standing ovation. It was touching.

Patti found the event moving enough to cry about it. "Speech!" someone called out.

"I don't know what to say, but, here goes. I was able to do what I did because Blanche believed in me . . ." cheers for Blanche, "and because I believed in others. Also, because I made a promise to a victim's mother that I wouldn't allow her daughter's death to become a cold case."

Patti burst into fresh sobs. Blanche comforted her.

"This experience has taught me," Lou went on, "that truth may live in unlikely places, and that there is more out there, as Shakespeare said, than was dreamt of in my philosophy."

There were hoots from the crowd. "Give us a break!" Tubby yelled. Lou mustered his dignity, and went on.

"I will never be as quick to dismiss a source of information on prejudicial grounds as I have in the past. I'm not sure I can convince you of this just by saying it, but be sure to check on a story before writing it off because you have misgivings about the source.

"And now, before Blanche sees my expense report and commits bodily harm on me, I'd like to thank you all."

More cheers.

After a few minutes of backslapping and handshaking, Lou and Blanche sneaked off to her office and closed the door. Lou filled her in on the latest developments.

"So," Blanche opened, "we have an exclusive on the details of the case." She frowned. "This doesn't help us much as a weekly. Knight can't hold on to this stuff from week to week."

"I don't know if it's a problem," Lou replied. He doesn't have to update the press every day."

"Well, we'll just deal with it. We have your insights, which no one else will have."

"Blanche," Lou blurted, "I met someone."

Lou could see the conflicting emotions playing out on Blanche's face.

Composing herself, she said, "Lou, I think this is wonderful. I am very happy for you. Patti will be ecstatic. May I ask who it is?"

"Her name is Hilda Truax, and she's the editor and publisher of the *North Coast Clarion*, in Seagirt. She was of enormous help in providing information, and I told her she would get credit in the story. Is that okay?"

"Of course. What's she like?"

"She's about my age, maybe a little older, hair a silver-white, cute figure. She's smart and cynical, funny. Completely dedicated to her paper, and to journalism. She reminds me of you, really."

Lou noticed the twinge on Blanche's face. It passed in a moment.

"What are you planning?" she asked.

"Truthfully, we are not a *we*, yet. She has no idea that I have any feelings for her, and I don't know how she feels about me. I need to speak with her."

Blanche nodded. "Go back to your office and call her. I'll make sure your article is edited and I'll get to work on the cover. Have her call me about the logistics of simultaneous publication, editor to editor. Talk to you later."

"Thanks, Blanche. For everything."

A few minutes later, Lou was on the phone with Hilda. She repeated the same kind of genial abuse Blanche had dumped on him.

"Look, Lou, I'm not saying I own you because we slept together, but I do worry when you run off and I don't hear from you. Gar Loober mentioned he had heard from you, but told me nothing."

"Hilda, do we know each other well enough?"

There was a pause.

"What are you getting at?"

"I enjoy being with you. I had a great time crawling around on the floor with you that night, and even more fun later."

Lou blushed as he said that, glad she could not see him.

"I wonder if we know enough about each other to try to be, uh, together." Lou's voice trailed off.

"Lou, you live in Portland, and I'm a couple hours' drive away. Our relationship will have to go slow for that reason alone. Let's see what happens."

"Hilda, that makes sense to me. I have no dating skills, and I hardly know what's appropriate any more."

"Now, the girls at the Dunes Café are having a party in a couple days, you know, to celebrate the arrests, and whatnot. Think you can make it?"

"Try and keep me away. Oh. Call Blanche Perry, she's the editor. She wants to talk to you about publication and making sure you and the *Clarion* have the proper credit for your participation."

"Can you transfer me? No time like the right time."

"I'll try, but I can't vouch for the phone system, or my ability to use it."

"Talk to you soon, Lou."

Lou diddled the phone, and punched in Blanche's extension. The rest was up to the technology spirits. As he made ready to go home, the phone rang.

"Lou Tedesco."

"Lou, this is Tom Knight."

"Hi, Tom. To what do I owe the pleasure?"

"Not much of a pleasure, I'm afraid. Interpol picked up Wheelock, but the Mexican government won't extradite if we insist on going for the death penalty. They don't have it there and don't support it anywhere."

"What are you gonna do?"

Knight sighed. "What can I do? I want the guy to stand trial in Oregon, but execution is out of the question. The law calls for the death penalty here."

"I know someone who will be pleased."

"Who's that?"

"Velma Korta. She told me she would fight execution."

"The vic's mother? Huh! Go figure."

"Tom, there's a party in Seagirt soon, to celebrate. It would be nice if you could put in an appearance."

"Hmmm . . . Yeah, that could be good. Maybe I'll do a full-fledged press conference. It'll look like, what? Closure?"

Lou wrinkled his nose at the word.

He gave the DA the location, and rang off. He wanted to check on the progress of the issue, and go home to think.

5. Publish, and Be Damned

When the *Stumptown Weekly* hit the street, the headline was not much more subdued than the one Lou suggested.

"Reporter Breaks Seagirt Murder Case! Apprehended Suspect Confesses and Names Accomplice!"

The *North Coast Clarion* came out the same day, with more of a local perspective.

The *Stump* story featured a sidebar interview with Hilda Truax and an exclusive statement from the DA's office in Waldorf, and put the two weeklies under the media deluge for weeks. TV news programs scrambled to get Lou, Hilda, and Blanche. They did talk radio, National Public Radio pieces, and were featured in stories in big-city papers. The *New York Times* did a series called "The Weekly Press in America," and the *Stump* staff got their pictures in the *Washington Post.*

Both Blanche and Hilda got offers to sell their papers to media giants, or to go to work for them. Both declined politely and then lived with degrees of regret for months afterward. Blanche got a regular gig on a local radio station as a commentator.

Each got many more subscribers, some of whom stayed on after their year lapsed. Fifteen minutes of fame perhaps, but exhilarating nonetheless.

Lou himself was offered jobs with the *Oregonian*, both Seattle papers, and the *San Francisco Chronicle*. Working in a city with a National League baseball team was a powerful inducement, but he turned them all down.

The party in the Dunes Café in Seagirt was a day after the story was published, and three days after Calvin Wheelock was delivered to Oregon. Lou and Blanche drove out in her Mercedes, which she had detailed to look its best. She wore what for her was very conservative clothing: a business suit, although high styled and short skirted. Blanche dragged Lou off to buy a snazzy new suit and he looked very dashing.

When they got to Seagirt, the Dunes was surrounded by cars and media vehicles.

"I guess Tom Knight called his press conference. It's a madhouse." Lou made a face.

"Come on, Lou! This is totally cool. You're gonna be famous."

"I'm not sure I can handle any more than we have now."

They had to park a few blocks away, and Blanche swore at the damp wind roaring off the ocean as they ran to the café. When they burst in the place was packed, and they got a standing ovation.

"This is getting to be monotonous," Lou whispered to Blanche.

"Take off your damn girdle and enjoy yourself," she whispered back.

Hetty Conrad walked up to them.

"Hi, Lou!" and she gave him a big hug. "This must be Blanche Perry. Welcome." Then, she hugged Blanche.

More cheers from the crowd.

"I think the whole town is here," Hetty said to them.

Ronnie and Connie, looking more like sisters than mother and daughter, waved and blew kisses.

"Say something, Lou!" Phyllis yelled.

"Yeah, Lou," Blanche said under her breath, "say something."

Lou flashed her a look, and turned to face the crowd. He saw Carla Higgins and her kid brother, Jack Narz and Lucy Persson, who seemed very friendly with one another, Velma Korta, and Hilda Truax, standing with her arms folded and a wry expression on her face.

He did not see Anthony John. He found it curious that the entrepreneur wouldn't be exploiting this opportunity. He did not see Jean, but he wasn't surprised. She never liked what he was doing.

There was a man standing next to Hilda who looked vaguely familiar, but who Lou couldn't place. He wore a gray suit and his weathered face shone with a kind of triumph.

Blanche elbowed him in the ribs. He focused, and held up his hands to quiet the crowd.

"Friends, I am very happy to be here today." Cheers.

"I would never have been able to accomplish anything without the help of your neighbors in this little town. First, Velma Korta." More cheers, and Velma blushing.

"Velma's loss, and her belief that justice could be done, are what kept me on target and honest through this whole effort. I wish there were more like her. And, Carla Higgins." Cheers.

"Carla's exceptional memory for her customers' video rentals gave me the first inkling of where to look. She took a big chance helping me, because she cares more about doing the right thing than playing it safe. Another exceptional person."

Carla covered her face in embarrassment, and Velma came over to hug her. The crowd went wild.

"And, the women of the Dunes Café." Lou decided to be magnanimous. "They were a constant reality check, and a source of nourishment, both literally and figuratively. Thank you, all." Cheers and raised hands.

"Jack Narz and Lucy Persson. Jack was willing to try anything to get at the truth, and he found it in a place where no one could have imagined it. And Lucy. She may have a gift of second sight and a house that looks like a wizard's cave, but a more level-headed and compassionate person can't be found. Jack? Lucy?" Lou gestured toward them, and the cheering resumed.

"Hilda Truax, a true gem. She knows more about this town than anyone alive, has great personal integrity, and is the true daughter of Chuck Truax in every way. I could not have done this without her."

Hilda gave a modest wave. Lou could feel Blanche tense up next to him.

Lou looked around. "There are a couple of others . . ."

Gar Loober walked in at just that moment.

"And, here is one of them. Deputy Gar Loober, a great cop."

Lou shook a beaming Gar's hand. The crowd found new energy to cheer.

"Gar could have, maybe should have, thrown me out of his office many times. After all, I'm hardly more than just a broken-down restaurant critic. Instead, he listened to me, and chose to give my story a fair hearing. And, he brought to bear the resources that only the police can. It's really his victory."

Gar acknowledged the ovation with a shy smile. In his way, Lou thought, he's as good as Knight.

"And, there's DA Tom Knight. He had no reason at all to take me seriously, and, in fact, on at least one occasion, did throw me out of his office."

Polite laughter from all.

"But, once he was convinced, he got the job done. I suspect he will be here later."

"And, Blanche! Everyone, this is Blanche Perry, my editor. But, she is also one of my oldest friends, and the daughter of the best friend I ever had. Without her belief in me, her playing devil's advocate to my wild ideas, her support for my articles . . ."

"And, mostly my willingness to finance this obsession,"

she said wryly. The crowd laughed, and Hilda checked Blanche out.

"Yes, and that, too," Lou chuckled, "I would never have been able to do this. Blanche!" He gestured, and the crowd responded.

Lou stopped for a moment. He looked around, again.

"There's one other person I would like to thank, but I don't know where he is. That man is Jim Twitchell, known as Nutty Bud. Not only is he not nutty, he is, in many ways, the most important piece in this jigsaw puzzle. He saw, and was threatened by, the young men who are, uh," he looked at Gar, "*alleged* to have done the murders." Gar nodded.

"He gave me the most useful clues and ways to approach the case. He didn't have to do anything about this. He really didn't owe this town much. He's lucky to be here, wherever he is, because he would have been a forgotten victim if things worked out differently. Jim, here's to you, wherever you are."

Oddly, there were no cheers. The man in the gray suit came forward, extending his hand.

"Lou, thanks for everything."

Lou was stunned. "Bud? Jim?"

"No, not Bud any more. Today is the third day I've been sober and I owe a lot of this to you," he turned, "and to Hilda, who pulled my sorry butt off the beach and sobered me up. Thanks to you both."

As they embraced, the party began in earnest.

As the crowd circulated around the room, Lou noticed a keg of beer in one corner of the café, over where the tables were, and wine on ice. He smiled to himself, grabbed a couple of flavored soda waters, and sought out Jim Twitchell.

"Drink, Jim?"

Jim took the bottle with a smile.

For the next few minutes, Lou gave the former homeless drunk a sincere pep talk about staying sober and offered to provide assistance and support if Jim ever felt weak or that he needed just one little snort.

Then, Lou asked, "Jim, what was your relationship to Chuck Truax?"

Twitchell laughed. "I wondered when you were gonna get around to that. Chuck was angry about the way that old Art Wheelock had turned Seagirt into his private political toy."

"And so, he gave you the development issue?"

"Yes and no. I actually got wind of it from Chet Green."

Lou was amazed. "I thought Chester Green was Wheelock's creature."

Jim nodded. "Yup, but he was also a big drinker, and when he drank, he ran his mouth. When I told Chuck, he did some of what he called legwork, and came up with the whole story. Chuck told me that, if Art had gotten his way, Seagirt would have a different place, full of shopping malls and ticky-tack high-rises. Art planned to move to his estate, anyway. He apparently couldn't even stand the thought of living in a place like this was gonna become."

"Why didn't Truax run for office himself? Why did he recruit you?"

Jim laughed. "Chuck was afraid that he would become a politician. Something about power corrupting. You know that saying."

"I do. And he wasn't worried about you?"

"Lou, I have always had one ambition in the world, to have a business that required not much work and paid me just enough to live. My hardware store was just that. Bein' mayor was too much like work."

"Was Wheelock aware that Chet Green had let the cat out of the bag?"

"I don't know, but Chet always felt guilty about it. He drank a lot more after his term as mayor."

Gradually, people noticed that Lou and Jim were off together talking, and began to come over to see them. Lou shook lots of hands, got pats on the back, and got kissed by women he had never met. Jim got effusive praise and promises of dinner invitations.

After a half hour, or so, Lou was able to slip away. He

saw Blanche and Hilda head-to-head, deep in an intense conversation. The whole idea scared him, and he avoided going over. Spotting Gar's head above the crowd on the other side of the room, he walked over.

He picked up Gar's voice in mid-sentence.

". . . my police work. I have to say, though it pains me to do this, that Chief Green was not much of a help with this case. I never believed it would come to this, but I'm thinkin' of running against the chief in the next election. This is just between you and me, okay? Keep it under your hat."

Lou smiled. Ambition had entered Gar Loober's life.

At that moment, the door flew open, and DA Tom Knight entered, hangers-on and media members trailing him. The place became bedlam for a while, until Knight set up in a corner with the help of the media techs, and called for quiet. The TV lights went on and the DA was in his element. After a round of greetings, the great man spoke to the crowd.

"Ladies and gentlemen, if I may . . ." He waved his arms, and his staffers quieted the crowd discreetly.

"Thank you. First, I want to congratulate the Seagirt police for their tireless efforts in this matter. When it seemed like the murders would pass into the cold-case file, Deputy Loober's persistence kept it on the front burner. This is first-rate police work, and Gar deserves a round of applause. Is Gar here?"

The crowd cheered, and Knight beckoned Loober into the spotlight. Gar moved with his best aw-shucks shuffle, and shook hands with the DA. Knight waved for quiet.

"Deputy Loober, I would like to thank you personally for your efforts. It is literally true that you closed this case."

Gar acknowledged the applause, and spoke into Knight's mike.

"Thank you, DA Knight. I felt like I couldn't look myself in the mirror if this heinous," he pronounced it hee-nee-us, "crime went unsolved.

"I only wish that Chief Green could have been more help. He has lots more police experience than I do, but for some reason he wouldn't get involved. I'm thinking that he might be gettin' a challenger in the next election."

More cheers. Knight looked uncomfortable, but knew better than to stand in the way of political ambition. He raised Gar's hand like a heavyweight champion.

Gar walked back into the crowd amid backslaps and a chant of "Gar! Gar! Gar!" Knight called for quiet.

"As you may know, Calvin Wheelock is now in custody." Cheers. "The only regret that I have in this case is that I had to take the death penalty off the table to get information from Phil Troy . . ." Boos. ". . . and Mexico won't extradite a death penalty case." More boos.

"Now, now. The trial begins next week, and it should be open and shut. As unsatisfying as it is to feed and house these two *alleged*," his voice dripped venom, "killers for the rest of their miserable lives, we can be comforted by knowing that they will never have the chance to do anything like this again."

Cheers.

"This case was an unusual case, in many ways. But, it is certainly the first time in my experience that a case was solved because a newspaperman made a promise to a grieving mother that he felt honor-bound to keep. With all due respect to the members of the media, I seldom use the word honor in the same sentence with the word newspaperman. The last time I even heard it was when I attended the memorial service for Chuck Truax as a kid.

"Something about this town brings out the best in the fourth estate, and whatever it is should be bottled and distributed to media outlets around the world. Lou, come up here."

Lou was beginning to tire of the brouhaha, but he wasn't about to deprive the folks of their show.

Knight stuck out his hand. "Lou, thanks." The crowd erupted in yet another cheer.

After they settled down, Knight went on.

"I can't discuss the case with Lou because he may be called as a witness, but I can congratulate him on his intelligence and persistence, and admire his ingenuity. And, most of all, we can be thankful for his honesty and personal integrity.

"Lou, please accept the thanks of a grateful public servant."

"And ours, too!" yelled Hetty Conrad.

Knight leaned over to whisper in Lou's ear, "And the thanks of the viewers of one of the funniest evidence videos we ever saw."

"Just promise me that you won't send it to every DA in the country," Lou whispered back. Knight just smiled, then turned to the crowd.

"One thing I can tell you," Knight said, "because it was reported in the media, is that Calvin Wheelock was asked why they did it." He paused, wringing all the drama out of the scene. "Wheelock replied, 'For the hell of it.'" Knight made a face, and the crowd lapsed into a shocked silence.

Then, pointing at Lou, "Hey, we're here to celebrate. Let's hear it for Lou Tedesco!"

As he acknowledged the crowd's approval, Lou noticed that Lester Green had come in, and was making himself as inconspicuous as possible. Despite that, people came up to him and scolded him, their fingers wagging in his face. Green seemed to ignore them, his demeanor as impassive as a statue.

His eyes were fixed on Lou.

Knight was calling the crowd to order.

"Okay, okay, people. I don't want to stop the festivities any longer. Enjoy yourselves, and I will head back to Waldorf to prepare for the trial. Thanks again."

Knight shook hands with Lou once more, smiling for the photographers, and managed to shake almost every hand in the room on the way out. He left trailing his entourage and the media, suddenly making the room bigger, and then music came from somewhere and people started to dance.

Lou went over to the refreshments, and grabbed another soft drink. He was aware of Lester Green's eyes on him all the way. He shrugged it off.

A tap on his shoulder made him jump. It was Velma Korta.

"Hello, Velma."

"Lou, I can't thank you enough. Nothin' will bring my baby back, or poor Larry, but the guilty will be punished, and they will not be killed by the hand of man. 'Vengeance is mine, saith the Lord.' And, I hate to admit this, but they will suffer more livin' their lives in a cage than they would with a quick death."

Velma blushed a furious red, and hung her head. "Lord help me for thinkin' that. I'm ashamed."

She recovered after a moment. "This is the best I could have hoped for, and it's your doin'."

"Oh, Velma, I was just . . ."

"No modesty, here, Lou. Gar would've let it go. Knight, too. Lester never got started on it. And another thing. It brought Jim Twitchell back from his livin' hell. I've already invited him to my church and he agreed. He don't have anyone, and neither do I. We can be each other's family.

"And you. You will always be family to me."

Velma gave him a hug, which he returned.

"One more thing." Velma giggled. "Look over there."

She pointed across the room as discreetly as possible.

Lou laughed out loud. "I don't believe it! It's Chloe, and she's combed out her hair. Twice, in just a few days."

"Been a long time comin', Lou." She squeezed his hand. "Call me sometime, Lou. And, come visit."

"I promise."

She smiled. "Your promise is as good as gold."

Velma went off to talk with her new convert. Lou turned around, and faced Hilda and Blanche, arm in arm and looking smug.

"I'm in trouble now."

"Well, I can't imagine what you mean," Blanche mocked, in a singsong voice. "I've just been filling Hilda in on the facts of life, you know, one editor to another?"

"And I've been a very apt pupil," Hilda added. "I'm on the verge of a breakthrough, I think."

"Editorially speaking, of course," said Blanche.

"Of course." Hilda nodded.

"Of course," echoed Lou. "So, do I have a chance, here?"

The women looked at each other.

"If you mean by that," Blanche said, "a chance for a richer, more complete, and happier life, you have a one hundred percent chance."

Lou raised his hands in surrender. "Okay, okay. What are my orders?" He clicked his heels, and snapped to attention.

Hilda looked at Blanche. "You're right. He can be housebroken." Then, to Lou. "As you were, for the immediate future. Rome wasn't built in a day."

"At least you've given me the distinction of being a major project. I would hate to think that I was a pushover."

"Blanche needs you back in Portland for the next issue," Hilda said. "After that, well, let's just say that the plans are in the planning stage."

"If I wrote that," Lou said, "either of you would strike it out as redundant."

"And don't you forget it," Blanche replied. "Right now, my new friend and I need a glass of wine and a consultation. See you later."

Lou watched them as they sashayed for the refreshments and imagined the genesis of dire conspiracies.

The party went on for a few more hours. The people of Seagirt needed the release and it was just a good party. Connie, dressed to kill, was vamping Gar Loober, who did not seem to be put off by the idea. Anthony John and Gar Loober: all of a sudden, two eligible bachelors in town.

Lou felt the need for some fresh air and quiet. He noticed that Lester Green had left, probably to do his job. Green was adequate for the day-to-day policing a town like Seagirt needed but, if the town was about to undergo a growth spurt, as rumor had it, he might not be able to handle it.

"Not my problem," Lou said aloud, and sneaked out the door. The weather was not ideal, but the cool, damp air was refreshing and even the chill was invigorating. Lou walked toward the beach, figuring he would take a look at the ocean, and head back into the café before he caught his death.

A block away from the beach, Lou felt something cold and hard press into the back of his neck.

"Keep walkin', Tedesco," said a gruff-voiced Lester Green.

Lou froze involuntarily. He got a brutal poke from what he guessed was a gun.

"I told you to keep movin'." Lou could smell booze on the chief's breath.

Lou started walking.

"Lester, what are you thinking?"

Green poked the gun barrel harder. "Don't you call me Lester, you bastard. You don't know me. Address me as Chief."

"Sure, Chief. Whatever you say. What is this all about?"

"I thought you knew everything, Tedesco. Such a goddamned smart-ass. You don't know nothin'. Head over to those dunes, there, just past the benches."

"Chief, all I wanted was to find the killers. Velma Korta and Jack Narz deserve that."

They were approaching a set of dunes beyond which, Lou recalled, was a sloping hill down to a tidal creek. It was perhaps fifty feet to the bottom.

"Don't you think they deserve that?" Lou pressed, unsure of how to handle the situation.

"All I care about is what I deserve. I been wipin' this jerk-water town's butt for years, and I get jokes behind my back. Okay, I can live with that. What do these yokels know, anyway?

"But you, Tedesco, you and that Judas deputy, you wanna ruin me, make me lose my job. What am I gonna do then? I'm almost sixty. Get a job as a rent-a-cop at some shopping mall? Not a chance. I go out at least with a pension.

"You even wanted to take that away from me, along with everything else I lost because of you."

"Wait a minute," Lou protested. "What did you lose because of me? Everything you did was your choice. You chose not to see the evidence, you decided not to investigate Wheelock and Troy. What's my fault?"

"You don't know nothin'. Stop here."

They were standing on a bluff overlooking the drop to the creek. It was high tide, and the creek was full of bone-chilling water. Lou was beginning to understand what Green had in mind. He started to turn around, and Green stopped him.

"Don't move. I don't want you to know when it's coming, but it's coming soon. I may not have much of a life left, but you don't have none.

"I was set for life. I was gonna move to someplace warm, where it don't rain six months out of the year, and you screwed me."

"I don't understand why you can't still do that," Lou said. "If you could afford to do that before, what's changed? You'll weasel out of the nonfeasance rap. People will be so glad to get rid of you, they'll give you early retirement."

"See," Green hissed, "you *really* don't know nothin'. Old Art Wheelock promised me a bunch of dough to keep his precious baby out of the slammer. He ain't so happy now. He told me to suck swamp water. Jean and me coulda settled down nice."

"Jean? What does she have to do with this?"

"My girlfriend, Tedesco. She's been tellin' me everything you said down at the Dunes. She ain't happy when I look bad, and when she ain't happy, I ain't happy. I was gonna pin it on some bikers. I had it all figured out. I just didn't figure on you and Judas Loober. I'll take care of his ass later."

"What are you gonna do, push me? Even an old fart like me could survive falling down there and live." Anger was replacing Lou's fear.

"Whaddaya think I am, an amateur? Loober told me about why you had the booze and poison. Very cute, and it gave me an idea. I got a bottle of vodka, and a real bottle of cyanide. You'll drink one, then the other. Then, you go over into the creek. You'll either die of exposure or poisoning. Don't make no nevermind to me either way. Dead is dead."

"People know I don't drink."

Green laughed, an ugly, raspy croak. "Once a drunk, always a drunk. I know, 'cause my daddy was a drunk. You just been at a party for hours. No one there will be able to say whether you had a drink or not. So, you drank, and you kept your word about the poison. Everybody knows you always keep your word, right, Tedesco?"

"Before you get rid of me, Lesss-ter," Lou dragged out the chief's name, with a snide tone, hoping to anger the man enough to distract him, "indulge me. How much effort did you really put into this case? Did you do any real police work?"

Green mustered what professional pride he had. "Ran down that kid with the wallet. And, I interviewed that punked-out bimbo of a waitress."

"That's when you still thought you could pin it on bikers. You weren't looking for a solution, just an acceptable answer, one that would get the heat off you. You're a sorry excuse for a cop, Lesss-ter."

"And you're a dead man, Tedesco. You just ain't quite there, yet. I'm gonna enjoy this."

Lou stiffened, his fists clenching and unclenching. He wasn't about to go without a fight.

"Lesss-ter, you can't make me drink that, Lesss-ter. You aren't man enough."

Lou heard a thud. Then, silence. He couldn't hear the chief's raspy breathing.

"Lester?"

He turned around. Lester Green was face down in the sand. Velma Korta stood a few feet behind him holding a baseball bat.

"Velma! What . . . ? How . . . ?"

"I saw you go outside, and I wanted to talk to you once more before you left. Then, I saw Lester. I knew that Hetty had a bat put by for protection, so I grabbed it and followed you. I heard everything Lester told you, and I'll repeat it to Gar Loober.

"I guess we're even, now. May the Lord forgive me."

Lou put his arm around the tiny woman.

"I'm not keeping score personally, but I'll bet you just got a gold star from the man upstairs." He laughed, "Baseball been berry, berry good to me."

The next afternoon, back in Portland, Lou walked from his loft to the *Stumptown Weekly* office. He had been in Seagirt later than he'd planned, dealing with the aftermath of Lester Green's meltdown.

Much to Gar Loober's credit, he had treated all concerned with courtesy and professionalism. He was especially sensitive with Green, explaining later that, despite the gravity of the chief's crime, he had been mentored by the man and owed him something for that.

Lou was impressed once more with the human capacity for compassion. And he was also happy to see Lester Green behind bars. Lou thought, not without irony, that Lester's future was secure, living off the largesse of the taxpayer.

Old Arthur J. Wheelock was also going to have to answer for his obstruction of justice, bribery, and corruption activities. Tom Knight sounded more than professionally pleased at the thought. Art Wheelock had been sullying Northwest life and politics for many years, and there would be widespread rejoicing at his fall.

When the case came up, Velma gave her testimony in a restrained and dignified way, but was vehement in all the right places. It had not escaped her that the man Seagirt had entrusted to uphold the law had almost caused her daughter's killers to elude justice. She was morally offended, as much as outraged and angry.

Hilda Truax had struggled to retain her professional distance as a journalist as she observed these proceedings. This was not only a great local story, it was in some sense a vindication of her father's quiet crusade to bring down a dirty political machine, and she felt the emotion of it. Art Wheelock was no Tammany Hall, but Seagirt wasn't exactly New

York City, either. It was only a matter of scale, not essential difference.

The first issue of the *Oregon Weekly*, the North Coast Edition, so named by the co-editors, would feature the whole story, going back to the Jim Twitchell-Chester Green election, and tracing the history of the pernicious Arthur J. Wheelock, and his minions and political heirs.

The last edition of the *Stumptown Weekly*, prior to becoming the *Oregon Weekly*, Portland Edition, was being set up, and would feature a long piece by the editor on the involvement of the weekly in helping to bring the machine down.

Lou had spent the night with Hilda. Blanche crashed in the guest room and the two Portlanders had driven back to town the next morning. Blanche went right into the office but insisted that Lou get a few more hours of sleep. Lou was happy to comply.

And now, he was on his way to work, feeling better than he had in years. On his arrival, the staff began to cheer, but he told them, "If I hear one more 'hip-hooray,' I'll run away and join a monastery."

"Hip-hooray!" shouted Tubby, who was promptly drowned in catcalls and noogies administered by the staffers. Lou went to his office, and found a mound of pink phone messages. He spent the better part of an hour going through them, and making a small pile of those he cared to follow up.

Then, he filled his coffee cup and wandered over to Blanche's office.

"Knock, knock, boss lady."

Blanche had been hunched over her desk, deep in concentration, and jumped when Lou spoke.

"Oh, hi. How you feeling?" she asked.

"Never better. You must be exhausted."

She stretched. "Well, I had all this nervous energy, and I thought it might be a good idea to make use of it. Got an enormous amount of work done, too."

"I hope this merger, if that's what it is, works out."

"I have no doubt that it will. Hilda is my new hero and role model. And, I'm glad she's going to be in the family."

Lou held up his hands.

"Whoa! We moving a bit fast here?"

Blanche batted her eyes. "Why, no. We discussed the merger quite extensively. It's in everyone's best interests."

"You're way too slick for me. I'm not even sure what we're talking about, anymore."

"I do have one serious question for you. Now that this is all over, would you like your old beat back? Restaurant reviews are much easier than rousting murderers and taking unscheduled dips in mountain lakes looking for evidence. Plus, Tony Bennett is touring, and we can score tickets."

"Thanks, but no. I have a few phone messages on my desk I'm considering. One is from a woman who claims to have proof that a guy on death row is innocent. And, there's an unsolved murder in Gresham that looks interesting."

"Heaven help me, I've turned you into a crusading investigative journalist. There's a special place in hell for people like me."

"I'll join you there, eventually. One more thing. Get the Tony Bennett tickets. I have someone I want to take."

"You got it. Now, scram, while I finish this masterpiece."

"Later, boss lady."

"And, dammit! Don't call me boss lady!"

Lou headed back to his office. He had a couple of calls to make.

Blanche got up and closed her door. She sat at her desk and thought things over. After a minute, she began to cry.

6. What's Playing at the Bijou?

The next weekend, Lou went back to Seagirt. He wanted to spend time with Hilda.

After a seafood dinner and a long talk about the news business, they went to bed. Content at first just to cuddle, Hilda's proximity began to excite Lou. He was glad to know he still had the capacity to be aroused.

The next morning, Lou and Hilda sat around on her back porch doing not much and enjoying it. He wore a threadbare and patched bathrobe that had belonged to Chuck Truax. She had thrown an old flannel shirt over her diaphanous nightgown. All was well.

Then, a look crossed Lou's face.

"Uh-oh. Penny for your thoughts."

"I knew you'd ask. We don't have this thing resolved." Lou sipped his iced tea.

"What's left? Calvin and Phil did it. Lester covered it up. Case closed."

"Who sent Henry Collins after me? What happened to those bikers? Who planted the poison in Green's coffee?"

"Who put the 'ram' in the 'ram-a-lama-ding-dong?' "

But, despite her joke, Hilda's face now mirrored the same look.

"Let me get my notes." Lou went back into the house.

Hilda raced off to spike her iced tea with bourbon, and sat in all innocence when Lou returned. Lou flipped through the notebook, stopping to read the scrawls from time to time.

"Okay, all we know is that someone with an English accent called Collins a lot, and that he often went out after the calls. Those calls could literally have come from anywhere.

"Reminds me of *The Manchurian Candidate.* You know, 'Would you like to play some solitaire?' Something like that."

"You know, between your obscure music references and your movie quotes, you might drive me nuts." Hilda cocked an eyebrow.

"You get to know me long enough," Lou muttered, "and there'll be plenty of other things to make you crazy. I haven't started on baseball, yet." He dove into his notes.

"I suppose that's what I get for hooking up with a movie freak. Speaking of movies, I should do an in-depth interview with Anthony John. Interesting young guy. Unusual name, too. Like an actor."

"What?" Lou's head snapped up.

"I said, Anthony's name is unusual, it's like a stage name."

Lou turned pages furiously. "Ronald Colman." He shook his head and laughed. "Lucy Persson strikes again!"

"Hey, I'm the one with the spiked drink. What the heck are you babbling about?"

"Lucy told me she got a strong image of Ronald Colman . . ."

"Yeah, so?"

"So? I'll tell you so. One of Colman's best roles was as an actor who was doing *Othello*, and his stage personality started leaking into his real life. He began strangling women offstage, like Othello did to Desdemona. Colman won an Oscar for it."

"That's taking the Method a bit far. So what?"

"The title of the movie is *A Double Life,* and the character's name is . . ."

"Don't tell me. Anthony John."

Lou stood up. "I need to talk with Mr. John."

"I'll go with you." Hilda stood up.

"The hell you will! If he's really responsible . . ."

Hilda put her hands on her hips. "And who saved your candy ass when the aforementioned bikers tried to kick you into the Pacific?"

"Okay, okay. Don't forget your blunderbuss. We might need it. Now, I'm getting in the shower."

Hilda took off the flannel shirt, and let her nightgown fall to the floor. "I'll go with you."

This time, there was no objection.

"You think we should call him?" Hilda was checking the magazine in her pistol.

"I love it when you brandish your weapon like that. Hell, no. Element of surprise, and all."

"What if he isn't there?"

"We'll surprise him another time."

"Sounds like a plan."

Hilda and Lou went through a checklist, like commandos before a raid. They established a cover story, interviewing Anthony for an article. They even developed a battle plan in case things went south.

Convinced that they had it covered, Hilda and Lou left the house. A few minutes later, the phone rang. After four rings, Hilda's answering machine kicked in.

"This is Hilda Truax, editor of the *North Coast Clarion.* Leave me a message." *Beeeep!*

"Lou, are you there?" came Gar Loober's panicky voice. "Hilda? If you're there, pick up. Aw, jeez . . . I been calling everyone I could think of to find you two. Listen, if you get this message, don't, repeat, do *not* hook up with Anthony John. I'm on the road, and I'll be back as soon as I can."

The machine switched off, and the little red light blinked.

Lou and Hilda sat in silence as the car moved into downtown Seagirt. Weekend crowds were just beginning to fill up the town as families and singles wandered the streets eating ice cream and sipping drinks, savoring the last days of summer. The weather was looking like it might clear up.

They drove up to the Bijou, closed in the early afternoon. There was no telling whether Anthony was in, or not.

"Are you ready to do this?" Lou asked.

"Hasta la vista, baby." Hilda patted her handbag.

Hilda parked, and they walked up to the front of the theater. Lou cupped his hand on the glass and looked into the empty lobby.

"I don't see anything."

"It's a big place, Lou. He could be anywhere in there."

"Yeah, or not in there at all. Maybe we should draw him out, so he doesn't have the home-field advantage. He knows this theater like you know the newspaper office."

"Lou, are you getting cold feet?"

Lou turned to look at Hilda. "Well, to tell the truth . . ."

"Hey, you two," Anthony's voice boomed out. Lou and Hilda jumped.

"What are you doing sneaking around here?" His tone was light and jokey. "You'll have to buy tickets just like everyone else."

Hilda and Lou exchanged looks.

"Hi, Anthony," Lou said, "we just got a wild hair to come over and see if you had time for an interview."

Anthony looked at his watch. "Hmmm. How long will it take?"

"Twenty minutes, half hour, maybe?" Hilda replied.

Anthony walked over to the front doors, and unlocked them. "Make yourselves comfortable. I'll be along in a minute. I'm out here on trash patrol and anything else I can spot that needs attention. Want a pop?"

"Nothing for me. Hilda?"

"I'm good," she waved the offer away.

"See you in a minute." Anthony turned and walked away.

Hilda and Lou settled on the Naugahyde bench in the

lobby. Hilda looked around. "I almost hope we have the wrong idea about him. This place is wonderful."

"Well, maybe we should just ditch the pretense and ask him."

"Nah." She shook her head. "I like the game, at least for a while. If it goes nowhere, we'll ditch it."

"Okay, but . . ."

"Hey, you two, good to see you. Amazing story about Chief Green, and all. Who knew?" Anthony walked into the lobby from somewhere near the theater auditorium. He ambled over to the snack counter and drew himself a soft drink. "Sure I can't get you anything?"

Hilda and Lou demurred again.

Anthony sat on a nearby bench. "So, what would you like to know?"

Lou nodded at Hilda. "How's the theater doing?"

Anthony knocked at the bench's wooden base. "Very well, so far. I'm aware that the novelty may wear off and that the thing might not sustain itself during the winter. I may have to close down from October to May. We'll see."

"How do you choose your films?" Lou asked.

"Good question, for which I have no real answer. At this point, it's a combination of my favorites, my instincts, and what's available.

"You'd be surprised how hard it is to find usable prints of some of these old films."

Hilda threw Lou a look. She wanted to go for it. Lou nodded.

"Anthony, Lou and I are crazy about Ronald Colman."

He sipped his drink. "Yeah, me too. Lou and I discussed this. I'll try to get his favorites."

"How about mine. Do I get a chance to pick one?"

"Of course."

"I'd love to see *A Double Life*. Interesting plot, a killer whose stage life begins to affect his real life. And coincidentally, his name is Anthony John."

Anthony smiled. "Remarkable coincidence, isn't it?"

"I don't think it's a coincidence," Lou said. "But, I can't

figure out what your role, no pun intended, has been in this. "You are, of course, involved in this?"

Anthony shook his head. "I'm disappointed, Lou. You managed to figure out so much of this. Can't make the last leap?"

Lou looked at Hilda. "I don't know, I've got a few half-baked ideas floating around."

"Now's the time, Lou," Hilda chimed in.

"Absolutely," Anthony agreed. "If not now, when?" He was taking this in good humor, Lou thought.

"Okay, Valerie Collins talked about a man on the phone with an English accent, and I'll bet it was your best Colman impression."

"Whoa," Hilda sat upright, "that starts a chain of thought."

"Go on." Anthony was smiling a broad smile.

"So, you used Henry Collins to get to me. We know he wrote the threatening note. He certainly tried to kill me. That wasn't nice, Anthony."

"Sorry." he shrugged, "Henry was expendable, and you were getting annoying."

"Annoying? I was after Calvin and Phil. Why should that annoy you?"

"You'll have to guess." Anthony was enjoying this.

"Why a double life?" Hilda asked.

"There you go, you're getting warmer." Anthony rubbed his hands together.

"Green was never able to run down two people: Stud Dunham and Freddie Fleer," Lou rubbed his chin. "I'm guessing that you may be one of them, and you can't be Dunham, because folks would recognize you. You might be Fleer, with a makeover."

"Damn!" Hilda jumped.

"Did you ever get to Alaska, Freddie?" Lou asked

Anthony sipped his drink. "Freddie Fleer was a pathetic lump. Anthony John is a vital young man. I was happy to leave him behind. Please call me Anthony.

"And, yes, I made it to Alaska, stayed about a year, hated

it, hated myself, and the church lost me. I thought it over, and split for Seattle. I lived on the street for a while, picked up some odd jobs, and went to community college. I discovered that I had a talent for software design.

"Within a few years, I had a big job with a dot-com startup, and, I made a small fortune selling out to you-know-who, and decided to refurbish my image. I became a gym rat, indulged myself in custom-made clothes, and got these nice blue contacts. The rest, about the movies, is accurate, just the way I told it at the opening."

"So, if I have it right," Lou said, "you were rich, still young, had a new life in Seattle, and had managed to leave Seagirt behind. So why come back?"

"Three out of four, Lou. I never managed to leave this place behind. I always knew I'd come back. What I didn't know is what I'd do.

"A couple of years ago, I developed the master plan. I hated Shelley for killing the baby."

"Some attitudes die hard, huh, Freddie?" Hilda's face was a mask of contempt.

"Freddie's dead, Hilda, in the grave with Shelley and the baby."

"So," Lou probed, "you came back to take your revenge against Shelley?"

"Not really, not at first," he mused. "I came back to find her and ask her to make amends, to marry me. It wasn't until I found out about her and Larry that I decided there was no hope for her." He frowned. "She was a hopeless little Seagirt girl."

"I never even spoke to her."

"Did anyone recognize you?" Hilda asked. "You've been here almost a year."

"Henry Collins. Spotted me the first time I went in for groceries. It was why I got him involved. He was a sorry excuse for a man: lousy dead-end job, unhappy marriage, although I felt sorrier for Valerie on that note. She used to be a nice girl, if a bit wild. Marrying Henry turned her into a bitter little nag." He shrugged. "That's why I have no regrets about Henry. He reminded me of what I would have become if I didn't escape."

"How did you convince him to do what he did?" Lou picked up the questioning.

Anthony grinned, and rubbed his fingers together. "Money. Simple greed. That SUV was the clincher. Unfortunately, his temperament made him as much of a liability as an asset.

"You haven't asked the obvious question." Anthony was warming to the game.

"Okay," asked Lou, "did you have anything to do with Larry and Shelley?"

"You can do better than that, Lou."

"Did you convince Calvin and Phil to kill them for you?"

"Good. Yes."

Anthony was in control, forcing a step-by-step pace, and that made Lou nervous.

"Come on, Anthony. Tell us how. Was it money with them, too?"

"Uh-uh, no, and I bet you knew that. Phil and Calvin are stupid and always thought they were better than the rest of us, so I just appealed to their pathetic vanity. I told them that they were really sharp guys, and that Calvin being a cop, and all, they could do the perfect murder."

"And, you fed them that miniseries as a motivator?"

"Yes!" He spread his arms, as if to embrace Lou. "Very good, Lou. I even watched it with them once. I provided encouraging commentary."

"Did they know who you were?"

"Never guessed. Not the sharpest tools in the shed, those two."

"So, they agreed to kill two people? Just because you asked?"

"Well, I *was* very persuasive, Calvin still had a bug up his ass because Shelley dumped him for Freddie the Freak."

"And then, she dumped you, Freddie," Hilda said. "Why? Because you insisted that she carry Calvin's baby?"

"Hilda, you are beginning to piss me off. Freddie is no

more. You know, like Monty Python says? 'He is a dead parrot.' I am Anthony John."

"Anthony," Lou asked, "did you try to get Green into it?"

"That was odd, wasn't it?" Anthony/Freddie mulled for a moment. "All I know is what I heard around town, what you turned up about old man Wheelock, and all that. I was completely separate from all that. I used Calvin, and his daddy tried to keep his name out of it. Quite a little story, there.

"Too bad you'll never get to write it."

"I don't know . . ." Hilda looked him over. "I kind of like our chances." She took her pistol out of her purse.

"Hilda!" Anthony exclaimed with delight. "Excellent! A pistol-packin' mama. I heard about your rootin'-tootin' escapades from my phony bikers."

"They were yours, too?" Lou was astonished.

"Oh, yeah. A pair of laid-off millworkers. Bought them all that nice biker drag, told them to mention Stud while they kicked the crap out of you. It really took him aback when you said his name first.

"They're long gone, and truthfully, I know not where."

"Lou," Hilda sneered, "it's time for Freddie to save his breath." Anthony frowned, and gave Hilda a dirty look. "He's gonna sing himself hoarse for Gar, as soon as we get his nasty ass down to the police station."

"Oh, Hilda, I'm *so* sorry, but I made other plans. You'll have to forgive me. Dub?"

Dub Gordon stepped out of the auditorium holding a shotgun.

"Howdy, folks. I guess you need to come with me."

"Dub! How . . ."

"How did he get all that information?" a smug Anthony asked. "Where did he get that post card? Phil Troy couldn't stand Dub. There was no reason in the world he would send him a card, except that I called them and asked him to do it. Some money exchanged hands.

"And, Dub is the one who let himself into your room, Lou. Did you know you can get into those rooms with a screwdriver? He planted that phony cyanide. Our brave cops are both away from the station for long stretches, every day. It was easy to drop it into the coffee pot, right, Dub?" Dub grinned and nodded. "I thought we would get rid of Lester and his Gomer Pyle deputy at the same time. Funny when that stuff turned out to be bogus. We tried." He gave a big theatrical sigh.

"Oh, and Hilda? Mind putting that gun on the floor and kicking it away?"

Hilda was not happy, but she complied.

Lou scratched his head. "Did you have all this planned out from square one?"

"I must admit my plan needed some work, on-the-spot improv, so to speak. Nice that I had those two to do the job. Their relationship is so, um, *peculiar* that I counted on them to be at each other when the end came. A weak link, I'll admit, but the gamble paid off."

"And Dub, what's your angle"

Dub grinned. "Told ya I was investing in that gas station. Had to get the money from somewhere."

"Jeez," Hilda muttered, "is there anyone in this damn town who *isn't* for sale?"

"Like I said," Anthony stood up and stretched, "I've got other fish to fry. Dub, my lad, time to take these members of the press to their final deadline."

Dub chuckled, and gestured with his shotgun.

"Wait," Lou said, "What makes you think that Troy and Wheelock won't bust you to the DA?"

"Lou, give me some credit, here. There's nothing to tie me to them, no physical evidence. Everything was cash on the barrelhead or worked on their credit cards. Nothing to make the connection. Their word against mine, and I'm a respected member of the community."

"Wrong. There's one thing." A voice came from somewhere in the theater.

Dub looked panicky. "Who's there? Show yourself."

"It's Gar Loober, Dub. Now, put that shotgun down, real slow, and I mean now."

Dub swung the gun toward the sound of Gar's voice, and

the sound of a shot reverberated. Hilda shrieked, and Dub went down like a sack of potatoes. Blood flecked walls and floors, and ran from the hole in Dub's chest.

At that instant, Anthony dove for Hilda's gun, his long arms and fingers groping for the weapon. He came up with it and aimed it at Hilda's head. He was no more than two feet from her. She looked at him with disapproval.

"Hold it right there, Deputy Dawg. I will kill this woman. Now, come out, come out, wherever you are, and drop your gun."

Gar emerged from behind one of the large auditorium doors. He held his gun high in the air.

"Just drop it, and kick it away. Do it!"

Gar put the gun down, and kicked it across the floor. He spoke quietly.

"Now look, Anthony, or whatever your name is . . ."

Lou began to move slowly, angling for a new position.

"Lou!" Anthony yelled, "move away from us. I don't want you doing anything noble."

"Where should I go?" he asked in real bewilderment.

"I don't care! Over there, by the trash. Fitting, somehow. Now, Deputy Dawg, how did you find me? Satisfy my curiosity."

"The nine millimeter you bought for them to use. You were too smart to let Calvin use his police weapon, so you acquired one at a gun show, where there are no records to worry about."

"How the hell did you know that?" Anthony was starting to sweat, in part from rage.

"I know," Lou said. "Your dead pal there, Dub. He told me and I passed it along to Gar. He even mentioned it was in Waldorf."

"Idiot! I can't believe he . . ."

"Wasn't him, Anthony," Gar said. "It was you. You used a phony name and all, but when I showed a picture of that Glock around to the gun dealers who were at that show, you got ID'd right off. 'Tall guy, nice clothes, bright blue eyes.' Hell, Lester Green coulda figured that out."

Lou began to look around for something to use as a weapon. All that he could find was a large bulb, a burnt-out marquee bulb on the trash pile. He palmed it behind his back. Hilda noticed Lou's move.

Anthony's attention was on Gar's story, and he was beginning to come apart. There was no predicting what he'd do if he felt cornered.

Hilda caught Lou's eye, nodded slightly. She began to mouth "one, two," locked on Lou's eyes, he nodded. "Three!" she yelled, Anthony started, and Lou pitched a perfect strike at Anthony's chest. The heavy bulb hit home with a smack, and dropped to the floor, where it exploded with a boom and a spray of glass.

The bulb was big, not enough to knock Anthony down, but enough to shock and stun him for a moment, and the noise startled him. In that moment, Hilda kneed him in the groin. Anthony doubled up and reeled back, falling on the floor in a near-fetal position. Gar pulled a pistol from an ankle holster.

Anthony shrieked, and fired wildly. Gar stopped him with one shot. Anthony twitched briefly, and died sprawled on the floor.

Hilda yanked her thumb in the air. "Yer out!"

"Hilda," Gar said, "remind me never to piss you off. We're shorthanded. Wanna be a deputy?"

"Thanks, Gar. Couldn't've done it without you. Oh, yeah. Nice pitch, Lou."

"Like I said not too long ago, baseball been berry good to me."

"Do you need us any more, Gar?"

"I'll need to take statements later. I'll call you."

"Let's go, Lou. We've got an appointment with a word processor. And I have one with a bottle of bourbon."

Lou looked around the theater. "Last picture show? Too bad."

Lou took Hilda's hand, and they walked out to the car. When they got there, Hilda broke down in tears. Lou comforted her for a while, then said, "Hey, it could be worse. Connie's prospects are down by fifty percent."

Hilda began to laugh.

Back in the lobby of the Bijou, Gar Loober began to shake violently. He had never fired his service weapon and now had killed two men in one day. When he had regained control, he walked out to his car to call in the state police for assistance.

He was the only cop in town.